LAKE

8/21

CRESCENT

CREATURE X MYSTERIES

Roanoke Ridge
Lake Crescent

J.J. DUPUIS

LAKE

CRESCENT

A CREATURE X MYSTERY

DUNDURN
PRESS

Publisher and acquiring editor: Scott Fraser | Editor: Allison Hirst
Cover designer: Laura Boyle
Cover image: istock.com/wingmar

Library and Archives Canada Cataloguing in Publication

Title: Lake Crescent / J.J. Dupuis.
Names: Dupuis, J. J., 1983- author.
Description: Series statement: A creature X mystery ; 2
Identifiers: Canadiana (print) 20200305662 | Canadiana (ebook) 20200305689
  | ISBN 9781459746480 (softcover) | ISBN 9781459746497 (PDF) | ISBN
  9781459746503 (EPUB)
Classification: LCC PS8607.U675 L35 2021 | DDC C813/.6—dc23

We acknowledge the support of the Canada Council for the Arts and the Ontario Arts Council for our publishing program. We also acknowledge the financial support of the Government of Ontario, through the Ontario Book Publishing Tax Credit and Ontario Creates, and the Government of Canada.

Care has been taken to trace the ownership of copyright material used in this book. The author and the publisher welcome any information enabling them to rectify any references or credits in subsequent editions.

The publisher is not responsible for websites or their content unless they are owned by the publisher.

Dundurn Press
1382 Queen Street East
Toronto, Ontario, Canada M4L 1C9
dundurn.com, @dundurnpress ✔ f ⓞ

This book is dedicated to my father, Denis Dupuis, whose love of the island inspired me to set the story not far from the town he called home.

On the dark bottom of the great salt lake
Imprisoned lay the giant snake,
With naught his sullen sleep to break.
— Adam Oehlenschläger, "Thor's
Fishing," translated by
Grenville Pigot

PROLOGUE

CLYDE RENGEL, THE TECHNICIAN FROM THE Marine Institute at Memorial University, lowered the remotely operated underwater vehicle over the side of the boat, letting it slip into the gentle, brackish waters of Crescent Lake. A cloud of bubbles appeared on the monitor as the ROV sank down into depths too cold for divers.

Our film crew had come to the edge of North America, to the island of Newfoundland, in search of Cressie: a giant eel that has haunted this still and serene lake from before the time of the first European settlers. The day before, a fishing crew claimed to have caught a ten-foot-long eel, impossibly big for these waters, in the very spot the ROV was now descending toward. We seemed close to uncovering the eel's lair.

"We'll be looking for caverns," said Dr. Willoughby, a marine biologist from the fisheries department we'd invited along to consult on the local wildlife. "Big ones from the size of that eel. Keep an eye out for fish bones and the shells of crustaceans. A conger is a big-time predator, so we should find evidence of its feeding behaviour."

Gulls squawked as they hovered over cresting waves. I found the sound of water lapping against the rocks soothing. Despite the biting chill, I felt alive in a way that I hadn't felt before. My lips were dry and my fingertips were freezing, but I wouldn't have traded the sense of adventure for anything.

As a chilling rain fell, the wheelhouse became a popular destination. Captain Phil pressed himself against the wheel to accommodate all of us. My team and I, with the exception of Clyde, who was controlling the remotely operated vehicle scanning the bottom of the lake, crowded around the monitor to watch the images being transmitted from the underwater world of greens and whites.

There were lines etched into the lake bed, and a round piece of metal jutted out of the muddy bottom. As the ROV approached a wall of rock, Clyde eased it down toward the opening of a cavern. The stone walls, smooth and round like billowing curtains frozen in time, narrowed in at the cave entrance. White particles floated in the water. The sandy bottom of the lake rose slightly, exposing something that undulated like a dorsal fin.

Then the ROV stopped.

"We've hit a snag."

Clyde pressed the button that reversed the tiny black propellers on the side of our miniature yellow submarine, then directed the craft forward again. But the ROV was still snagged. He kept on reversing then going forward again, like he was snowed into his driveway, but the ROV wouldn't break free. The camera jerked and a cloud of silt covered the lens.

"Let's reel her in. Dr. Laidlaw," Clyde said, motioning for Duncan to take hold of the crank. He then leaned over the edge of the boat, reached down to the surface of the lake, and took hold of the neon-yellow cable. He began pulling it up with a long, smooth motion. "Easy on that tether," he kept saying. "Easy ... easy."

The screen revealed nothing but clouds of bubbles and silt kicked up from the lake bottom. Clyde and Duncan continued slowly reel in the ROV, soon joined by our cameraman, Chris. The rest of us, except the captain, were pressed against the gunwale, offering feeble assistance before settling into the role of spectators.

As the top of the ROV broke the surface of the water, I saw that something else had followed it up. A fold of blue rose from the rippling water, then collapsed and slumped against the hull of the *Darling Mae*.

"Goddamn," Chris said, looking over the gunwale, the yellow tether gripped tightly in his hands. Chris and Clyde seemed to freeze.

Danny waved his hand in front of my face, a plastic Canadian twenty-dollar bill folded between his thumb and forefinger. "A bet is a bet, Reagan," he said.

"Ah hell," I said, looking at what we'd pulled up.

ONE

The first reports of these mysterious lake dwellers can be traced back to precolonial Native American legends, which warned of the Woodum Haoot (Pond Devil) or Haoot Tuwedyee (Swimming Demon), both of which purportedly dwelled in the lake. Since the early 1900s there have been numerous reports of encounters with these creatures, and not all of them have been pleasant.

— Rob Morphy, *The World's Strangest Lake Monsters*, August 20, 2015

DAD'S INTEREST IN MYTHS, MONSTERS, AND cryptozoology had started with episodes of *In Search of …* when he was a boy growing up in Wyoming in the 1970s. Each week brought a new mysterious phenomenon to explore: Could plants respond to people's thoughts? Did ancient Phoenicians visit New Hampshire? Were the images carved into the Nazca plains made by or for extraterrestrials? But nothing held Dad's imagination hostage like the mystery animals — Bigfoot, Nessie, the swamp monster of the Louisiana Bayou. It took years to gestate, but when he came back from the Gulf War, he was obsessed. He started taking road trips with army buddies, visiting dark forests and quiet lakes, looking for creatures that conventional science scoffed at. Sometimes he'd take me along. But as the trips, which usually took place on school days, became more frequent, he usually ended up driving off by himself, leaving Mom and me waving in the driveway.

Eventually, he acted as if he were still travelling, even when he was at home. He crashed on the couch or slept on the air mattress in the basement. His relationship with Mom became more that of lodger and host than husband and wife. He gave up looking for substantial employment altogether, opting to make just enough money to pay for his expeditions.

But for all his research, all his hours sleeping on hard ground and cooking over a campfire, the only things he had to show for it were a collection of blurry photographs and overflowing boxes of notebooks. When Dad took off, the notebooks were all that was left of him. Mom couldn't bear to throw them out.

Every entry in those notebooks began the same way. The name of a monster, or *cryptid* if you're in that community, was written in capital letters, my dad tracing each letter in blue ink multiple times and underlining it with the same thickness. Then came pages upon pages of background — everything Dad had picked up at the local library or from TV documentaries. Finally, the entry became a journal, marked with the dates and times of his own explorations.

When I was a girl, I had no idea how far he drove on those trips. Only looking back can I compute the distances between Washington State, where we lived, and places like Point Pleasant, West Virginia, and Lake Champlain, Vermont. He even crossed the border into Canada, which seemed to have as many lake monster legends as it had lakes.

Dad's last complete entry was about a lake monster called Cressie that supposedly lived in Lake Crescent on the island of Newfoundland in eastern Canada. Though Dad had written pages of background information about Cressie, there were almost no notes about his visit there. The only thing he had recorded, in the margins of the notebook, was the location and departure date and time for the ferry from North Sydney, Nova Scotia, to Port-aux-Basques, Newfoundland. The date he'd jotted down was one week after the last time I ever saw him.

I remember the day he left. Mom tore into him right there as he was packing the station wagon, her voice resounding through the trees that separated our property from the neighbours'. Dad never came back inside the house after that. He didn't hug me or kiss the top of my head, just gave me his half salute and smiled. Soon, the back of the station wagon disappeared as the road curved around the splayed-finger branches of the evergreens. I never dared to cry in front of him, saving that for later, once I was sure he was long gone and I was in my bed, a pillow muffling my sobs.

I wonder how far he got before realizing he'd left his notebook behind.

Our expedition to Crescent Lake would be a wild goose chase. I knew that going in. But the terms of my deal with the TV network stated very clearly that I could pick any cryptid anywhere in the world to cover in our second episode. So, why not Cressie?

You couldn't tell it was late April when we landed. The Deer Lake airport was thoroughly dusted with snow, and high winds whistled through the automatic doors as the oil patch workers ahead of us went outside to greet their waiting loved ones. We were officially one month into spring, but this part of Newfoundland had apparently missed the memo.

The season, however, seemed to change sometime during the hour-and-a-half drive to Robert's Arm. The sun was out, and it truly felt like a spring day, though with a definite chill in the air. I was surprised to see the harbour nearly empty, with the fleets of fishing boats already out on the water.

I suppose they had to get out on the water as soon as the opportunity presented itself. Gone were the days when, as Captain John Cabot's crew remarked, the sea was "full of fish that can be taken not only with nets but with fishing baskets." The catch each individual boat can now expect has, in the past few decades, decreased significantly.

Much of the island of Newfoundland is a scar left over from the ice age, the soil having been scraped off into the oceans long ago by the receding glaciers. The harbour at Robert's Arm was cradled by tree-covered hills that rose up to the rocky cliffs, as if protecting it from the ocean that swept in through a narrow gap. The main road led to the docks and boats; smaller roads criss-crossed up and along the hills, leading to houses, huts, and cabins nestled among the wind-swept trees and lichen-covered rock. Forces of nature left their fingerprints all over this landscape, and though it was weathered and cracked, it refused to break.

This was a beautiful wild place, but I was just too tired to fully appreciate it. I hadn't had a moment to truly rest since we'd left Silver Spring, Maryland, hours earlier.

We dropped off our luggage at the Lake Crescent Inn, had a late breakfast that included lots of coffee, then climbed right back into the two rental vans. Our schedule was tight, and we had to get started.

Robert's Arm was a picturesque town, with old houses dotting the shore and aluminum boats with outboard motors and other pleasure craft listing gently in the harbour. It was also eerily still but for the odd sign of life now and then: a car would appear for a moment, then disappear behind an outcropping of trees; a small aluminum boat with an outboard engine would tear through the water, then vanish just as quickly as it had arrived.

After we parked, I got out and stood gazing out over the water, breathing in the cool sea air. I noticed a huge building perched on the hill at the edge of the narrow peninsula that pinched the bay before it flowed out into the ocean. The peaks of its roof and the chimney jutted up over the trees like a castle guarding the entrance to Robert's Arm. At the bottom of the hill, the trees opened to reveal the entrance to a driveway. The road that curved around the bay ended there, and on the side opposite the driveway was a dock that looked lonely so far from the others.

"Interested in a spot of ghost hunting?" someone whispered in my ear.

I'd been in a trance and started at the interruption.

It was Duncan Laidlaw, a British paleontologist who'd joined our team for this expedition.

"It does look like a beautiful old place. But look where it is. Like it was built by someone who wanted to lord their wealth and power over everybody else," I replied.

"I imagine that was precisely the idea. Why it was built up there, lording over all the other houses in town. Probably comes with a dungeon for deformed heirs or something of the like," he said, laughing.

Duncan and I turned and walked down the dock toward a white-and-blue fishing boat, patches of paint peeling off it like diseased skin. Next to the vessel stood a hunched man. I assumed this was Phil Parsons, known locally as Captain Phil. We'd arranged for him to take us out on the waters of Lake Crescent in his boat, the *Darling Mae*. The purpose being to search for giant eels.

"Captain Phil?"

"That's me," he said, removing his Greek-style cotton fisherman's cap and walking across the dock, hand extended. "How d'you do, my dear?"

"I'm well. And you?"

"Fit as a —"

He was drowned out by a boat engine chopping through the water. Soon, a large white fishing boat pulled up next to us, rocking the dock with its wake. Twice the size of the *Darling Mae*, the vessel looked as though it had arrived fresh from the showroom. I could see the name, *Tide Queen*, written on the hull, the white water churning beneath it.

Captain Phil tugged on the bill of his cap and looked over at the man piloting the craft. He was a big guy, built somewhat like a cartoon lumberjack, a refrigerator-and-a-half wide at the shoulders and sporting a straw-blond beard that resembled brush in a vacant lot. He reminded me of Gaston from *Beauty and the Beast*. The resting smirk on his face gave me the impression he was used to getting his way.

"Morning, Jimmy," Captain Phil said. "Folks, this is Jimmy O'Donahue."

"You're looking for Cressie?" the man asked, looking at me and ignoring the captain entirely.

"We're shooting a documentary," I said.

"That's the same thing, isn't it?"

"It's a distinction of degrees," I said.

"I can sure help you find it. Better than him, anyway."

"I'm just taking them around the lake, Jimmy," Captain Phil said patiently.

"Cressie can swim faster than his little dinghy, that's for darn sure," Jimmy said, scoffing. "Why don't you bring your gear aboard my boat, I'll take you around."

"Do you know much about Cressie? Ever seen it?" I asked, raising an eyebrow, curious if there was substance behind Jimmy's bluster.

"Me? Sure, I've seen it. I know where Cressie lives and where she feeds. For the right price, I can take you there."

Jimmy was twelve feet of ego in six feet of man-boy, and I trusted he wouldn't screw me over like I trusted a piranha not to bite. "You dance with the one that brought you," I said. "We hired Captain Phil. We'll stick with Captain Phil."

Jimmy folded his arms across his barrel chest. "I'll catch Cressie myself, then. Then we'll see where things stand."

There was a tell behind his smirk, the way he didn't blink, like he was trying his hardest not to break eye contact with me.

"Good luck," I said coldly.

Jimmy nodded at a man standing on the bridge of his boat, and the propellers of the *Tide Queen* started up again. As it pulled away, Jimmy continued to stare at me. I stared right back, like it was some kind of game of chicken. Stillness is the difference between thinking you're the alpha and being the alpha, as Dad used to say. Jimmy turned away as the *Tide Queen* sailed on toward the middle of the bay. My muscles, from my scalp to my calves, relaxed.

"That guy is something else," I said to the captain, trying to be polite.

Captain Phil took a long drink of coffee, then wiped his mouth with the back of his sleeve. "His dad is an important man in this town. There's a lot for him to live up to." He shrugged. "All the young folks 'round here are frustrated. The jobs just aren't here like they used to be."

"I guess you're right," I said, turning and walking down the dock to join the rest of my team.

Back at the vans, the three of us who would regularly appear on camera — Saad, Lindsay, and I — fastened GoPros to our headgear and mics to our clothes. Chris unloaded his camera gear with the help of Clyde Rengel, the sonar and ROV technician. Dr. Duncan Laidlaw consulted some notes on his tablet.

Those of us who would be on camera, as well as those who were blogging, strapped cameras to our heads. This had sounded like a cool idea in the planning stages but now felt silly to me in practice. But the point was to document the entirety of our expedition. None of that *whoa, did you see that?* garbage you usually got from similar shows. Everything would be caught on tape. Our format was simple: investigate cryptozoological phenomena using skeptical scientific methodology. The goal was to make the science as interesting as the sensationalism.

Danny LeDoux, the producer sent by the network to keep us on track, sat with the door open, his legs out on the gravel, drinking coffee from a thermos and eating a granola bar as the rest of the us worked busily around him.

Danny screwed the lid back on his thermos, then took a travel-size bottle of Listerine from the inside of his jacket. He took a swig, gargled it around his mouth, and spat it out on the ground outside the van. He then walked toward us, but only after giving himself a quick look in the mirror on the passenger door and fixing his hair. Danny wasn't going to be on camera; it was just his vanity to never have a hair out of place.

"Our adventure begins," he said.

I fought the urge to roll my eyes.

"Here's the game plan, folks," Danny continued. "Today we're going to head out on the water and see what we can see. Any questions?"

Danny spoke with such conviction that I almost believed that he had done all the legwork to set this up. Aside from using the network's travel adviser and signing for the vouchers, Danny was a producer only in name. I was the one who'd chartered the *Darling Mae*. I hired Clyde Rengel to operate the ROV. I rented the vans, made all the necessary calls, and even drafted the itineraries for Lindsay, Saad, Duncan, Chris, and myself. He had the experience, I'd be the first to admit that, but there was a limit to how much undercutting I'd tolerate. The deal was very clear: it was my show to do my way. Danny was to advise only when necessary.

Danny went on. "We need conventional footage on top of the high-tech stuff — the side-scanning radar and ROV shots. We'll be laying some traps throughout the lake, so we can shoot that. We should be back in by early afternoon. Then we'll split up. Laura and I have witnesses to interview once we're back on dry land."

"What if we don't find anything interesting today?" Lindsay asked. "We can't live blog nothing."

"Doesn't matter. Today is Duncan's show. Background and context, fish stories," Danny said. "The two of you can go out with the ROV tech — he's also a camera guy — and talk to the locals. Try to make that interesting."

"We're doing a science show, not a monster show," I said. "We need to provide some actual scientific methodology."

"Like devoting days three and four to fieldwork with Dr. Willoughby and his students? That was just the price for getting him on the show," Danny said.

Dr. Willoughby would demonstrate to us, and the audience, how fieldwork was conducted, how eels were caught and measured, and how we'd go about drawing out a large eel if one were residing in Lake Crescent.

"Regardless of that —"

"Agree to disagree," he said. He brushed the front of his shirt, looking down at it as if gauging the development of his paunch. "Science or no, we need a good story."

•   ●   •

Due to its size, the *Darling Mae* was moored on the side of Robert's Arm that faced the Atlantic Ocean, not on the lake itself. We'd have to sail out of the harbour, along the coast, and up Tommy's Arm River into Lake Crescent.

The *Darling Mae* pulled away from the dock slowly, kicking up a trail of bubbles in the green water. The nose of the boat pointed away from the town and toward a shelf of exposed rock, upon which an uneven row of black spruce sat like softball trophies.

It was, to use the cliché, smooth sailing as the *Darling Mae* careened toward the mouth of the bay. The old mansion I'd noticed earlier was still visible on the starboard side. Its imposing position on the hill guaranteed it to be the first house seen by any vessel entering the harbour. Short trees with thick trunks surrounded it, providing a natural windbreak from the gales and gusts blowing in off the bay, but none grew tall enough to block out the building's majesty.

"She's a real beauty," Captain Phil said, following my eyeline. "That's the Showalter place."

I'd learned that Sir Leland Showalter was an English lord who'd moved to Canada after World War One to oversee a logging empire. His name kept coming up in my background research on the town. He'd been like a king on this part of the island, staying in what amounted to a castle when he wasn't in England on his family estate or in Ontario, where he bred cattle. I should have figured this was the place he'd built.

"Impressive," I said.

Saad, my best and perhaps only friend, slid up and stood by my side, the wind ruffling his short black hair. He remained silent as I took one last look at Showalter House as the pointed roof disappeared behind the high, rocky cliffs as we left the bay and entered the open ocean.

"This looks familiar," Saad finally said.

"Exposed rock and evergreen trees? Yeah. Feels just like home."

"I meant it feels like last time," he said.

I realized then that he wasn't talking about our university days, but our misadventure about a year ago at Roanoke Ridge in Oregon.

"They don't have Bigfoot in Newfoundland," I said.

Saad smiled, a playful look in his brown eyes.

Thoughts of the majesty of Showalter House faded as the first icebergs came into view, an invading armada in the distance. We gathered at the aft section of the boat and watched as they appeared to shrink with distance. Coves of varying sizes sliced into the coastline. The *Darling Mae* wove between small islands, staying close to shore as though there were a ledge we might fall over. We cut through the narrow passage between tiny Raft Island and much larger Pretty Island, emerging at the mouth of Tommy's Arm River, which snaked wildly on the way to Lake Crescent, which itself was about six miles long.

We passed beneath the Tommy's Arm River Bridge, the lake ahead a thin, curving gash in the earth that funneled west under the George Baker Bridge to a section called the Narrows.

It was easy to picture the history here: pirate ships skulking behind the rocky outcrops; Beothuk fishing parties in birchbark or animal-hide canoes; floating logs destined for the paper mill.

Captain Phil brought the boat parallel to the rocks and the shore. Chris and Clyde took what looked like a black torpedo from a crate, fawning over their toy as they did so. Duncan and Dr. Willoughby came over and joined in on the fawning. After Lindsay joined their circle, Saad and I clustered around the equipment with the others.

Chris focused his camera on Clyde.

"This little beauty is going to show us what the bottom of this lake looks like," Clyde explained. "Side-scan sonar. She emits pulses that bounce back from the lake bottom and give us measurements of what's down there. The data it collects will be transmitted to a laptop that Dr. Willoughby will be monitoring on the bridge."

We parted to let the white-haired Dr. Willoughby pass on his way to the covered bow. He powered up his computer as Clyde leaned over the railing and lowered the side-scan sonar into the water.

Captain Phil, from his post at the wheel, watched us for a moment, then turned back to the waters ahead. I noticed a dreamcatcher hanging from the ceiling, above the throttle next to the radio. I decided to join Dr. Willoughby inside.

As I watched, a black-and-white image appeared on the computer screen. It was bisected by a white line, one half displaying the data from the port side, the other from starboard. The portside screen was dark, formless, but the starboard side displayed two long white scars that tracked like the readout of a heart monitor, except for the fact that the broken lines ran vertically and not horizontally.

"Those are deep crevasses at the bottom of the cliff-side there. They look promising," Dr. Willoughby said to me, then looked into the camera I was wearing and added, "Eels prefer to live in caves and among rocks. The deeper the better."

"But not, like, deep enough to crush a sub or anything?" I asked.

He spoke directly into the camera again, raising his bushy salt and pepper eyebrows. "Some species of eel live at the edge of continental shelves and beyond, at depths of four thousand metres."

I did the math in my head. "That's thirteen thousand feet!"

"Impressive, isn't it? But around here we only get freshwater eels, *Anguilla rostrata*. The water doesn't get that deep in the lakes here."

"So, you don't expect to find a giant eel in this lake?"

"I would love to. That would make my whole career, not to mention help me get some of my funding back." He looked me right in the eyes. "Government cutbacks.

"But I wouldn't bet on finding anything out here," he continued. "The best we can hope for is a larger ocean eel that got lost while spawning. It's possible that a conger or a moray, once lost here, wouldn't have to divert resources toward spawning anymore, and might end up growing larger and larger. But the odds of that are one in a million. I'm not holding my breath."

"We're all set here, I see," Duncan said, bending at the waist to get a better view of the sonar readout. "I guess we can rule out some of the usual sea serpent suspects: giant squids and oarfish."

"That's correct," Dr. Willoughby said.

"How about a population of conger eels that have somehow become lost while spawning?" Duncan asked.

Dr. Willoughby shot me a glance, a *great minds think alike* look on his face.

I smiled and raised my eyebrows.

"We really can't rule that out," he said. "Eels make such a remarkable journey to spawn in the Sargasso Sea, it is possible that some have lost their way and wound up here. They'd easily become the apex predator in this ecosystem."

"Could a larger species of eel have been introduced to the lake? An invasive species?" I asked.

"That seems unlikely. It's possible that new species may invade these waters as the oceans warm. Striped bass, blue crab, tarpon, and American lobster have all been reported in habitats farther north than they've traditionally lived. It's possible we might start to see American congers here. However, the American conger only gets up to two metres long. That's just over half a metre longer than the American eels found here already."

"That's not even close to what the eyewitness accounts of Cressie say," Duncan said. "How about the European conger?"

"Given how far the European conger travels to spawn — around six thousand kilometres in some cases — I can see a small number getting lost. Even then, the longest ever recorded was only three metres."

Duncan pulled up his sleeve and checked his watch. "History has taught us that Europeans crossed extraordinary distances to access the fisheries of Newfoundland. Perhaps that applies to eels as well."

"Glaciers scraped the fertile soil from this land and deposited it into the sea," Dr. Willoughby said. "That's why the coastal marine life thrived here for millennia. The fanciful part of me believes that these might be the right conditions for a giant eel."

We traversed Lake Crescent's perimeter slowly, marking down the places most likely to host an eel — spots with rocky overhangs, deep crevasses, or caverns. I could picture a large serpentine creature undulating through the frigid water of the ocean, working its way up to the rays of sunshine penetrating the water, between the icebergs and up Tommy's Arm River.

"I can waste entire afternoons staring out my window, imagining what might be possible if the circumstances were right," Duncan said, mirroring my thoughts. "I lose entire days that way sometimes. Speculative biology is a hobby of mine." He turned and smiled at me. "Did you know that Heuvelmans had nine categories of sea serpents?"

"Bernard Heuvelmans, the French-born, Belgian-raised, so-called father of cryptozoology," I explained, so the camera could pick it up.

"Yes, him," Duncan continued. "Super-eels is one of his categories. And perhaps the most plausible, unless you're partial to super-otters. Most later crypto-zoologists have built on Heuvelmans's work. Some have given super-eels the binomial *Ceticonger longus* and subdivided the super-eel family into two groups, megacongers and titanocongers."

"How large are these eels supposed to be?" Dr. Willoughby asked.

"From what I've read, megas are supposedly in the ten-to-thirty-foot range, titanos range from thirty to a hundred feet."

"What do they base these measurements on?" I asked.

"Eyewitness reports and legends mainly," Duncan said. "It's remarkable, the level of speculation that you find in online discussions. Some cryptozoologists claim, for example, that the titanocongers have adopted a whale-like method of filter feeding. It seems I'm not the only one enthralled with speculative biology."

"Where did that idea come from?" Dr. Willoughby asked, fascinated. He leaned forward, resting his elbow on the table beside the laptop, watching Duncan curiously.

"Sightings of these beasts swimming with their mouths open. I suppose the alleged similar lengths between these creatures and cetaceans must have something to do with it, too. But titanocongers are thought to dwell mainly in the deep ocean. Cressie would likely fall into the megaconger category."

"What I'd give to identify and name an eel that big," Willoughby said, chuckling.

"*Ceticonger willoughbii*," Duncan quipped.

"That'll be the day!" Willoughby said with a smile. "Although it's quite against protocol to name a new species after yourself."

"Then you'd better hope *I* discover the creature first," Duncan said, "so I can name it after *you*."

"What an honour that would be, Dr. Laidlaw," Willoughby said, mock-bowing.

Although there was no denying that we had become cryptozoologists by merit of making a television series like *Creature X*, we were still going to apply conventional methods of field biology in our search. I hoped to acquaint the monster-hunter audience with how science actually worked, even if only on a subliminal level. Which was why we were fortunate to have Dr. Willoughby on board. His expertise and authority were necessary to conduct the survey of the lake. Since we were operating on the hypothesis that Cressie was indeed a species of eel, and not an ancient marine reptile or unnaturally large fish, Dr. Willoughby advised us on the traditional methods of surveying a lake's eel population. That meant that, after making our way to the centre of the lake, Dr. Willoughby tied the impaled corpses of a trio of herring with a wire to a crab trap. Then, with help from Dr. Laidlaw, he tossed the whole thing overboard. When the ripples settled, all that marked the trap's location was a round red buoy bobbing on the lake's surface. If a large eel had made Lake Crescent its home, it was unlikely the herring would last long.

"So, finding a large eel — or even a population of large eels — in this lake is not outside the realm of possibility?" I asked.

The two scientists looked at each other. Neither seemed to want to be the first one to answer. Duncan was never one to shy away from speculation; perhaps he was deferring to the expert in the field. I could tell Dr. Willoughby was concerned with sounding crazy on camera.

"No, I suppose it's not outside the realm of possibility," he eventually responded noncommittally.

Duncan went on. "Another element that adds credibility to the theory that Cressie is an eel is that eels have incredibly long lifespans."

"What do you mean?" I asked.

"Sightings of many cryptids go back generations. We therefore have to assume that, if they do exist, there must be breeding populations of them. There can't be just one of each. With an eel, however, it is possible that one rather large individual could live through multiple human lifetimes."

"Like the Brantevik eel," Dr. Willoughby said.

"The Brantevik eel?" I asked.

"In the town of Brantevik, Sweden, in the summer of 1859, a young boy released a European eel into a well," Dr. Laidlaw explained. "That eel reportedly lived in the well until August of 2014. Can you imagine that?"

I glanced over at the screen, at the murky waters below us, and shivered.

T W O

Now, while Crescent Lake does reportedly host freshwater American eels, these are normally under five feet long. Divers from the Royal Canadian Mounted Police ... allegedly surfaced on the lake with "descriptions of giant eels as thick as a man's thigh."
— Dr. Joe Nickell, *Skeptical Inquirer*,
July/August 2009

CRYPTIDS, MONSTERS, FOLK CREATURES, whatever you want to call them, often have one incident, one image, or one video that elevates them from a local phenomenon to a national news story or an international sensation. Although the legend of a creature in Loch Ness dates back to the sixth century, apparently spotted by St. Columba, it wasn't until the "surgeon's photo" of 1934 that the Loch Ness monster became world famous. The same can be said of Bigfoot. Although Indigenous Peoples had legends of the Sasquatch, and there were many supposed encounters between settlers and "wild men" or "ape men," it wasn't until the Patterson-Gimlin film came out in 1967 that Bigfoot reached celebrity status. Although there have been no pictures or video taken of Cressie, its "big break" came in the 1980s, when a team of RCMP divers were probing the icy waters of Lake Crescent to recover the victims of a plane crash. It was widely reported that the divers were unable to get close to the wreckage, as a swarm of eels "as thick as a man's thigh" prevented them from recovering the bodies. It was that moment that compounded all the Native American legends about pond devils and the folklore the European settlers and their descendants had spread about a giant eel in the lake.

After spending the morning on the water, we returned to town and split into two groups. Doctors Willoughby and Laidlaw, accompanied by Lindsay, Saad, and Clyde, were to follow the map I had made to the sites of several famous Cressie sightings, shoot some footage of the surrounding area, and speculate on the behaviour reported by the eyewitnesses. Danny, Chris, and I hopped into one of the rental vans and drove to the RCMP detachment in Springdale. There, a media liaison officer was going to meet with us to discuss the plane crash and the team of divers that supposedly encountered the unusually large eels.

We didn't expect or need much footage from our interview with the officer. The show was supposed to be more of a guerilla-style documentary, to make the audience feel as though they are on the expedition with us. But Danny thought the "fanboys" at home were more likely to "swallow" the plane crash story if it came from "a man with a badge and a gun." He even warned me not to first mention the eel story during the interview.

The Springdale detachment of the RCMP was housed in a grey two-storey building at the base of a tree-covered mountain, its well-maintained lawn set against a landscape of greenery that grew wild and free.

The constable at the desk, a woman who looked a decade older than me, watched us come in the front door with an expression on her face as mean as any guard dog I'd ever seen. Instead of greeting us, she raised her eyebrows, clearly bidding us to state our business.

"We're here to meet with Sergeant Deloitte," Danny said, smiling like a salesman.

She kicked away from her desk, her chair rolling across the tile floor several feet. Her eyes landed on some distant target.

"Roy," she shouted. "Roy!"

Sergeant Deloitte appeared and led us back to his office, which was nice in a sterile sort of way. The only item of any personal significance was a picture frame sitting just off the blotter on the desk, opposite his computer. I couldn't see what the picture was of, but assumed it was of his family — a wife, two, maybe three kids.

The sergeant sat back in his chair and looked from me to Danny to Chris and his camera. He was red faced, and I couldn't help but notice his neck was pinched by the collar of his uniform, folds of flesh pouring over the sides. But he had a friendly manner and a firm handshake and seemed like Norman Rockwell's idea of a cop.

"'Ow are you all doing this morning?" he said. He spoke with his head tilted back, his voice starting high at the beginning of the sentence and falling low by the end. "Isn't this something? A real 'ollywood film crew sitting on the other side of me desk."

"I'm afraid we're not that glamorous," I said. "We were just hoping to ask you some questions —"

"About a plane crash, as I understand it. But I'm afraid there isn't much to tell. I 'ad a look through the files. We don't 'ave any record of a plane crash in Lake Crescent between 1977 and 1997."

On his desk was a stack of file folders half a foot high. I stared at them, because what else could I do? I had really hoped to use the plane crash to create a narrative. This could really put a damper on my plans.

"I kept the files out in case you wanted to look for yourself. They're old enough; it's not improper to show them to you."

"Thanks, but no thanks," Danny said, eager to get back on the road. "We shouldn't take up any more of your time."

We were all quiet until we got to the van. Chris took the wheel for the drive back to Robert's Arm. Danny, in the passenger seat, stared out the window at the rugged scenery. His face betrayed no expression, but I wouldn't put it past him to be able to stare out at such majesty and not be impressed.

"That really threw a wrench in my plans," I said.

"We'll just get a couple of locals to repeat the stories they've heard. It'll probably be better than the truth, anyway. More colourful," Danny said. He took out his phone and began ticking away at the tiny keyboard. "Entertainment comes first. If you can slip something educational in the back door, good for you. But you can't teach someone anything if they're falling asleep."

"I was hoping for more than just footage of people telling dramatic stories," I said. "I was hoping to track down eyewitnesses, like those RCMP divers. We need to ascertain the exact location of the incident. Everything I've read online is vague. If we can't prove this incident even occurred, we've lost an entire leg of the Cressie legend."

"We've still got the interview with that local Cressie expert, Beaver Cannings. Maybe this Beaver guy will be able to point us in the right direction."

"His name is *Beave*, not *Beaver*," I corrected.

"Maybe we can get Wally and Eddie Haskell on camera, too," Danny said. "Wait, you're probably not old enough to know what I'm talking about, are you?"

Danny was the kind of man who resented being treated like he was no longer young and virile, but he lorded the fact that he was my elder over me as though this amounted to wisdom attained only through pilgrimage, vows of poverty, and other religious rites.

"First, I know *Leave It to Beaver*," I said. "Second, you're not much older than I am. That show was off the air before you were born, too."

We took Highway 390 around Halls Bay, one of the many fingers of the Atlantic that held Newfoundland in its grasp. Aside from the powerlines that ran parallel to the highway, only the mouth of the odd gravel driveway reminded us that we weren't the only people on this part of the island. There were patches where the shrubbery thinned out and the evergreen trees stood like fenceposts, holding back the untamed wilderness.

The road curved and we came to a bridge that spanned a river. A shrub-covered mountain filled the passenger window. The odd car began to appear on the horizon, then another and another as we came to a stop at the Trans-Canada Highway, where we waited for a caravan of tractor trailers to pass before making the turn.

At the turnoff to Robert's Arm, we continued along Highway 380. The hydro poles along the route leaned at odd angles, like grave markers on the rocky hillside. The shrubs and trees eventually fell away, revealing Lake Crescent to our right. In some stretches, the lake was only a few feet beyond the guardrail; in others, walls of rock that had yielded to dynamite when the highway was built rose up beside us. It was truly beautiful country.

When we came to a small gravel parking lot that grew out of the shoulder on the passenger side, we turned in and came to a stop. A statue of Cressie, looking more like a dragon off a Chinese food menu than an eel, faced us, indicating that Robert's Arm was just around the next curve.

The local authority on Cressie was a man named Theodore "Beave" Cannings. He was Lake Crescent's answer to Adrian Shine, the naturalist who's made the pursuit of Nessie his life's work. We found him pacing by the lake under the gaze of the Cressie statue. There were no other vehicles around, so it was a safe bet he'd walked here from town. It wasn't far, and he probably knew a shortcut.

Beave appeared to me to be the Canadian stereotype, with his plaid jacket and a hat with earflaps. His hands were in his pockets, and he pushed his shoulders up high, like he'd caught a chill. I extended my hand as I approached, but Beave ignored it, choosing instead to engulf me in a hug like a long-lost relative. His clothes were steeped in day-old body odour. I heard change jingling in the pockets of his jeans.

A strong wind blew across the lake, rippling the water. It wasn't hard to imagine dark humps breaking the surface, maybe even a head rising up on a goose-like neck.

The interview with Beave was intended to be the introduction to the episode. Hopefully, it would provide background and a little context. When Beave introduced himself he spoke with a thick accent, and though I could understand him clearly enough when we'd spoken on the phone, I envisioned the need for subtitles for our TV audience.

He was a godsend, though. He'd been the first call I made as I reached out to experts on Cressie, and he was the first to answer. He also seemed by far the most knowledgeable. Unlike my dad, Beave had only the one interest, only the one monster, and he was more than happy to help. Like a border collie, he'd rounded up all the living eyewitnesses to the creature. He provided me with contact information, the locations of significant sightings, and overall had saved me a ton of legwork. Because of that, I was going to make sure that Danny didn't edit his interview to make him look like an unhinged and lonely old quack.

When Chris stepped up, Beave shook his hand, pumping it several more times than was necessary. But when our burly cameraman began clipping the mic to him, his tough, shop-worn layer peeled away. He froze stiff, didn't even breathe until Chris stepped back. Afterward, he looked over at me and smiled, showing the gaps in his teeth. Beave looked so boyish; it was heartwarming. It was people like him who made me want to find one of these cryptids, maybe name the species after them.

"I've lived on the lake here me whole life," he began. "Growing up, y'always hear stories 'bout creatures in the water from the older folk. Those stories go back to the earliest days of settlement here, and even before. The Natives used to talk about swamp devils or pond demons in these waters. Said the creature could change shape; pretend it was a woman and lure men to a drowning death.

"In modern times, the first local to see the beast, far's I know, was a lady by the name of Grandmother Anthony. Saw it one afternoon when she was out berry-picking. That was 'round the turn of the century. Since then, Cressie's been spotted dozens of times. Two woodsmen back in the fifties saw the thing not far from here. Well, these fellas saw what they thought was a boom log floatin' loose. The pulpwood industry was a big deal back in those days, y'see. They went out on the water to reattach it, when the thing suddenly rolled over and dove deep to the bottom of the lake. Those men didn't waste time getting back to shore, no two ways about that.

"Most famous story about Cressie has to do with a snowmobile accident. This was many years ago. Mountie divers came to recover the bodies. But when they dove into the dark waters, they were met by a mob of eels as thick as yer thigh. The eels attacked them and forced them out of the water."

Danny cocked his eyebrow as our eyes met. Beave saw this and misread it as a sign to stop talking.

"It was a snowmobile accident?" I asked. "We'd heard it was a plane crash."

"It was most definitely a snowmobile," he said, looking down at his boots. "I knew the fella; it was a lad I grew up with by name of Lou."

"What was his last name?" I asked.

"Fenton, Lou Fenton."

Danny, who was standing beside Chris, nodded, his arms folded as he looked to see what the camera was shooting. Beave had given us the break I'd hoped to get from Sergeant Deloitte.

We filmed Beave for the better part of an hour. He warmed up to being on camera and it felt to me as if I were watching someone's granddad tell a story. Beave relaxed his shoulders, took his hands out of his pockets, and forgot that he was being recorded. Afterward, Chris took wide shots of Beave standing by the water, the ripples flowing toward him as if being summoned. The camera followed as he walked over the grass along the shore, glancing over to the water occasionally or staring off pensively. I didn't see the point in any of it, but I deferred to Danny. He wanted the human connection — the mystery that is ostensibly at the bottom of a lake but is really a mystery deep inside of us. I'd prefer to shine the light of science on those mysteries rather than nurturing them. But I understood that Danny had made a career out of TV, and his expertise was to be respected.

"Have you always lived here?" I asked when they returned, the breeze from the lake blowing tendrils of hair across my face.

"For near ten years, I worked down in St. John's. The fishery was suffering and the mill had closed, so I decided to live with me sister and see what kinda work I could find in the city."

"When did you become interested in Cressie?"

"Since I was just a little one, standing on the shore, skipping stones across the lake. It's like I could feel Cressie down there, you know?"

"That's interesting," I said. "But you've never seen Cressie personally?"

"Can't say that I have. I'm just waiting for my turn."

"But you believe there's a creature living in the lake?"

"A lotta people has seen it. Good people. There's gotta be somethin' to it."

"Well, I look forward to meeting some of these people," I said.

"It'll be my pleasure taking you 'round to meet 'em," he said.

"Can we give you a lift back to town?"

"Wouldn't want to cause no trouble," he said. "It's not far, anyhow."

"At least back to the inn then?" I asked.

Beave nodded.

Beave sat in the back of the van, taking stock of all the gear we'd brought with us.

Past the signs indicating the town and the two others beyond it, we came upon the Cressie Gas Bar and Supplies. Between the gas pumps and the building itself, at the end of the parking lot, was a gravel road that led to the Lake Crescent Inn.

"You can get just about everything you need on this little stretch of road," Beave said, indicating the gas station and convenience store, then a pharmacy a little farther east.

As our tires crunched along the gravel road past balsam poplars and pin cherries, I looked between the seats and through the windshield to where Lindsay and Saad were just getting out of the other van. Both stood there looking toward the inn, not moving. Saad glanced over his shoulder as we pulled in, then said something to Lindsay, who started slowly toward us.

As we came closer, I could see a black sedan, a light blue coupe, a minivan, and some pickup trucks, all parked in front of the inn. As far as I knew, we had the whole place to ourselves, save for the owners.

"What's all this?" Chris asked as he slowed the van to a crawl.

"Folks around here are the friendly sort," Beave said.

Chris edged us up behind the other van, parking as close as he could to its bumper to avoid blocking the driveway. There was a crowd of townsfolk gathered on the front lawn. Two folding tables were set up in a line in front of the front window, a banner that read *The Robert's Arm Ladies' Auxiliary Welcomes You* hanging behind them. I counted six women, between fifty and seventy years old, standing near the tables in a line, like a diplomatic envoy waiting to greet us. Fred and Mary Williamson, the proprietors of the inn, stood on the front steps with a small woman with hair dyed orange red like a sunset and a tall, lean man in a green wool sweater.

"Is this a —"

"Welcoming committee," Danny said, giving himself a look in the rear-view mirror.

Crap, I thought. We hadn't had a single moment to rest since deplaning, unless you counted sitting in a rented van filled with video equipment, and I longed to just flop down on a bed and pull a pillow over my face. "I didn't think those were real, that they were just something they talked about in old movies," I said.

"Get ready to soak up the small-town charm," he said. "The glad-handing and the small talk takes some getting used to, but it's still one of the best parts about shooting on location — the locals love you."

"The food looks good," Chris said meekly, staring out over the steering wheel.

"I'd bet it is," Beave piped up from the back.

I turned my phone on, using its camera to give myself a once-over.

Danny opened his door, puffing his chest out as he stood up. "Smiles, everyone," he said.

Chris took his baseball cap off and laid it on the dashboard. He ran his fingers through his black hair, recently dyed to hide the grey. He got out of the car, tugged his fleece down past his beltline, and looked back at me. "They won't bite," he said.

Beave came around the front of the van and paused, looking toward the tables, the food, then the front steps of the inn. It was as though some witchcraft, some line of salt sprinkled on the earth, prevented him from getting any closer. "Guess I'll see yous tomorrow," he said, making his way toward a path that led through the trees in the direction of the town.

"Ah, sure," I said. "Don't you want to …"

Beave raised a hand and kept walking until he entered the narrow gap in the trees, the tips of branches scraping at the sleeves of his jacket. He was hunched over and hobbled a little as he walked. I pictured a life of rough weather and hard labour for a man like that, but it was all speculation and imagination. He could have been an accountant for all I knew.

Chris hung back a little, giving me time to catch up. He stayed a half-step behind me the whole time, maybe out of courtesy or just habit as a cameraman. Danny moved down the gravel driveway, not hurriedly but with a grace I didn't know he was capable of. The woman with sunset-orange hair, wearing a black turtleneck, dark jeans, and a thick orange vest that resembled a life jacket, approached him. Was Danny's almost-superhuman schmoozing power the result of his career choice, or was it an innate ability that had allowed him to succeed in his field? It was a question that popped up from time to time as I watched him in his element. Me? I was still adjusting to being the centre of attention.

"And this is the star of our show," I heard Danny say. "Not to mention the brains behind it." He swept an arm in my direction as though he were parting a curtain that separated the woman and me.

"How do you do?" she said, taking my hand. "I'm Mayor Dunlop. Maureen. Welcome to our town."

"Thank you," I said. "Laura Reagan."

There was a look on Danny's face that said *I can't take you anywhere*, but I ignored it.

"You have a lovely town here," I added.

"Thank you. Laura, I'd like you to meet John O'Donahue."

The man in the green sweater had been standing patiently, so still you'd have thought the inn had sprouted up around him. He was quite handsome for his age, definitely what you'd call a silver fox. He extended his hand to me in a slow, dignified manner, as though he was the kind of man who might have tea with foreign dignitaries.

His hand was warm, a sharp contrast to the cool air blowing in from the Atlantic.

"Laura Reagan," I said again. "Pleasure to meet you."

O'Donahue had perfect posture, well-coiffed grey hair, and features that looked as if they had been carved from wood. But there was a sadness in his brown eyes that his polite smile couldn't hide. "It's my pleasure," he said. He didn't have the same accent as Sergeant Deloitte or Beave. He enunciated each syllable the way a newscaster or a stage actor might. He was not imposing, and he made sure to position himself out of the way of the mayor, a move that seemed deferential to her office.

"We hope you'll take advantage of the hiking trails around the lake," the mayor said. "They're some of the finest on the island, you know."

I nodded and looked around. Chris, Lindsay, Saad, and Duncan were talking with members of the ladies' auxiliary, a table of baked goods between them.

I turned my attention back to the mayor. "Yes. Sorry … I hope we'll have time to see all the sights, but I can't promise anything. Our schedule is very tight."

"I'd love to show you the Hazelnut Trail personally," she said. "I'm especially proud of it."

"It may not seem so at first glance," John added, "but there's a lot to see here. This town has an interesting history. There's a lot more to Robert's Arm than sea monsters." There was no mockery or malice in his voice — just the same steady, polite tone — yet something about the comment made me curious.

"So, I take it you've never witnessed Cressie yourself?" I asked. "Either of you?"

Mayor Dunlop stuffed her hands into the pockets of her vest. "Can't say that I have," she said, before turning to John.

"The folklore of Newfoundland is as rich as any other former colony of the British Empire. We have our own legends here — fairies, sea monsters, pirate treasure, haunted shipwrecks. I've never put too much stock in any of them, except as evidence of a lively culture. And the truth is we've had enough tragedy in this town, enough real hardship, that a monster in the lake is hardly necessary." He looked down at Mayor Dunlop, locking eyes with her only briefly before lifting his gaze back to me. "Excuse me," he said, taking a step past me before stopping and turning back to me. "It was a pleasure to meet you, Miss Reagan. There's so much to see and appreciate here; I'd love to show you around."

"How can I say no to that?"

He smiled, his gaze dropping to his feet for a second.

I couldn't quite get a read on him. There seemed to be something beneath the surface of his hospitality, but I couldn't tell what.

"Oh yes, and I almost forgot, I would be delighted to host you and your team at my home for a St. George's Day feast."

"Oh yeah. I read about St. George's Day when I was researching the island," I said. "Unfortunately, we're flying out Sunday."

"Although the feast is traditionally held on the Monday," John said, "we do things a little differently here. Are you available Saturday evening?"

"That's a very nice offer, but I wouldn't want to put you out. I'm sure a large crowd of TV people would be a tight fit."

Mayor Dunlop smiled at O'Donahue, and he looked back at her with a mischievous gleam in his eye. There was an inside joke there somewhere.

He tugged at the bottom of his sweater and smiled widely. "Well, I may have to move a chair or end table, but I'm sure I can find the room."

"You've seen Showalter House? By the mouth of the bay?" Mayor Dunlop asked.

"Yes, I have," I said. "It's marvellous."

"Well, that's John's humble abode," she said.

"Really?"

John nodded. "When I took it over, it was in shambles," he said. "You can imagine what our weather does to a century home when it isn't properly maintained."

"I can only imagine. It looks to be in pristine condition now, though," I said.

"Then you must come over and see the interior."

Our shooting schedule gave us some wiggle room, taking weather and other anomalies into consideration, and we'd likely be done by Saturday dinnertime.

"I'll have to confirm it with my producer," I said, "but it should be fine."

"Splendid!" He gave me a shy smile before turning and continuing on in his slow and controlled manner toward the sweets table. Although he was a lithe man, closer to being frail than sturdy, he moved with a quiet confidence. I noticed that the others seemed to swirl around him deferentially.

"Nobody is more passionate about Robert's Arm than John O'Donahue," Mayor Dunlop said. "He's a one-man historical society."

"I don't doubt it," I said.

"Mayor Dunlop, let me introduce you to the rest of the team," Danny said, stepping in and whisking her away.

Their departure seemed to create a tangible wake, one that engulfed me. I stood there for a moment, watching the little get-together as though it were playing out on the other side of one-way glass.

A voice cut through my reverie. "It's lovely to get the chance to speak more than a scant few words to you, dear."

Mary and Fred, the proprietors, had broken away from the crowd, reclaiming their spot near the front steps of the inn.

"Likewise," I said, not really knowing what to say.

"We hope you enjoy your stay here," Fred said.

"This is quite a breathtaking spot," I said, looking around. "This might turn out to be more like a vacation than work."

"We like to make all our guests feel that way," Fred said, hoping for laughs.

Mary gave him a short, playful elbow. "Fred means we don't usually get guests out here hunting Cressie. Just fishermen and hikers."

"Fishermen," Fred scoffed.

"American tourists," Mary clarified.

They seemed like a nice couple, about retirement age, who had earned their wrinkles and now the chance to enjoy the life of quaint country inn proprietors.

"Have you spent a lot of time out on the water?" I asked Fred.

"Only three-quarters of my life," he said. "I fished cod for a living before this."

"How about Lake Crescent itself?"

"Oh sure. Lived in Robert's Arm all my life."

"Have you ever seen Cressie?"

"Oh, I've seen things moving in the water out there that could have been big, but it's hard to tell with nothing to compare it to."

"Fair enough," I said. "How about you, Mary?"

"I know people who have — good, reliable people — but I've never seen anything like a giant eel."

"Beave Cannings is the man to ask about Cressie," Fred said.

"Yes, we spoke to him before coming here, actually," I said. "He's very knowledgeable. He mentioned a snowmobile accident that happened on the lake back in the eighties. Do you remember it?"

"Sure, we heard about it," Fred said, like it was a sale at the local department store.

"It must have been a shock to the community," I said.

"People falling through the ice is always a tragedy," Mary said. "But that sort of thing happens a lot on this island, as you can imagine."

"And maybe sometimes it doesn't happen at all," Fred said.

"I don't understand what you mean," I said.

"What my husband means is that there was some question as to whether old Pop Fitzcairn saw what he thought he saw that night —"

"It must be two, three hundred feet from Pop's bridge down to the lake," Fred said. "And this was in the black of night. To not only see the riders, but to be able to identify them? Seems like a stretch to me. Always has."

"Sorry, what bridge?" I asked.

Fred laughed and explained to me that around those parts, a bridge refers to what we would call a porch.

"You think Pop Fitzcairn made it up then?" I asked.

Fred shrugged. "Lou had been ruffling feathers around town, him and that girl of his. They owed money —"

Mary looked at him sharply. Airing the town's dirty laundry to a guest probably wasn't the best business strategy. She turned and gave me a knowing smile.

"Fred's not alone in his thinking. The RCMP sent divers down, but they didn't turn up anything — no bodies, not even a snowmobile."

"Legend has it that the search was called off due to the divers encountering large eels," I pressed.

"As thick as a man's thigh?" Mary said. "We've all heard that one. It seems to me that they just gave up, if I remember clearly."

"I know three people who swear that there was a hole in the ice before sundown. How anyone could have missed it, even in the dark, is beyond me," Fred added.

"So then, what happened to the victims, Lou Fenton and the woman he was with?"

"Sarah somethin' or other," Fred said.

"Tindall, Sarah Tindall!" Mary said, looking pleased with herself. "Seems to me more like she just picked up and left. Probably went west to Toronto or Vancouver or some such place. People come and go from here all the time. They go away for work, they go away to hunt. Half the houses in this town are empty half the year. Only the old folks stay put. At some point she left and just didn't come back."

"Do you remember the date of the snowmobile accident?" I asked.

"*Supposed* snowmobile accident," Fred added.

They looked at each other before looking at me and shaking their heads.

"I thought you was here about Cressie?" Fred asked.

"I am," I said. "It might not seem like it, but this is all related. Part of my job is to try to pin down the local legends about Cressie and understand their origin. When I first started researching Cressie, I read that RCMP divers encountered abnormally large eels when looking for the remains of the pilot of a plane that crashed into the lake. It turns out it wasn't a plane crash, but a snowmobile accident, so that's one aspect of the story clarified. If I can determine the date of the accident, I can reach out to the RCMP and maybe interview the divers and confirm whether or not they saw anything out of the ordinary."

Mary nodded. "That's very interesting, dear. You're like a detective."

"In a sense, I suppose I am," I said, smiling.

A grey sky moved in over the trees at the far edge of the property. The yellow birdhouse that hung from a steel pole in the grass between the inn and the stone walkway seemed to dim and fade as the sunlight retreated across the lawn. The weather here could turn on a dime, I knew, with several currents converging on the island and cold air flowing down from the Arctic.

Saad caught my eye and moved in a wide arc around the small crowd and toward me. He looked tired and moved a little clumsily. He was in the habit of going to bed well after midnight, and not accustomed to being up before eleven in the morning. When I was running ScienceIA and Saad worked for me, his schedule didn't matter. But TV was different than running a website.

"Didn't sleep much?" I asked.

He shrugged. "My niece is starring in a school play. I had to watch her practise over Skype."

I didn't know the exact time difference between Canada and Pakistan, only that it's significant, swapping day for night.

"It must be hard to maintain a relationship with them when they're so far away."

"It's like my nieces are totally different every time I see them."

I looked over at Danny, who was standing beside Lindsay, eating a blueberry tart and schmoozing with the mayor and our hosts. He made a big production of sampling the tart.

"I picked the berries myself," the lady behind the table said, her words carried to me on the wind.

Danny nodded a lot as he chewed that first bite, then held the tart in the air and gestured toward me.

"Did you see Mr. O'Donahue leave?" I asked Saad, ignoring Danny.

"The older gentleman? No."

"Hm. That's weird. He doesn't seem the type to leave without saying a formal goodbye."

"Do you think that means I can disappear, too?" he said, stifling a yawn.

"I'll cover for you."

"Thanks, but if you're staying, I better as well."

"We'll try to wrap this up soon."

THREE

More "Cressie" sightings in Newfoundland

The alleged sighting of a mysterious creature has reignited talk of whether Newfoundland's Crescent Lake has its own version of the Loch Ness Monster. Reports of "Cressie" sightings in the lake near Robert's Arm about 400 kilometres north-west of St. John's on Notre Dame Bay go back over half a century.

— CBC News, August 14, 2003

THE INN SEEMED LARGER IN THE SILENCE. The welcome wagon had gone, and with it any illusion that Robert's Arm was a bustling town a short drive from an urban centre. After connecting to the inn's Wi-Fi, I searched for news stories about the snowmobile accident but came up empty. Small-town newspapers tend not to digitize their archives and put them online, and the accident would've have taken place long before the local paper had a website.

Lindsay had been the first to duck out of the greeting party. I'd have given even money it'd be either her or Saad. Maybe staffing my team with intellectual introverts would end up making boring TV, but I trusted them both to do the kind of work I wanted on the show.

Lindsay's suitcase sat open on her bed. She was taking out her clothes and arranging them neatly in the dresser of our room. I thought to tell her she could use more than the bottom two drawers — my intention was to live out of my suitcase, and just throw my dirty clothes in a plastic grocery bag.

"I haven't had a roommate since freshman year," I said, smiling, trying to act like a warm, friendly person.

"Huh," Lindsay said, shifting clothes around in the drawer to make more room.

"How about you?"

Lindsay closed the drawer with a squeal and a bang. "This is not where I saw my life going," she said.

"That makes two of us."

In my wildest dreams, I never imagined I'd be producing and starring in a cryptozoological documentary series for a cable network. What I'd given up to get here was days spent sitting in my apartment posting stories to my website. Lindsay, on the other hand, had lost more. When she and two other female students at the University of Washington were harassed by their Ph.D. adviser, they'd filed a Title IX complaint, which led to an investigation. Lindsay, who was until then primarily a crusader for science education and communication, shifted her attention to the issue of the harassment of female science students. It was still a huge problem, according to a 2014 study in which 64 percent of female anthropologists and other field scientists reported that they'd experienced some form of sexual harassment in their workplaces. Lindsay's shift in focus didn't make her any friends in academia, and she took a step back from finishing her Ph.D.

When we first met at the Roanoke Valley Bigfoot Festival, Lindsay and I got off to a rough start. There was no doubt in either of our minds that she was the smarter of the two of us. She made no attempts to hide it, either. But when she left the University of Washington after the investigation, I had to offer her a job.

"I guess I should thank you," she said. "For this opportunity. It'll look good on my resumé."

"You might even have a little fun," I said.

Lindsay undid her braid, wearing the hair band as a bracelet as she combed her fingers through her hair. She looked out of place here, like a technicolor character in a black-and-white movie. She was supposed to be in a southeast Asian jungle studying the mating habits of gibbons or something, not in a remote corner of Newfoundland looking for sea monsters. "Don't get carried away," she said, giving me at least the hint of a smile. "I'm still a little surprised you picked me for this."

"To be honest, I didn't really like you at first. You humiliated me that first night we met. But I knew you were smart. I knew you were going to make something of yourself. Then I heard about the stand you took. That was brave. I thought to myself, *I need a smart and brave woman like that on my team*. Between the two of us, we could inject a dose of feminism into this show, at least subliminally, like it might just diffuse over the airwaves."

"Speaking of the airwaves. Come on, *Creature X*? Really?"

"It wasn't my idea to call the show that."

"*Creature exxxxx*," she said, drawing out that last syllable. "*Creature X!*" She raised her hands and curled her fingers into claws.

"I know, right?" I said.

She shrugged, then smiled. "Although, at this point," she said, "I'm not above saying *Wait, what's that over there!* to any rustling bush or blurry figure."

"Yes, you are," I said. "That's why I brought you on."

Lindsay smiled. It was like she tried not to but couldn't help it.

We weren't out to make the typical sensationalist open-ended time-waster. I wanted real science to engage my audience as I had done for years with my website.

Suddenly, I wasn't feeling quite so tired. Problems outside my control had that effect on me, like they made steam in my stomach powering a turbine of uneasy energy. "Want to go for a walk?"

"I'm feeling pretty exhausted," she said, then, as though compelled by a sense of obligation or manners, added, "Rain check?"

"Sure," I said. "I just need to clear my head, you know?"

Following the lake's edge, I walked until the sky grew so dark the water in the distance was the same colour as the grass, like charcoal in the moonlight. There was no beach or boat launch that I could see, just trees, grass, rocks and then, abruptly, water. As the moon rose higher, seeking to establish dominance in the night sky, it added a silver glow to the tops of waves otherwise invisible.

The surface of the water broke. There was a quick popping sound, followed by a sucking noise. I shone the light from my phone over the lake but saw nothing other than concentric ripples spreading outward.

The ocean breathed cold air down my neck. Branches on the trees waved in silent panic as they stood on the shore before the abyssal black water of the lake. The isolation of the remote town on this island felt quantifiable. The ground felt hard beneath my feet, like it still hadn't thawed out. The grass was stiff and bristly. The chill was energizing, but I just wanted to curl up under the covers and go to sleep.

Inside, the inn was nice and warm. It felt almost like an old-time Christmas, complete with Danny LeDoux haunting the armchair in the living room like the ghost of Jacob Marley.

"There's nothing here," he said as I came in, not looking up from his tablet.

"How do you know that?"

"I just do. I can feel it. I have a nose for what makes good TV, and we're not finding it here."

My blood was suddenly boiling and a flame of defiance burned in me. I wasn't about to let Danny smugly dismiss my first time out as leader of this team. "Twenty bucks says we'll find something sensational," I said, as though possessed.

"You're on," he said. "My bet is the people here made the whole thing up for the tourist dollars. In fact, I bet half of the monsters we hear about were dreamed up by local chambers of commerce."

Back in the room, I found Lindsay in the bathroom taking out her contact lenses. Her long dark-brown hair was tied up in a loose, sloppy bun, and she wore flannel pants and a blue T-shirt. On the front of her shirt was an anthropomorphized pi symbol holding a microphone and accompanied by a speech bubble that said, *Stop me if I'm repeating myself.*

I wanted to talk to her. I wanted to talk to someone, anyone, but it seemed like unburdening myself to someone who was technically my employee might mean giving up any sense of authority. And by the time I even thought about taking a chance, anyway, Lindsay was on her bed, laptop on her knees, headphones in. She was watching a video, the flickering images reflected in her glasses.

Then came my turn to stand in the bathroom, in front of the mirror, to remove all the makeup I'd caked on for my new career in showbiz. My skin wasn't used

to the abuse: I was breaking out. I changed into pyja-
mas, brushed my teeth, and settled into bed.

The floorboards creaked in the hallway. Someone —
probably Chris or Danny — was sneaking out.

F O U R

In the local oral tradition, sightings of
Cressie go back to the turn of the century
when one of Robert's Arm's first residents,
remembered today as "Grandmother
Anthony," was startled from her berry-
picking by a giant serpent out on the lake.
— R.A. Bragg, *Beothuk Times*,
Summer 1993

THE NEXT MORNING, I MET CAPTAIN PHIL
aboard his ship. When I'd left the inn, the rest of the
Creature X team was still in bed or having breakfast.
I decided to walk to the harbour alone, breathing in
the air, taking in the sights, letting the sounds of boats,
birds, and the shouts of fishermen engulf me.

Captain Phil sat on the railing of the *Darling Mae*
drinking coffee from a thermos, staring out across the

gently rippling waves, his eyes narrowed. I expected him to make a wise or enigmatic observation about the sea, but instead he just wished me a good morning.

"How goes the Cressie hunt?"

"We're still looking," I said.

"In a hundred years of sightings, nobody's even taken a picture of the thing. Can't expect to hook it in a couple days."

"What's your take on Cressie, Captain Phil? Real or imagined? Have you ever seen it?"

"No, not me. I know plenty of folks who swear by it being out there, though."

"But between you and me, what's your honest opinion?"

"Well, I know people on the island who are convinced they've seen fairies in the woods — honest-to-goodness fairies." He leaned in closer, wide-eyed, the smell of coffee on his breath. "What I think is that people who get tired of staring at water, rocks, and trees all day start seeing more than what's out there, whether it's fairies or giant eels or pirate gold."

"Pirate gold?"

"Every so often we hear about some old artifacts being found on the island, usually farther south, and all the treasure hunters come out of the woodwork, thinking it must be one of the hideaways of Peter Easton or Jack Brill or some other notorious pirate."

"How likely is it to find buried treasure on the island?"

He wiped the sides of his mouth with the back of his hand, his bristly stubble unlikely to scratch the leathery skin of his hands. "Just where she is in the ocean and her shape, Newfoundland was a great place to launch raids on vessels travelling to the New World, then hide with the booty after. We had our fair share of pirates, it's true. But I ain't found any treasure yet, and I don't know anyone else who has, neither."

"There is a fascinating history and culture here," I said.

"You can sure say that."

"Your point about people seeing what they want to see is exactly why I want to talk to trained observers, people less likely to mistake a log in the water for a giant eel. Like police officers, for example. When we visited the RCMP detachment in Springdale, we asked about a plane crash that brought the RCMP divers, and they said they had no records of the incident. Beave Cannings told me later it wasn't a plane crash, it was a snowmobile accident."

"And he'd know," Captain Phil said. "No one goes gaga for the whole Cressie story like ol' Beave." He took a long sip of coffee. "They say that Cressie makes big holes in the ice. They can be very dangerous. Folks use the lake as a highway when it freezes over. You can look out on the lake any winter's night and see the lights of the snowmobiles as they zip across."

According to my dad's notebook, Cressie wasn't the only Canadian lake monster blamed for mysterious holes in frozen lake surfaces. Old Ned, as the story goes, breaks holes through the ice in New Brunswick's Lake Utopia.

"Have you seen them?"

"I've seen the holes," he said. "I've never seen what's making them."

"Do you remember the RCMP sending divers out to search for snowmobilers?"

"I remember that night, the accident, sure, and the Mounties. But I don't know anything about no big eels." He leaned back a little, setting the thermos on the railing of his boat. "All's I know is the talk in town and what I saw from my window. I'd fallen asleep on the couch watching the Canadiens stomp the Leafs in overtime. The missus saw the commotion outside — the town had one ambulance and one fire engine, just like now — and she came into the den to wake me up. The next day I heard Pop Fitzcairn saw a snowmobile fall into the black water around midnight. He said it was a man driving and a woman holding his waist. Pop once told me he could still hear her scream, even years later."

So, the snowmobile fell through a hole in the ice. Did that particular aspect of the Cressie legend begin with this accident? Or did the accident just help perpetuate it? I wondered.

"Is the man who witnessed this still around?"

Captain Phil pointed over my shoulder. "Pop? He lives on the lake side. Crescent Avenue splits into Tommy's Arm Road. Gotta go all the way to the end of the paved road and follow the gravel one as it winds up through the trees."

"How long did it take for the RCMP to arrive?" I asked.

"Can't be sure," he said. "All I know is by the time they sent divers down, it would've been more of a search and less of a rescue, if you get my meaning. No one could survive in those waters long."

"Do you remember the exact date of the accident?"

Assuming my goodwill with the RCMP detachment was running on empty, I didn't want to call Sergeant Deloitte and have him dig through dust-covered filing cabinets unless I could narrow down the search for him a little.

"Sorry," he said. "Memory's good, just a little short, like the rest o' me. They never found any bodies. The current's strong under the ice. But Lou's got a marker in the cemetery. It'll have the date on it."

"I didn't see a cemetery in town."

"It's down the road a ways. The Methodist United Church cemetery on Pilley's Island."

"Is it far?"

"Oh, 'bout a ten-minute drive. Five if my wife's driving," he said, the shadow of a smile playing at the corners of his mouth.

"If you don't mind my saying so, the accident doesn't seem to have been a big deal. What I mean is, for such a small town, the tragic death of two residents seems like a distant, foggy memory. Maybe I just haven't spoken to the right people. I guess you and Lou weren't close."

"I knew him to say 'good day,' and I knew his family. The whole town did," he said, wiping his hand across his mouth again. "Lou'd been having some trouble around town. He couldn't find work ... and his house caught fire a while before the accident. I think most folks just assumed he'd taken off for greener pastures."

"And since no body was ever recovered …"

"I think it was easier for most folks to believe he and that girl had just run off."

Shortly after the crew came aboard, we set sail, so to speak, cruising around the lake as we'd done the day before. Captain Phil was more talkative, as if he had expanded his skill set to include tour guide. Duncan and I stood on either side of him; Saad, Lindsay, Chris, and Clyde looked out over the port side at the town and the trees and rocks that rose out of the water. Danny was on the bridge with us, though seemingly lost in thought. Dr. Willoughby continued his sonar survey of the murky depths.

"That there is Devil's Cove Head," Captain Phil told us. "Lots of legends about that spot. A strange pile of rocks was found behind there a while ago. A man named William Anthony dug 'em up and found a tomb filled with artifacts. They were handed over to the RCMP, only to be shipped to a museum in St. John's. But they were mislabelled, and no one knows exactly what happened to them."

"That happens all too frequently," Duncan said. "Artifacts or specimens get lost in the shuffle, as it were."

As we careened at a gentle pace, the odd speedboat ripped through the water ahead, creating a wake for our bow to cut through. Captain Phil brought us to the traps we'd set the previous day, and Duncan and Dr. Willoughby checked the herring in each. All the bait was untouched. If there was a giant eel in Lake Crescent, it wasn't biting.

Finally, the *Darling Mae* turned back at the mouth of Tommy's Arm River. As we slowly drifted back toward town, Chris filmed the hills, evergreen trees, and rocky cliffs. We cruised the stretch of coast that brought us back to the bay and the harbour. No one expected to spot a giant eel, so we sat back and enjoyed the ride. Captain Phil pointed out all the coves as we drifted past, naming each one but not providing any explanation as to how they ended up with names like Measles Cove. Then the land narrowed, as if a giant thumb and forefinger were pinching the route to the harbour.

"What's going on there?" Danny said, pointing to the approaching dock.

Raised voices travelled to us over the water. Soon, we could see that the boat moored in the harbour was the *Tide Queen*, captained by Jimmy O'Donahue. Danny motioned to Captain Phil to bring us in.

A westerly wind was blowing ripples across the water's surface as a small group of townsfolk gathered by the edge of the lake, chatting loudly among themselves.

Jimmy O'Donahue was standing on the stern of the *Tide Queen* with a megaphone, looking like a modern-day P.T. Barnum. I couldn't make out his words, more from the distortion than distance.

O'Donahue's two sidekicks knelt down to pick something up from the deck. They seemed to struggle, blowing hard and wheezing as they stood upright again, then squatted like Olympians. When they stood again, they held between them an object that was long and grey, the sun shimmering off its slick back.

It was a massive eel.

"I give you Cressie!" O'Donahue yelled dramatically as the two men teetered back and forth, the boat listing gently. "Proof that we got some giant eels 'round here."

"No way," I muttered, stepping onto the dock and approaching the *Tide Queen*.

Chris took position to my right, camera hoisted on his shoulder. The residents of Robert's Arm present looked impressed but not awestruck. If Jimmy was expecting fanfare, he must have been disappointed.

"That's a big eel there, boy," an old fisherman said, seemingly to himself.

Other fisherman stepped off their boats and came over to get a closer look. A blue pickup truck pulled over on Main Street, and a man and a woman got out to witness the spectacle. Even the doors of the United Church opened, the minister standing with his hands on his hips.

The creature was maybe seven feet long. Not a world record by any stretch, but much bigger than the local eels. The area behind the head to about the middle of the body was thick and fat, almost like a human torso. The rest of the eel was its long, sleek tail. Its jaw was slack and its mouth hung open, as though astounded it had been caught by the likes of Jimmy O'Donahue.

"I'd like to examine it," I said, making my way through the crowd.

"Last I checked, you weren't interested," Jimmy said loudly. He flashed what my dad would've referred to as a "shit-eating grin." His two cronies on the deck of the *Tide Queen* smiled back at their leader, chuckling their subservient chuckles.

"So, you're just going to, what, keep that eel all to yourself? Maybe mount in on your wall or have it for dinner? Come on. Let us look at it."

"Certainly, little lady. Certainly. Have a good, long look."

Dr. Willoughby sidled up on my left side, cupping a hand over his eyes and squinting at the eel.

"I meant properly examine it. I'd like Dr. Willoughby to take a look."

"That can be arranged," Jimmy said.

"It's a conger, all right," Dr. Willoughby said. "I can tell that much from here."

"Have you ever seen one in these waters?" I asked him.

"Not in fresh water," he said. "Eels follow ocean currents when spawning. They tend not to deviate from them."

"Then you're in for a special treat. I caught this eel in the lake, no ocean currents there," Jimmy said.

"Can my team examine it properly?" I asked again.

"Everything is negotiable," he said. "Why don't you come aboard? We'll work something out."

· ● ·

Jimmy agreed to a closer examination of the specimen but with one stipulation: we could not damage the eel in any way — it had to be returned to him in pristine condition. That created problems for us, because I wanted to dissect the animal. First, it would make interesting video. But second, and more importantly, it would help us determine if the specimen was indeed from Lake Crescent. Its stomach contents held the key to its habitat and lifestyle. If we found ten pounds of mackerel in its gut, we'd know it wasn't living in fresh water. Also, dissection would tell us if the eel had been recently frozen. If Jimmy O'Donahue was perpetrating a hoax, he may have carted in a frozen eel. Small ice crystals in the tissue would give that away.

But if he was telling the truth, it would be a huge discovery. Lake monster sightings from all over the continent would be given a lot more credibility, not to mention the ramifications for conventional marine biologists. How might such a discovery change how science views these watersheds?

But there was no way Jimmy was being honest. I wasn't going to let myself hope he was sincere, not for even a second. I can make room in my worldview for coincidence, but not a guy like Jimmy O'Donahue catching a conger eel in Lake Crescent on the second day we happened to be in town.

F I V E

In the early 1980s, a huge hole appeared in the ice covering the lake. With no reasonable explanation for this phenomenon, residents believed that Cressie was the most likely culprit.

— Downhome,
September 26, 2008

DANNY LEDOUX SAT DRINKING A COFFEE and swiping through the pictures of the eel Jimmy O'Donahue claimed he'd caught in Lake Crescent. A dozen shots of the animal had been uploaded to the community Facebook page within an hour of Jimmy's spectacular revelation. We had reporters calling the inn to speak with us, one from the local newspaper and one from the public radio station. The press was good in the long term, since it built interest in the

Cressie phenomenon, but bad in the short term, since we wanted an audience coming to our website and TV program, not the Newfoundland press.

Danny's jacket hung on the back of his chair. He was also looking over the footage Chris had shot of the eel, his tablet open next to his laptop for a side-by-side comparison with the Facebook images. He tapped his left temple and furrowed his brow a little, so deep in contemplation I wasn't sure he knew I was there.

I cleared my throat. "He wants five thousand dollars to rent the eel," I said. "And to show us where he caught it."

"Yeah, that's, like, nothing," he said, tapping the screen of his tablet. "Why come to me about this? You have control of the discretionary spending."

"If we're getting scammed, the amount doesn't matter," I said.

"This is TV. Everybody is scamming somebody. Five thousand bucks is cheap. Walk with me."

He stood up, set his tablet on the table, and slipped his jacket on.

"Should you phone the network?" I asked. "The legal department might have something to say about this."

"You're a big girl, Laura, it's time to start making big-girl decisions."

I searched for a response, my inner censors bleeping out expletives as I did so. But before my anger relented and I was able to walk and talk again, Danny left the room, the screen door clapping shut behind him.

We started around the outside of the inn, toward the gazebo and the lake beyond it. I was playing catch-up, following the scent of his aftershave. Evening grosbeaks looked like Christmas lights, their golden bodies and black-and-white wings fluttering among the branches of the evergreen trees. A silver fox brazenly jogged along the grass at the edge of the property before disappearing into the trees. Despite its name, the fox's lean low body looked black in the shadow of the forest.

Danny broke the silence. "Once, to get a shot of a coyote hunting and tracking a rabbit, I rented a coyote from a game farm and bought a rabbit from a pet store. Obviously, the cute bunny who'd never seen a predator in its short life didn't last very long, even against a canine with little real-world hunting experience."

"That's —"

"Despicable? Unethical? Selfish? That's the game, Laura. Do you know how long it takes to get really dramatic footage? The kind that boosts ratings?"

"No," I said.

"Time is money. We don't have enough of it to make programs that people really want to see. Sometimes we have to get creative. Did you know that Disney Studios once shot a documentary where they forced some lemmings off a cliff to show that they committed mass suicide?"

"That's a myth," I said. "Some species of lemmings try to migrate en masse across large bodies of water. None of them commit mass suicide."

"People didn't know it was a myth then. And yeah, Disney was exposed more than twenty years later, but what matters is the Oscar that *White Wilderness* won in

1958, not some investigative journalism people don't care about."

"So, you want a big eel carcass, regardless of our inability to prove its provenance?"

"No, I want the story, and I want footage of that eel's ugly corpse, preferably hung on a hook next to you so we can see the lovely host of *Creature X* being dwarfed by this monster. If we can prove it's a hoax, even better. It worked for us last time. Show the audience how clever you and the team are. Do some science, like you're always going on about."

I stared at Danny.

"What?" he asked.

"Nothing."

"Nothing?"

"I'm just a little surprised," I said.

"About my negotiable morality?"

"No, I just would never have thought you'd let yourself get played for a fool."

He shrugged. "I'm not such an egomaniac that I'd throw away a good thing when it lands in my lap," he said. "That money is just more economic stimulus for this town. I'd say the town could use it. You don't want to shell out five grand? Fine. Negotiate."

"Jimmy won't even permit us to dissect the eel," I said.

"Too bad. Remember what that alien autopsy tape did for Fox in the nineties? I'd love footage of a sea serpent autopsy."

"Necropsy," I said.

"What?"

"Autopsies are for humans. Animals get necropsies."

"Just get some footage we can use," he said, his eyes flaring with impatience.

We had no lab in which to examine the eel, and none of the locals were exactly volunteering their dining rooms, but we were given the okay to conduct our examination in an old fish flake across the road from the harbour. It didn't look like much from the outside, just an old wooden shack covered in sheets of fake-brick siding in various stages of peeling. Behind the siding, the walls were constructed of wooden boards so old they'd faded to grey. All we needed, however, was space, a flat surface, and electricity — the latter obtained via a power line that led from a nearby hydro pole to a rusty metal one attached to the roof of the hut.

It would be a tight squeeze inside with all of us, our equipment, and the giant eel, which was all the excuse Danny needed not to cram inside the fish flake with the rest of us. Instead, he and Lindsay decided to walk the road that curved around the lake, shooting video of the surrounding terrain, the trees bent almost horizontal from the stiff wind. Although they moved slowly, like tourists taking in the sights, I couldn't help but notice them meandering toward the van; knowing Danny, there was a good chance of a coffee run in the near future.

While Saad and Duncan carried the eel, which was wrapped in a canvas tarp, Dr. Willoughby opened the padlock with a key the mayor had provided. Captain Phil arrived shortly after, almost hobbling a little, carrying a work light attached to an orange extension cord. I'd never paid attention to the way he moved over dry land.

Once inside, the captain set up the light. Saad and Duncan laid the canvas over the wooden table in the centre of the room. Chris set his camera up on a tripod in the corner while Saad and I fastened GoPros to our headgear. We wanted to record every aspect of our investigative procedures.

Duncan did the honours, peeling back the tarp with a magician's flourish. The noxious stench of fish filled the room instantly. Saad and I reflexively brought our hands to our faces, but Duncan and Willoughby had known it was coming.

"The trimethylamine oxide in fish that allows them to maintain fluid balance is broken down by bacteria after death. Hence the smell," Duncan said matter-of-factly.

"Good to know," I said, my voice muffled behind my hand.

"I find it unlikely that an eel this size would have ignored the bait in all our traps," Dr. Willoughby said. "Such easy meals are hard to turn down."

"Look at the swelling around the pectoral fins," Dr. Willoughby said, pulling the light closer.

"Air trapped in the swim bladder?" Duncan asked.

"This is something else. Eels have the remarkable ability to draw in water through their mouths and filter it through the branchial cavity. This specimen seems to have a large amount of water stored in that cavity."

Saad, Dr. Laidlaw, and Dr. Willoughby began pulling rubber gloves over their hands. The creature's mouth was open, and its cold dead eyes stared up at me. Dr. Willoughby began examining it with a magnifying glass, starting with the mandible as Duncan measured it from tip to tail.

"It's a conger, all right," Dr. Willoughby said. "European."

"How can you tell?" I asked.

"The brownish-green colour and its size are dead giveaways," he answered.

"Not to mention that the dorsal fin is much longer than the anal fin in *Conger conger*," said Duncan, "as compared to *Conger oceanica*." He pointed at the long ridge that ran along the eel's back starting just behind the pectoral fin, then looped his hand around the tail to the fin on the underside to make his point.

It was a haunting specimen, I had to admit. *Atavistic* was the word that jumped to mind. A relic from a bygone epoch.

Saad gently poked and prodded the eel with his gloved finger, paying special attention to the swollen branchial cavity. "We have to get the water out of this thing," he said.

"Why?" Dr. Willoughby asked.

"It'll tell us where the animal came from."

"The salinity," Duncan said, nodding.

"How are we going to test that?" I asked. "Do you have the right equipment?"

Saad stared at the deceased eel as though he was hoping it would turn, look up at him, and provide the answer. The others looked at Saad expectantly — he'd already proven to them how clever he was, time and again. Yet I feared that they expected too much from him. How often did a problem like this pop up?

"Dr. Willoughby, do you have a conductivity meter by chance?" he asked, falling back on his background in chemical engineering.

I should have known better than to doubt him.

"Of course," Willoughby replied. "I use one for electrofishing."

"Excellent," Saad said.

"Electrofishing?" I asked.

"It's a means of sampling fish populations in rivers. We submerge a cathode and an anode, DC electricity flowing between them. This drives the fish toward the anode and allows us to determine which species are in the vicinity and how dense their populations are."

"We'll need a plastic container to empty the branchial cavity into, and another one the same size to store a sample of the water from the lake for comparison," Saad said.

"Fresh water shouldn't conduct electricity at all, whereas salt water would have a high level of conductivity. Right?" I said.

"Exactly."

"Keep in mind the water in Crescent Lake has a higher level of salinity than most lakes," Dr. Willoughby added.

"Still, the conductivity meter should be sensitive

enough to distinguish between brackish water and salt water," Saad said.

"How do we get the water out of the eel?" I asked.

"We vent it," Dr. Willoughby said. "Same way you get the air out of a fish's swim bladder."

The team spent the next several minutes scrambling to assemble the necessary tools: a syringe, the conductivity meter, two plastic containers, and a sample of lake water. We all then offered gloved hands to hold the eel while Dr. Willoughby made an incision tiny enough that we hoped Jimmy wouldn't notice. Never mind that he'd be able to watch us performing the procedure when the show eventually aired. The cloudy water drained in spurts into a plastic jug as Dr. Willoughby pressed around the incision. Duncan held the mouth of the jug to the incision, collecting the fluid.

Saad took the conductivity meter and waited for it to calibrate for the temperature of the water, a process that took half a minute. Then he tested the lake sample as his baseline.

As we waited, I found the smell had become too much. Or maybe it was all in my head. The space inside the fish flake was claustrophobic.

"Compared to the sample of water from the lake," Saad said, "the water we extracted from the eel has a much higher level of salinity."

"So, we've been had?" I said.

"I'd say so. The lake water tested as having a conductivity of twenty-eight millisiemens per centimetre. The water from the eel was fifty-three."

"I knew there was something fishy going on," Duncan said.

"Oh, please, don't," I said, shaking my head and smiling.

"This is a fine kettle of fish," he continued.

"Stop!" I pointed my finger at him like it was loaded.

"Fine," he said. "So, do we confront O'Donahue about his little fish story?"

"That's the five-thousand-dollar question," I said.

I stepped outside and over to a patch of dirt road where a streak of sunlight poured through the trees, swinging my arms to savour the space outside the confines of the fish flake. I inhaled long, deep breaths of fresh air, then pulled out my phone and keyed in Danny's number.

Instead of a greeting, I heard the sound of a long sip.

"It's a hoax," I said. "I'm gonna confront O'Donahue."

"Atta girl," he said. "But wait until after he takes you to the spot where he supposedly caught it. Let's get some ROV footage first. We are storytelling, after all. We need some suspense: murky water shots, stock footage of eels, the whole thing. Then, at the end of the day, science will win and the truth will come out."

The sound of tires crunching over gravel alerted me to a grey sedan slowly rolling up. A man in a plaid shirt with a jacket over top got out and gave me a slow wave. Nothing about his lean frame, loose walk, or sandy hair said *reporter*, but my gut told me to be on edge.

"Danny, I think there's a reporter here."

"Don't say a word to him, and make sure the others don't either," he said before hanging up.

I slipped the phone into my pocket and, pretending not to notice the approaching reporter, opened the door of the fish flake and told the guys to stay inside.

"Good day," the man said with a muted Newfoundland accent.

"Hello."

"I'm with the *Nor'easter*," he said. "Lawrence Mercier."

"You got here quick," I said.

"You can imagine not a lot goes viral in this part of the country, and I'm based out in Springdale. It wasn't a long drive. You're Laura Reagan, the cryptozoologist, right?"

"I am Laura Reagan, but I'm not sure I'd call myself that."

"Can I ask you some questions?"

We had a protocol for reporters, lines I'd practised in my head but had never had to say out loud. "My staff and I are contractually obligated not to disclose any of what we see while filming to any media aside from NatureWorld properties."

"I just want to know a few things about that eel," he pressed.

"I get that. I'm not trying to give you a hard time, but I can't tell you anything. Neither can any of my people."

"What about Dr. Charles Willoughby? He works for the province. It's his job to talk to us."

"I can't stop you from calling the Ministry of Fisheries and putting in a request with his supervisor. I'm sure Dr. Willoughby will be more than happy to comply with whatever the ministry suggests."

Mercier opened his jacket and rested a hand on his hip. He seemed like a man who liked to communicate through a stare down.

I didn't move; I didn't look away.

"Ever heard the expression 'There's no such thing as bad publicity'?" he asked. "It seems like we'd both be helping each other out here."

"Nope, never heard that one," I said.

Eventually, he threw up his hands, turned, and headed off toward the harbour and the *Tide Queen*. I was sure Jimmy would give him a better soundbite, anyway.

S I X

"It is not impossible," said Professor Frederick Aldrich, director and professor of biology at Memorial University, Newfoundland, "that prehistoric animals might have been cut off by land formations, and assuming the ability of the animals to survive in this new environment, and not only survive but reproduce, creatures such as those mentioned may in fact exist today."
— John Braddock, "Monsters of the Maritimes," *Atlantic Advocate*, January 1968

THERE WAS NOTHING I COULD DO TO STOP Jimmy from chasing his fifteen minutes of fame.

He welcomed Lawrence Mercier with open arms, the two of them standing on the dock in the shadow of the *Tide Queen*. Pretending to swipe through my phone, I walked obliquely in the direction of the dock, moving near enough to overhear some of their conversation. It seemed as if Jimmy wanted me to hear him, though, so I cut the act and walked over.

Jimmy spoke in clichés, like a football star doing a post-game interview, his voice loud as he pontificated into Mercier's recorder. His friends aboard the boat leaned over the gunwale, watching Jimmy and trying hard to maintain straight faces.

I had an urge to expose Jimmy as a fraud right then and there, but I bit my tongue and stuck to the plan. I made Jimmy agree to show us where he and his cronies "caught" that conger, but there was no point in setting out on the water then, with so little daylight left.

I circled back to the fish flake, leaving Mercier in Jimmy's hands. It would be a better story, sensational clickbait likely to get picked up nationally, maybe internationally. Every ripple on Loch Ness caught on tape and every Blobsquatch photographed in the Pacific Northwest ended up on my newsfeed.

As I walked up, Duncan exited the fish flake and took a deep breath of the cold air rolling in off the Atlantic.

Saad was right on his heels. "I need to take a shower."

"Maybe more than one," Dr. Willoughby said, emerging behind him.

"Surely you must be used to the smell, Willoughby," Duncan said, "and it's only us amateurs who make such a fuss."

"I've spent two-thirds of my life mucking about with fish, either in the water, on a boat, or in the lab. And I can tell you there is a great distinction between tolerating the smell and getting used to it," said Dr. Willoughby.

Clyde and Chris were the last to emerge, with armloads of camera and lighting equipment. We all headed toward the vans we'd parked alongside an old stone wall, the soles of six pairs of shoes scraping across the gravel.

"See that man on the dock, talking to Jimmy?" The team stopped and looked over my shoulder like a meerkat colony on alert. "He's a reporter. Danny wants us to keep our mouths shut around him."

"I thought I heard someone talking to you," Chris said absently. "Showers, change, then chow time?" He slammed the back doors of the van after securing his gear.

"Splendid idea," Duncan said. "Anything but fish and chips."

"You might be out of luck," Dr. Willoughby said. "Around here at least. Though I guess we could drive into Springdale for pizza or Chinese."

"I have to run out to Pilley's Island first," I said.

The men looked at me curiously.

"There's a lead I want to follow up on after I tell Jimmy that we're finished with his eel."

After letting Jimmy know he could come and retrieve his prize, Duncan, Dr. Willoughby, and Clyde took one of the vans back to their motel. The rest of us took the other back to the inn, where we found Lindsay and Danny sitting at the dining room table, to the left of the front door.

Lindsay was on her laptop, Danny on his smartphone. They both looked up from their devices as we came in, clustering by the row of hooks to hang up our coats.

Chris kicked his boots off by the door and crossed the threshold into the dining room, heading toward Danny. The two men smiled at each other. Danny's body language changed around Chris; he stopped being "on" and instead behaved like a normal person around a long-time colleague who had become a friend.

"How'd it go?" Danny asked.

Chris gave him a thumbs-up. "Got some great footage."

"Alien autopsy?"

Chris nodded. "Alien autopsy."

The words took me back to the nineties, to watching the hyped-up "documentary" on the couch in the living room with Dad. "The rest of the team is meeting us here in an hour," I called out from the doorway, "for dinner."

"Where are you going?" Danny asked.

"Pilley's Island, just down the highway."

"What's there?"

"A graveyard."

"Spooky," he said, adjusting his glasses. "Have fun now."

Lindsay tucked her laptop into a black canvas bag that hung on the chair beside her. "I'll go with you," she said.

Saad sat in the passenger seat and Lindsay climbed in the back. I rolled my window up the moment the cold air rushed in as we turned onto the highway. The sun had made a difference of about ten degrees, its rays holding back the chilling effect of the ocean breeze, but as it waned, I'd begun to feel the chill in my hands and on the back of my neck.

"Do you find it cold?" I said over my shoulder to Lindsay.

"I'm dressed for it," she said. I saw her tug at the collar of her parka in the rear-view mirror. "I was born in Harbin," she continued, "which is the same latitude as Siberia. I'm no stranger to the cold. They call it the Moscow of the East. Partly because of all the Russian architecture left over from the construction of the Trans-Siberian Railway, and partly because the climate is more like what we think of as Russia's than China's."

"I'm getting cold just hearing about it," I said. "Saad, you lived in northern Pakistan as a kid, right? How does it compare?"

"I don't actually remember it. I was only three," he said. "I lived most of my life in Karachi, which is like American summer all year round."

We headed east down Highway 380, through Robert's Arm. It was a quiet drive along a desolate and winding stretch of road, with small trees, scrub brush, and power lines surrounding us on both sides. Where the highway turned into Pilley's Island Road, the view changed dramatically, with piles of logs on the right and exposed rock to the left, then into walls of green pierced through with turn-offs that led to gravel drive-ways. Ponds eventually appeared on either side as we crossed the bridge spanning Flat Rock Tickle.

Finally, we came to the church. It sat atop a hill, a white mid-nineteenth-century wood building with a brown roof and red-brown trim. A white picket fence stretched around it, enclosing the small cemetery in back. I had the feeling no new bodies had been interred here in decades.

We parked on the gravel shoulder and walked through the open gate, pausing to see if anyone would appear and ask what business we had there. But beyond the fence was only windswept wild grasses and the spray from the waves crashing against the rocks.

As we wandered among the grave markers, many of the names were familiar, names I had encountered while reading about the region: Anthony, Colbourne, Hewlett, Harris, Ryan. Each came with a short inscription, *In Loving Memory Of*, *Loving Husband and Father*, even a simple *Here Lies* — vain attempts to encapsulate the meaning of a life on a slab of stone.

We fanned out as though we had a game plan all along. Even in a remote place like Pilley's Island, there were a lot of headstones, two centuries' worth, and it would take some time to find the one we were looking for if we didn't split up. The sun was already low in the sky.

I quickly eliminated the tall obelisks with the names of entire families etched onto them, as well as the moss-covered stones so old and weathered that the names had been almost completely worn away.

"Most of these markers are from the eighties," Saad called out.

Lindsay and I joined him in the southeast end of the cemetery. There were more of the same familiar names, Colbourne (*In Memory Of*), Anthony (*Loving Husband*), and even an O'Donahue (*Beloved Wife and Mother*). A few stones in, Lindsay found the headstone of Louis Roger Fenton. His date of death was February 29, 1988. Below the date, it read, *May the Road Rise to Meet You.*

"He died on a leap year," Lindsay said. "Weird."

"You're right. That is a little weird."

"Think it'll help us find a giant eel?" Lindsay said, genuinely curious, taking out her phone and snapping a picture of the gravestone.

"It's better than nothing," I said.

Saad looked out over the other headstones. "You suppose many of these have no graves underneath them?"

"I'd think so," I said. "Given the number of fishermen lost at sea."

"The ocean giveth and taketh away," Lindsay said, her voice earnest. "It's like God to people who earn their livelihood from it."

We began slowly walking back to the car. The church stood between us and the road, the ocean at our backs and the dead beneath our feet. The desolation and loneliness of the place hit me all at once. It was like the earth could give way beneath our feet and we'd slide into the ocean as if we'd never existed.

At least we now knew Lou Fenton's date of death. My phone had no signal, so the information was useless in that moment. I'd call Sergeant Deloitte from the inn, where the reception was dependable.

On the drive back, in the growing twilight, we saw a tow truck hoisting a silver Ford pickup from the gravel shoulder. The front end of the truck was totalled, and shards of the shattered headlights twinkled against the road like stars as the beams of our headlights swept over them. A moose cow lay at the side of the road, motionless. I slowed down but forced my eyes to stay on the road. Her calves were likely somewhere in the woods, waiting for their mother to find them. I remembered what it was like, waiting for my dad to come home, then finally realizing that he never would.

The rest of the team had already gathered on the lawn of the Lake Crescent Inn by the time we turned onto the gravel skirt of the tree-lined driveway. There was one unexpected face in the group: Beave Canning, our Cressie expert and local guide. He stood beside Duncan with a look of boyish glee on his face and a gap-toothed smile. It must have felt like his moment — an American TV crew and real scientists coming to look for his obsession, picking his brain, availing of his expertise. I smiled. I wanted him to enjoy it. My father had experienced the same thrill through his friendship with Dr. Berton Sorel, the one credentialed anthropologist who shared his belief in Bigfoot, and that acknowledgement can mean everything to a person who has dedicated their life to the fringes.

"Fish and chips it is," Duncan said, the disdain in his voice pulling it down an octave.

"I knows a good place," Beave said, beaming.

"You guys go on ahead," I said. "Saad and I still need to clean up."

Beave gave us the name of the place. "Will yuz be all right to find us?"

"The vans have GPS," I said.

Saad took a quick shower by his standards, but I still beat him downstairs with time to spare. I called the number on Sergeant Deloitte's business card. The phone rang and rang until I got his voice mail, an automated female voice informing me I'd reached the voice mail box of, then a clip of Sergeant Deloitte saying his own name. I left a message. Maybe with a precise date and the correction about the snowmobile accident, Deloitte would be able find the files pertaining to the incident and provide us with the names of the divers who supposedly encountered the "eels as thick as a man's thigh."

Lindsay volunteered to drive, gripping the steering wheel tightly as we drove toward the ocean, determined not to share the fate of the Ford pickup. Set back from the road, with a gravel parking lot in front, was a wood-and-glass building; the sign for Fenton's Fish and Chips featured a blue fish leaping from the painted water on either side.

"Wow, Fenton must be a common name around here," Lindsay said.

"I guess so," I said.

The parking lot was nearly empty except for one sedan and a pickup truck. The restaurant itself looked closed, save for a silhouette passing by the window.

We parked and headed inside to join the others, weaving between the chairs and tables to the back, where the table they'd chosen offered a view out over the water. The whitecaps of the waves were all that was distinguishable of the black ocean. Saad connected another table and slid extra chairs across the floor. The otherwise empty restaurant echoed with our voices.

"Did you know that just two hours' drive from St. John's you can find fossils of the oldest known complex lifeforms on the planet — jellyfish-like creatures with the earliest known muscle tissues," Duncan said, seemingly out of nowhere, until I saw that he was looking down at a map of Newfoundland on his placemat.

"That's fascinating," Lindsay said.

He turned to her. "It really is. Not to mention the abundance of trilobite and crinoid fossils."

"It's a UNESCO World Heritage Site," I said.

"Indeed. This one island has four of them," Duncan said.

I could only think of two, offhand.

"So, into the murky depths," he said, looking over at Beave. "A genuine sea serpent this time."

"Bigfoot needs a break," I said.

"It's about time," Duncan said. "Bigfoot is good for you Yanks, but for maritime cultures in the North Atlantic, the sea serpent is king."

"Let's hope our audience thinks so," Danny said, head down as he scrolled through his phone.

"Come now," Duncan said with schoolboy excitement. "What's more frightening than the dreaded Jörmungandr, sea serpent and archnemesis of the Norse god Thor? Sea serpents have been the cause of sailors' nightmares for thousands of years. We even have cases of lake monsters acting as bad omens or portents of doom. Look at the Morag of Loch Morar, for instance. Not to mention the number of sightings cryptozoologists report."

"Why do you think there are so many sightings of sea serpent–like creatures?" Saad asked. "Why do these myths persist to this day? We don't talk about dragons or trolls anymore. Why sea serpents?"

"Water is the perfect medium for misidentification. Rarely is a creature or object still when it's on the water, with other objects nearby to provide perspective. Even the most seasoned fisherman might catch a fleeting glimpse of a species he's seen before and come back to shore thinking he's seen a sea serpent. Not to mention all the species he hasn't seen. Oarfish and pipefish are both rare and wondrous serpent-like creatures. Cetaceans, pinnipeds, logs, cephalopods, floating garbage, even otters are frequently misidentified as monsters of the deep."

Beave sat with his leathery hand around his water glass, staring down into it. He took deep, audible breaths. Most of the team, I believe, had forgotten that he was even there until he spoke. "I've got to disagree with you there, Doctor," he said, obviously holding a lid down on his frustration to stop it from boiling over. "The folks that 'ave seen Cressie may not have fancy schooling, but they're on the water practically each day of their lives. It's their way of life. You think a fisherman doesn't know the difference between a whale or garbage in the water and a giant eel?"

We fell silent as the waitress reached between us, placing bottles of beer and cups of coffee on the table.

"We don't always see what we think we see," I said, once she retreated to the kitchen.

"But sometimes we *do*," Beave insisted.

"So, on a scale of one to ten, what is the likelihood of finding a giant eel in Lake Crescent?" Danny asked. "You first, Duncan. Let's get the mainstream opinion."

"Getting down to brass tacks, are we?" Duncan asked, leaning back in his chair and looking up at the ceiling. "My completely unscientific guestimate would be four."

"Only four?" Danny asked.

"Bigfoot would be one, so four is really quite high," he said. "There is access to the ocean, so it is possible that a larger species of eel was lost while spawning, perhaps caught in turbulent conditions, or was brought here by fishermen. It has been theorized that fish, if they aren't spawning, put their energy to use in growing. I doubt that any eel would grow to the length we've heard reported here — some Cressie sightings describe the creature as being thirty feet long — but it is possible that a particularly large eel, with nothing nearby to compare it to, will grow a few feet in the mind of an eyewitness."

Danny nodded.

Beave listened politely, but I could read the dejection in the lines on his face.

"Now over to you, Beave, for the practice, not the theory. You live here, you've heard the eyewitness testimony, you know the lake. Out of ten, how certain are you that there's a giant eel in the lake?"

Beave smiled nervously as all eyes turned toward him. He hadn't come prepared to debate, and he was aware that anything he said would likely not sound as articulate as the comments made by the English paleontologist.

He turned his glass around on the coaster as though he were screwing in a lightbulb. "I guess it'd be silly to say 'Ten out of ten,' since I haven't seen the thing myself," he said quietly.

"Why don't you come along tomorrow?" Duncan asked. "It may improve your chances of seeing Cressie."

"That'd be fine, boy," Beave said, still but glowing.

The food didn't take long to arrive, with the brief waiting period spent looking out at the mouth of the bay and the rocky walls on either side. In the darkness, it became challenging to discern where the rocks and cliffs ended and where the ocean began. The backsplash of lights from the restaurant illuminated the shore then diffused into the night. Conversation petered out as the crew focused on eating, replenishing from the day and refuelling for the next.

I felt as though I was treading water in some ways, but as I took stock of the day's events, I realized I'd made some decent headway. We'd ascertained the exact date of Lou Fenton's death, a tangible fact we could investigate, and we'd shot some good footage of quality science being conducted. Tomorrow we'd investigate the spot where the conger eel had allegedly been caught. Then we could expose Jimmy's fraud. It had been a good day, and I knew where the investigation was going. It felt as though I could relax, maybe even get a good night's rest.

At first light, I peeked through the curtains at the sky, trying to read what kind of day was in store for us. I didn't like what I saw. Wispy cirrus cloud spread like mares' tails over the sky, as if they'd been painted there. "Mackerel scales and mares' tails make lofty ship carry low sails," as my father would say. It was a sign that rain was coming. If there were any other signs that indicated trouble would follow, I didn't see them.

I heard a car door slam and turned to look toward the driveway, where I saw John O'Donahue approaching the inn, a tall orange thermos in one hand and a bouquet of flowers in the other.

Lindsay stirred beneath her comforter as I left the room. I heard floorboards creak as I pulled the door shut, telling me that Lindsay had risen. Similar sounds came from the other corners of the inn as I padded down the hall. Alarms sounded, bedsprings squeaked, and floorboards creaked. Downstairs, soft whispers blanketed the inn like a fog.

The smell of Mary's blueberry muffins greeted my nostrils from the top of the staircase. As I descended the steps, I began to identify the voices and pick the words from the air. Mary and John spoke by the front door.

"I don't think they've woken up yet," Mary was saying. The conversation paused as John's gaze found me, then Mary's quickly after.

John raised the bouquet, pointing the mix of carnations toward me. They spanned the rainbow and were wrapped in yellow paper. Once I made my way down the stairs, John thrust the bouquet at me once more, but it still didn't kick in that they were for me.

"Please," he said. "Accept my apology."

I took the flowers.

He raised the thermos to shoulder level. "And I brewed coffee for you and your team to take with you today." He took a step closer, hanging his head a little.

"You really didn't have to; we have plenty of coffee here …"

John stood quietly, as if ready to be dressed down for a transgression known only to him.

"You have me at a loss, Mr. O'Donahue."

"It's John," he said. "Look, I'm sorry about my son."

"Your son?"

"Jimmy. I've heard all about his prank with the eel."

Captain Phil said Jimmy's dad was an important man in the town, but it was hard to believe that a brash show-off like Jimmy was the son of such a soft-spoken, articulate, considerate man. It seemed to defy reason.

"You're sure it's a prank?" I asked. "Did he tell you that?"

"He doesn't say much to me about anything. But I can tell you that no one has ever caught an eel like that in Lake Crescent, not for at least as far back as my grandfather's day. I don't understand why he does these things. If his mother were alive to see this …"

I shrugged my shoulders. "So far, Jimmy's prank has made for the most exciting footage we've shot. It was really brilliant, watching the team determine the eel wasn't caught in the lake."

John's gaze drifted up then back down to the floor. "I'm relieved that some good came out of it. Have you given any thought to Saturday? Dinner at my home?"

The truth was that I had been thinking about it, but hadn't found the time to mention it to Danny, Saad, Lindsay, or any of the others.

"I'm interested, and I know my team must be, too," I said. "But it's a little soon to make a commitment. I know it's not fair to keep you waiting. A lot of work must go into this sort of thing and you need to know the guest list well in advance."

"Nonsense. We can certainly manage it. I have an awfully large home for just my son and me. I like to fill it with guests every chance I get."

· • ·

We followed the *Tide Queen* out of the harbour, giving Jimmy a head start as he piloted his vessel toward an outcropping of rocks protruding from a clump of mossy earth and trees. Unlike most of the exposed rock surrounding the lake, which has been rounded and smoothed by millennia of exposure, these rocks jutted up like the spires of a gothic cathedral.

We'd passed by here the day before, and Dr. Willoughby had made a note of the location, as there looked to be a series of caves below the waterline, ideal for eels.

The *Tide Queen*'s engine was cut, and it drifted ahead of us, moving behind the outcropping until only the top of the boat was visible. It didn't strike me as coincidence that Jimmy just happened to find "Cressie" in the one spot where the whole escapade would be hidden both from people on the shore and other boats.

Saad and Lindsay stood in the shelter with their collars up. Danny sat beneath the cover of the bridge holding a hot thermos of coffee. The breeze was chilling, and a light mist began to fall, soon turning to freezing rain.

When we caught up to the *Tide Queen*, Jimmy was standing at the aft waving. "That's the spot," he shouted, pointing to a narrow passage between the outcropping of rock and the shore. "Good luck!"

"Stick around," I shouted back. "We're just getting started."

I knew from his expression that we wouldn't find anything. His smirk remained visible as the *Tide Queen* set off toward Tommy's Arm River. Confronting him would have to wait. Danny wanted some ROV footage, and I couldn't help but agree with him that we needed a narrative with some suspense.

Despite the miserable weather, the water was calm enough to deploy the ROV. Chris was practically salivating as Clyde Rengel took the unit out of its case. When it came to playing with new toys, Chris was a perennial child.

"We'll be looking for caverns," Dr. Willoughby said. "Big ones from the size of that eel. Keep an eye out for fish bones and the shells of crustaceans. A conger is a big-time predator, so we're likely to find evidence of its feeding behaviour in the area."

Gulls squawked as they hovered over cresting waves. The sound of water lapping against the rocks was strangely soothing. Despite the biting chill, I felt alive in a way that I hadn't felt before. My lips were dry and my fingertips were freezing, but I wouldn't have traded the sense of adventure for anything.

Clyde, wearing only the thinnest of rainslickers over his sweater, leaned over the side of the boat and lowered the ROV gently into the water, as if he were helping a child down off a swing. The ROV began broadcasting directly to the monitor set up on the bridge.

As the chilling rain continued to fall, the bridge became a popular destination. We crowded around the screen and watched the green-and-white images of the underwater world.

Silt floated in the murky green water — water that had looked so blue when we'd first arrived. There were lines etched into the lake bed, and a round piece of metal stuck out of the muddy bottom. As the ROV approached a wall of rock, Clyde eased it down toward an opening that looked as if it could be the entrance to a cavern. The stone walls narrowed, smooth and round like billowing curtains frozen in time. White particles floated in the water. The sand on the bottom of the lake was disturbed and rose up, exposing something that undulated like a dorsal fin.

Then the ROV stopped.

"We hit a snag," Clyde said. He pressed the button that reversed the tiny black propellers on the side of our miniature yellow submarine, then sent the craft forward again. But the ROV remained in place. He kept working the controls, reversing then going forward again, like he was snowed into his driveway, but the ROV wouldn't break free.

"Let's reel her in," Clyde said.

The ROV was tethered to a reel encased in black plastic on the deck. A detachable crank was plugged into the side of the case. Clyde pulled the crank back slowly, but it was hard to tell if he was turning it at all.

"Dr. Laidlaw," Clyde said, motioning for Duncan to take hold of the crank. He then leaned over the edge of the boat, reached his hand close to the surface of the lake, took hold of the neon yellow cable, and pulled on it in a long, smooth motion. "Easy on that tether," Clyde kept saying. "Easy … easy."

The screen now showed nothing but clouds of bubbles and silt kicked up from the lake bottom. Clyde and Duncan continued to reel the ROV in slowly, soon joined by Chris. The three pulled steadily with more force than the ROV's little rotors could hope to generate, but with the control of men knowing the value of the equipment. I went over to see if I could give them a hand, Saad and Dr. Willoughby followed.

"What the hell is that?" Danny asked. While the rest of us were trying to recover the ROV, he sat back in the covered area of the boat with his arms crossed, watching the transmission.

I turned back to the monitor just in time to catch what looked like a polished rock, or Styrofoam, or some kind of shell peeking out from the folds of what looked like a tarp. It could have been anything.

As the top of the ROV broke the surface, we saw that something else had followed it up. The fold of a blue tarpaulin protruded from the rippling water, then rose up and slumped against the hull, falling open slightly.

"Goddamn," Chris said, looking over the gunwale, the yellow tether gripped tightly in his hands.

"Ah hell," I said, looking at what we'd pulled up.

Wrapped in the tarpaulin, like a baby in its blanket, was a human skeleton.

"Captain!" I called out.

Captain Phil left the bridge and crossed the aft section, looking like a parent hearing his kids fighting. The rest of us stood stock still for the length of a few deep breaths.

Danny held his hand out to me, a plastic twenty-dollar bill folded up under his thumb. "A bet is a bet, Reagan," he said.

I swatted his hand and the money away. "Do we bring it aboard?" I asked Captain Phil.

"We have to untangle the ROV first," Clyde said.

"Bring it aboard," Captain Phil said, sighing.

Duncan reeled the ROV in slowly. Clyde and Captain Phil leaned over the gunwale and unhooked the tarp from the ROV. Lindsay, Saad, and Dr. Willoughby reached over to lend a hand.

"Grab the corners, both ends. Let's bring the whole thing over at the same time," Captain Phil said.

Duncan pulled up the ROV, quickly setting it to the side so the others could lay the tarp on the deck. Water trapped in the tarp spilled out, funnelled through the opening where the skull was exposed, and washed over our boots. The dark orbital cavities stared up at us like they might somehow suck in our souls. The tarp and skeleton were bound together with a worn bungee cord. Rope had been tied from the bungee cord lengthwise. A second coil of rope lay on the deck like a snake basking in the sun.

A small leather pouch had fallen out of the tarp and onto the deck. It was attached to a metal ball chain, the kind you see fastened to rubber stoppers in a bathtub, which was looped around the neck of the remains. The drawstring of the pouch had long since rotted away in the brackish water, and its contents lay half exposed.

"Is that …?" Danny adjusted his glasses to get a better look.

"Looks like gold," I said, kneeling down out of the gaze of the skull.

Something came over me, a swirling mix of shock and intrigue, that feeling of hearding a noise on the other side of the door and being compelled to pull it wide open.

Danny's voice snapped me out of it. "Don't touch anything," he said. "No legal trouble this time around, got it?"

The exposed edge of the gold piece was rounded, but not quite thick enough or smooth enough to be a ring. The pouch lay there limply at the end of the chain, tempting me to give it just a little nudge and set the gold piece free.

"It's round. Not like a ring, more like a coin," I said, peering closer.

I felt a chill on the nape of my neck. I stood up quickly and took a few steps back. I sensed something else looming over us, hovering just above the deck, watching us.

Beave was standing on the bridge, leaning against the bulkhead. He had the oddest look on his face. *Fear?*

Captain Phil threw a red buoy into the water. It floated like a lightbulb in a darkroom. Then he went to the bridge to radio the police.

This is just perfect, I thought. *Another body.*

On the trip back to the dock, the skeleton commandeered the aft section of the deck. We all gave it a wide berth. The rain continued, and we took shelter on the bridge, cramped into the tight space, no one speaking, all of us looking at anything but each other. Lindsay and I were no strangers to human skeletons; we'd both worked with them in university. Duncan certainly would have, too, same for Dr. Willoughby. But there was something different about dredging one up from the bottom of a lake. There was nothing anthropological or archaeological about it, just the seemingly violent action of exhuming a body from its underwater grave.

The waters turned rough as we passed through the stretch known as the Narrows, the point where the river flowed into the ocean. I couldn't look at the skeleton anymore, but couldn't take my eyes off that pouch. With every wave bucking against the bow, I found myself hoping that it would be just enough to shake the gold piece loose. Maybe there was something wrong with me, that compulsion to know more. *What was in the pouch?* That question was eating away at me.

As we sailed up the coast toward the mouth of the bay, the waves heaved the boat at odd angles, shaking loose everything but whatever was in that pouch. It was early still, but I could see that the harbour in the distance was empty.

A speedboat cut diagonally across the bay, perpendicular to us, leaving a frothy wake. We sailed directly into the ripples, the bow of the *Darling Mae* rising up before crashing down through the wake. It was just enough to shake the object free. It made no sound as it slid out onto the wet deck. It didn't clang or roll, it just lay there: a gold coin, bent in an S shape.

I ventured out and knelt down, staring at the coin.

"You really don't want your fingerprints on that," Danny warned.

"It's a coin," I said. "With what I assume is a coat of arms on it. It's twisted up badly."

"Too bad," Danny said. "It could be valuable in mint condition. I mean, more valuable than just its weight in gold — if it even is gold. We'll need a hell of a lot more gold than that if this thing shuts us down."

Sergeant Deloitte of the RCMP met us at the dock, his hands in his pockets. A young constable whose nametag read *Anthony* stood with him, drinking coffee out of a Styrofoam cup. Two paramedics waited behind them, the ambulance parked near the cruiser. The ambulance was not of the cube van style that I was used to, but more like an old van an uncle might have rusting away beneath a tree beside his driveway. A few locals had stopped their cars in the middle of the road and watched our approach. Like Charon traversing the River Styx, we were delivering the body as though it were a soul bound for Hades.

Captain Phil moored the craft, and we all stood back as Deloitte came aboard. Saad looked as though he was struggling to remain still, like he might put his hands up at the sight of the police. To Saad, a skeleton was still a body, a person who had died recently for all he knew, and the shock was evident on his face. Danny, on the other hand, looked almost disinterested. Overall, though, I got the sense that most of us were apprehensive, perhaps fearful of being treated like suspects. It was an unreasonable fear, sure, but that didn't make it feel any less real. I took a step toward the dock, Saad following behind me.

"Please stay where you are," Deloitte said, a hand held up like a traffic cop.

After the paramedics had removed the remains and loaded them into the ambulance, Sergeant Deloitte spoke with Captain Phil, flipping his pad open and making notes. The young constable smiled shyly when any of us made eye contact, and bobbed his head a little. He stood between us and the shore, as though one of us might make a break for it, glancing every few seconds toward the sergeant as if looking for instruction.

"And why that spot in particular?" I heard Sergeant Deloitte ask Captain Phil.

The captain shrugged. "Some of the boys caught a big eel 'round there. Thought it was a good place to look."

Sergeant Deloitte nodded, then looked at the young constable and made a scribbling gesture in the air with his pen, pointing to the rest of us.

The constable looked around for a place to set his coffee cup down and decided on the dock. He then took out a pen and notepad, and started by asking us all our names, how to spell them, our occupations, and where we were staying. The constable made careful notes of all our details, confirming them twice as if he might trip us up on some inconsistencies. He wasn't a Barney Fife type, but there was a youthful innocence about him that, coupled with his rural naiveté and burly frame, made him seem almost like a big kid playing cop.

"I'm sure I don't need to tell you not to broadcast this," Sergeant Deloitte told us. "The people around here will find out soon enough. Better they hear it through official channels."

Danny assured him that we could be trusted. He closed the distance between them and shook the sergeant's hand as though they'd just closed a billion-dollar merger. I was surprised he hadn't spit in his palm first.

"There's a reporter from the *Nor'easter* already in town," I said. "Lawrence Mercier." Both men turned to look at me. "I just wanted you to know, Sergeant, so you didn't think that we called him."

"I'll make a note of that," he said.

With that, the sergeant let us go.

Danny, trying out compassion for what might have been the first time in his life, decided that we were done for the day. No more filming or blogging or anything that resembled work. The rain had stopped, and the sky was now a bright grey. Although there were still several hours of daylight left, the crew was content to punch out early. We all decided to head back to our respective accommodations, with tentative plans to reconvene for dinner. I doubted that Sergeant Deloitte wanted to talk about the death of Lou Fenton at that moment, and it was certainly the wrong time to confront Jimmy about his eel. The ROV footage would have to be edited down to remove any hint of the body we found. Maybe Danny's fears would come to pass: maybe production would stop and the network would pull us back.

S E V E N

During the late 19th and 20th centuries, sightings of large seagoing creatures that seemed to defy explanation were regularly reported in newspapers and magazines, often generating considerable interest. Some were made by reputable people with good credentials and experience with regard to the observing of animals and marine phenomena.

> — Dr. Darren Naish, *Hunting Monsters: Cryptozoology and the Reality Behind the Myths*, 2016

I WAS EMOTIONALLY AND PHYSICALLY drained by the time we reached the inn, but it didn't feel right to give in to it somehow, so I managed to muster enough energy to project the appearance of normalcy. Maybe it was in my head, but a game face felt necessary; I was, in essence, the leader.

The team dispersed to their rooms, to their phones, tablets, and laptops. Lindsay went to take a shower, leaving me by myself in the room. I'd come upstairs without taking my gear off. Realizing that I still had the GoPro strapped to my head, I unfastened the black strap and was about to take the camera downstairs when I realized that it had captured footage of the entire incident.

Taking out my laptop, I turned it on and plugged in the camera, transferring the video onto my hard drive. I had come up with certain protocols for the show, in the event that we actually came across anything out of the ordinary. There was a procedure to follow, a chain of custody. Our footage and personal devices were supposed to stay separate. But if I had made up the rule, I reasoned, surely I should be the one to break it.

I was aware of the shower running as I loaded the software, opened the video, and cut to the section I was most interested in. I enlarged the best frame I could find showing the gold coin, which clearly showed the bottom third of it. I zoomed in and confirmed that there was definitely a crown near the top edge. The bottom portion looked like a coat of arms of some kind. It looked familiar, but I just couldn't place it.

I became so engrossed with the coin and the coat of arms on it that I didn't notice the shower had stopped running.

"That's the coin from the body?" Lindsay asked matter-of-factly.

"Shit!" I said, startled.

Overcome with curiosity, Lindsay sat down on the bed beside me, towelling her long black hair and leaning toward my screen. Her elbow lightly tapped my shoulder, the scent of her lavender shampoo filling the air.

I tilted the laptop toward her, since there was no concealing what I was doing. I thought it best to play it off as normal.

"The very same," I said. "It would be nice to identify it. Based on the uneven edges, my guess is that it's old, minted before the industrial revolution."

"Far older than the remains themselves ... and definitely older than the tarp they were wrapped in."

"Exactly. A souvenir, maybe? But a ball-chain necklace seems like an unusual accessory."

"With the coin being folded like that, I imagine its value must be sentimental."

"It just seems so odd to wear a piece of gold but conceal it in a leather pouch," I said.

Lindsay got up and walked around the bed, tossing her towel nonchalantly on the floral comforter. She put her glasses on, took her phone off the nightstand, and began tapping away. I continued to click through each frame of the video, trying to view the coin from every angle possible.

"The coin is Portuguese. Likely minted in 1708."

"Oh," I said. "Cool. How did you ...?"

"I googled 'gold coin Newfoundland,' which gave me nothing but images of the Newfoundland two-dollar coin, the only gold coin ever minted by a British colony, obviously before Newfoundland became part of Canada."

"Obviously," I said.

"Then I searched for 'gold coin found Newfoundland,' and this picture came up." Lindsay turned her phone toward me. The coin on the screen looked identical to the one on mine, except the one pictured on the phone was in much better condition and nicely polished. The familiar coat of arms on the coin was a variation of the one on the Portuguese flag.

Lindsay scrolled down to read the story. "There have only been two such coins discovered in Newfoundland, it says. One was from an archaeological dig of the Colony of Avalon, an English settlement south of St. John's. A Portuguese coin was found there, as well as a Scottish gold coin and the British currency you'd expect."

"And the second?"

"The second …" She continued to scroll. "The second came from a site suspected to be a pirate hideaway, on the coast south of here. It was dug up in the eighties when some artifacts were found on a construction site. The provincial government had the site excavated by archaeologists from Memorial University. It says they found gold coins from Spain, Portugal, England, and France, apparently."

"Wow. Real pirate treasure?"

"A handful of coins, it seems … not exactly what I'd call *treasure*. When the archaeologists dug deeper, they found a cave that stretched to the ocean. What looked like a promising find turned out to just be the scraps of one."

The reality of the situation set in. We weren't really talking about treasure here; we were talking about human remains that we'd pulled up from the bottom of a lake.

Lindsay set her phone down and sat quietly for a minute. "What do you think this means?" she asked, turning to me. "Will we be able to continue with the show?"

"I don't see why not," I said. "So long as we stay out of the way of any investigation. We have some good footage from the lake, the interview with Beave, the eel necropsy. We still have the interviews with the eyewitnesses and the survey of the eel population with Dr. Willoughby and his students. I think we should get everything we need, even if a section of the lake is cordoned off."

"How do you think that body got there?"

Maybe I shouldn't have said anything at all. I thought about letting her question fall to the floor and die. Past experience taught me that there are no good outcomes when you poke around a dead body, that you should keep curiosity on a leash from the get-go and let law enforcement worry about it. We were just there to search for a giant eel, after all.

"I can't imagine any natural or accidental cause of death that ends up with someone wrapped up in a tarp and left at the bottom of a lake."

Lindsay nodded and gazed absently at her phone. We sat quietly side by side, each wrapped up in her own thoughts. I felt a gravity pulling at both of us, the gravity of a mysterious death and all its implications.

I jumped when someone knocked on the door with staccato rhythm.

"Yes?" Lindsay said.

Chris opened the door, keeping his large hand resting on the knob, swallowing it. "The boss man …" He paused and looked at me. "I mean, Danny wants us to make a decision about dinner. Chinese takeout okay for you guys?"

Lindsay nodded.

"Sure," I said.

"Google Bojo's Restaurant, Springdale. The menu's pretty standard. Let Danny or me know what you'd like. We're driving into town in a bit."

I pulled up the menu on my laptop. I didn't have much of an appetite and settled on the chicken corn soup before sliding the laptop over to Lindsay. There was a soft clicking sound as she scrolled through the menu.

"Have you made it to Saad's room yet?"

Chris shook his head.

"I'll ask him," I said, standing up.

Saad was in his room with the door half open, watching *Arsenic and Old Lace* on his laptop. Unaware that I was watching him, his feet swayed back and forth, one resting on the other. There was a disconnect between his upper body, which was completely still, and his feet, which moved rhythmically. When I knocked on the doorframe, he lifted the headphones off and smiled.

"You hungry?" I asked. "We're ordering Chinese. Chris and Danny are picking it up."

He shrugged.

"I don't have much of an appetite either," I said.

"Not surprising, given the circumstances."

"I'm just getting soup," I said. "The place is called Bojo's if you want to check out the menu online. You should get something light at least."

I sat at the foot of the bed, and Saad brought his knees up close to his body, providing much more space than I needed. I know he didn't mean to treat me as though I were contagious, but that's how it felt. He was always keeping a distance between us.

"I have to ask," he said. "Why are we here?"

How could I tell him I chose Robert's Arm because I thought it might bring me closer to my father in some totally unreasonable way. That I hoped Beave would tell me about another Reagan he'd met who had come up from the States to learn about Cressie. Maybe Dad would have stayed here, married a local, and I'd find a half-sibling running around. Why *had* I come so far?

"I'm starting to ask myself that question."

It was a sombre meal, like a funeral with beef chow mein and chicken fried rice. Had the mood been lighter, I might have given Chris a hard time about screwing up my order, but I let it pass. We ate in silence, which seemed to call attention to every little sound — the pings of text messages, chairs being shifted on the hardwood floor, the peeling noise the skin of my forearm made as I lifted it off the plastic sheet that covered the white linen tablecloth.

Danny and I sat opposite each other at the heads of the oval table. The plaid curtains of the inn's dining room were closed and it felt like we were sealed in together, sheltered from any consequences that dredging up human remains might bring.

After dinner, Fred came to fetch us, his brow furrowed and an accusatory look in his eyes, as though we'd brought trouble to his house. There was a constable at the door, he said, requesting to speak to Lindsay, Saad, and me specifically.

We stood up and went out to see what he wanted. The others followed. The constable's empty hands, resting on his belt, dispelled any notion I may have had that he was there as an errand boy to deliver the RCMP report on the snowmobile accident. He asked if we'd mind coming with him to clear up a few things.

"Stay out of jail," Danny yelled as we put our jackets on and walked out the door. "And don't offer any footage to the cops until I talk to legal!"

We were only in the car for a couple minutes before we pulled up outside the Old Town Hall; the ambulance station was connected to it, and the town's one ambulance was parked in front of a garage door. The young constable opened the back door and led us inside. It was tight in there. The three of us hovered by the entryway, me standing shoulder to shoulder with Lindsay, Saad behind us.

On the floor, surrounded by a moisture stain, was the blue tarpaulin we'd pulled out of the lake. It was opened down the middle and the top of a human skull was visible. Sergeant Deloitte stood next to it, hands on his hips.

Saad, Lindsay, and I waited for a word or gesture to let us know that it wasn't a mistake, that Deloitte had actually sent for us.

"Thank you for coming out so late," the sergeant said.

"You're welcome," I said. "What's going on?"

He waved us closer and lifted the loose flap of the tarp, revealing the skeleton. "We have only one medical examiner for the whole province, believe it or not," he said. "And he's down in St. John's. Don't figure I can get him to rush up here before a holiday weekend without a little arm-twisting, and I don't want to ship the body south like the morning's mail. At least, not until I know what it is I'm dealing with. Then Constable Anthony here reminded me that you're anthropologists. My missus watches *Bones*, so I know you people don't all study monkeys in the jungle. Maybe you can tell me something about this skeleton."

"I'm not a pathologist or an MD," Lindsay told him, "but I can tell you about skeletons."

Sergeant Deloitte took one hand off his hip and gestured in a *by all means* sort of way.

Lindsay circled the bundled tarp, tilting her head.

I was relieved that Lindsay took the lead. It had been a while since I'd worked with any skeletons and I was happy not to have that pressure on me. She dove right in, no hesitation. She'd been presented with a problem and was wasting no time trying to solve it.

"Could you open it more for me, please?" she asked.

Deloitte peeled the flaps of the tarp back like it was foil wrapped over a burrito. The tube lights hummed as Lindsay ran her fingertips down her braid, almost stroking it, like it was her beloved cat. She knelt down and inspected the pelvis of the well-preserved skeleton.

The bones, still with a sheen of moisture on them, represented dead body number two for Saad and me. He kept his distance. Lindsay, on the other hand, didn't seem to mind. She was thorough, thoughtful, professional. I decided to follow her lead and dust off my own anthropology skills.

Despite the fact that the flesh had decayed and pulled away in the tide after what had to have been years of erosion and scavenging, the skeleton looked practically complete, probably because of the rope binding the tarp together.

"The skull looks to be female," Lindsay said. "The shape of the orbits, the lack of brow ridge, the rounded forehead, and the muscle-attachment markings are those of a woman. If I had to guess, I'd say she was in her twenties, based on the cranial sutures."

Lindsay worked her way down the skeleton. "The outwardly flaring hips, broad sciatic notch, and circular pelvic inlet also denote a female." She slowly side-stepped her way back toward the skull. "And she was white."

"How can you tell that?" Deloitte asked.

"The narrow nasal aperture, sharp nasal sill, and high nasal bridge," she explained. "The small teeth, notable crowding, and blade-form incisors are also consistent with European features."

"Then there's the mastoid complex," I interjected. "It's pointy and narrow, as you'd expect from someone of European ancestry."

"Laura is correct," Lindsay said, bending over and pointing behind the mandible and zygomatic arch. "The mastoid *process*" — I was proud of my contribution for all of three seconds — "is characteristic of a European skull." She drew a circle around it in the air with her finger.

"Can you tell what killed her?" the sergeant asked.

"I'd say this depressed skull fracture here," she said, pointing high up on the back of the skull. "You can tell by the shape and the skull fragments that the tissues were still moist and elastic when it happened."

"Any chance you can tell what caused it?" Deloitte asked.

"It's not as circular a wound as you'd expect from a hammer, and it's not as clean as an axe wound. The striking surface of the weapon was narrow and hard, but not at all sharp. I couldn't tell you what caused it."

After Lindsay had finished her examination and stood back up, Deloitte continued to look down at the skeleton, hands on his hips. Maybe he was waiting for more. Maybe he expected us to solve the case for him. "Can you tell how long she was down there?" he asked.

Lindsay shook her head, not taking her eyes off the skeleton. "I'm afraid to even speculate," she said. "The bones are exceptionally well preserved, likely because of the temperature of the water and its salinity. I once worked with a 12,000-year-old skeleton found in an underwater cave in Mexico that looked only a little more weathered than this one. If there is little bacterial action on the protein in the bone structure, then a skeleton can remain intact for ages in low-temperature, low-oxygen, neutral-pH waters."

"The tarp likely aided in the perseveration," I added. "Look at her teeth, though, the amalgam fillings. They rule out remains older than the nineteenth century. If further examination of her teeth reveal that she only has amalgam fillings, then we can assume she hasn't been to the dentist since composite fillings became more popular, as they look natural and don't contain mercury."

Lindsay nodded, pinching her chin between her thumb and forefinger. "That's a large window of time," she said.

"Was there anything else in the tarp?" I asked. "Any articles of clothing or personal effects besides that necklace?"

Deloitte adjusted his hat. "Not a thing."

"Other than the coin, there's nothing that can be easily dated, and the age of the coin definitely doesn't match the age of the tarp, bungee cord, and ball chain."

Deloitte narrowed his eyes at me suspiciously. "You saw the coin?" he asked.

"Yes," I said. "I didn't touch it, but I did get some video footage of it." I lassoed Saad, Lindsay, and myself with my index finger. "We were all wearing cameras. Everything we saw was recorded. I used that footage to identify the coin. Well, it was actually Lindsay who identified it."

"Can you tell me anything about it? All I was able to find out was that it's gold, Portuguese, and about three hundred years old."

I shrugged under his gaze. "That's all we know, too." I looked at Lindsay, then back to Sergeant Deloitte. "But it must have some significance if all her other personal effects were removed and that coin was left in place."

Deloitte bent down and folded the flaps of the tarp back over the skeleton, then looked at us with wide, wet-eyed seriousness. "She obviously didn't do this to herself."

"You were good back there, with the body," I said to Lindsay.

She shrugged. Her braid fell off her clavicle and swung around behind her. "I've worked with so many skeletons. Anatomically modern humans, Neanderthals, *Homo erectus*. Even several australopithecines. I was always taught to respect the specimens because they were once people, part of a community. The skeleton back there wasn't any different."

"Still."

"What an odd way to bind a body, though, don't you think?" Lindsay said, shifting topics. "You'd think that tying the ends of the tarp would make more sense, not just tying the centre and leaving the ends open like it was a wrap or taco."

"Wrap or taco?" I said.

"Sorry, I don't mean any disrespect."

"It's okay, I'm just thinking. What if there is something to that — the food idea?"

"I don't understand," Lindsay said.

"Me, neither," Saad added.

"Have you ever seen video of a whale fall? When a whale dies in the middle of the ocean, its body drops to the ocean floor. The body gets eaten in three stages. The first stage begins with the mobile scavengers — hagfish, sleeper sharks. Stage two brings the enrichment opportunists, animals that colonize the bones and other remaining organic matter, like *Osedax* — boneworms — crabs, giant isopods. Stage three is the sulphophilic bacteria that digest the lipids in the bones and in turn provide food for mollusks and other animals. Keep in mind, whales are a special case because they're so big, they can support an entire ecosystem. But still, the point is a dead body can provide food for several levels of the food chain."

"So, you think that the person who disposed of the body wanted the flesh to be eaten away?"

"It would certainly make the body harder to identify, especially if they feared that the body might be discovered sooner rather than later. The killer might have seen this as insurance."

"But there are so many other ways to identify a body. Dental records, for one. The teeth on that skeleton had clearly been cared for."

"Perhaps the person who disposed of the body had reason to believe those records would be difficult to find. Maybe the victim wasn't a local. If nobody around here was missing and a body turned up with no hair or skin, no ID, then whose dental records would the police compare the body's with?"

"I suppose that's more reasonable than my first thought," Lindsay said.

"What was that?" I asked.

"Someone using that body as bait."

Just then, I pictured the traps we'd set for Cressie. I wondered if we'd stumbled into an old horror film, one in which the inhabitants of an isolated and picturesque town sacrificed outsiders to their lake god. It was crazy — but then again, everything would feel crazy after you reel in a human skeleton while searching for a lake monster.

EIGHT

The mention of ice brings us to one of the oddities of Crescent Lake. Strange holes are often reported in the thick ice covering the lake during the winter months. It has been suggested that the holes are caused by tragic accidents such as snowmobilers falling through the ice.... Speculation abounds that perhaps the holes are caused by Cressie busting through the ice rather than people accidentally falling in.

— Denver Michaels, *People Are Seeing Something: A Survey of Lake Monsters in the United States and Canada*, 2016

DANNY SPENT THE NEXT MORNING IN damage control mode, sitting at the head of the dining table at the inn, surrounded by electronic devices. He tapped away on his laptop while simultaneously talking to the network and glancing over at his tablet. He even managed the seconds wisely enough to occasionally sneak in a sip of coffee and a bite of one of Mary's blueberry muffins. It was something to watch as I zipped up my vest and put my coat on; he was like a champion lightweight boxer staying in the pocket while dodging a flurry of jabs, crosses, and hooks.

"… Just clear it with legal, and make sure the laws here are the same as in the U.S. Great. Thank you, I've got another call coming in … That's fine. Email it to me." He paused, sipped some more coffee, and continued, unaware that I was standing there watching. He only had so much attention to go around. "Hello … yes, yes, there's nothing to worry about, trust me. We're just going to stick to the plan, okay?"

When Saad and Lindsay joined me, we made just enough noise to earn a glance from Danny.

"Yes … No, we're all going to come out of this smelling like roses."

He waved absently as we walked out the front door.

We headed toward the Robert's Arm public library, a five-minute walk from the inn. Since the local RCMP was now saddled with a suspicious death investigation, I wasn't counting on Sergeant Deloitte to dig through old files for me. We'd have to search the archives of local newspapers ourselves to uncover information about the snowmobile crash. We had the date and the names of the victims, but we didn't know if RCMP divers had searched for the bodies, or if there was any connection to eels.

The library was located on the first floor of the Old Town Hall, right next to the ambulance station. There was a faint wet-dog smell in the foyer, and it was quiet. The fluorescent lights made the inside of the library brighter than the grey morning outside. A desk facing the door sat empty, row after row of bookshelves on either side. As far as I could tell, the place was deserted. In one corner was a semicircle of little plastic chairs facing an old wooden one. Toys and children's books were scattered on the floor.

"Hello?" I called out.

There was no reply. After a pause, the three of us fanned out to look for microfilm or alkaline-buffered folders, the media in which old newspapers are stored. I headed toward the back.

"Good day," a voice, soft and measured, said quietly from my blind spot.

I turned to see John Donahue, his feet planted as though he'd been standing there forever.

"I hope I didn't startle you."

"I haven't been snuck up on in a while," I said, taking stock of my racing heart.

He smiled. "The librarian we had here when I was a boy, Mrs. Frobisher, wouldn't tolerate loud steps or any sound above a whisper. I guess I never got out of the habit of being quiet."

"That's a dying art," I said.

We stood there for the length of a few deep breaths, neither of us saying a word. I waited for him to mention the skeleton. It must have been the talk of the town.

"Now, what brings you to our little library?"

"We're looking for newspaper clippings from the area, going back at least as far as the eighties."

"We?" he asked, looking around.

I looked around but couldn't see Saad or Lindsay anywhere. "My team's around here somewhere," I said. "Anyway, I'm looking for some information about the history of this area."

His mood instantly lifted. John held his head high, his shoulders back. "It's providence that we've run into each other then. I happen to be something of a history buff when it comes to Newfoundland. Our town in particular. And not to speak ill of Fern — the librarian — but I probably know the library as well as she does. I spend many of my days here. Within these walls is the history of our town, a history that is rapidly disappearing, and the identity of the town with it. I fancy myself the curator of that history." He smiled, revealing perfect white teeth.

"That's great. I'd love to pick your brain," I said.

"It's yours for the picking," he said. "But I must warn you, once I get started, I never know when to stop."

"That works for me," I said. "I did a lot of background research on Robert's Arm and Newfoundland before we came, but I'm sure there's lots I don't know."

"Where should I start?"

"Not the very beginning," I said. "Let's start with the end of the Viking settlement and go until present day."

He chuckled. "The whole area north of here was a French fishery for four hundred years," he said. "They called it *le Petit Nord*."

"The Little North," I said.

"You speak French?"

"No, not really. I took some classes in high school."

"My family was one of the first to permanently settle in this part of the island."

"Are there any French branches on your family tree?"

"No, ma'am, Irish stock through and through. But the French paid my ancestors to stay in the area year-round to protect their fishing camps during the off-season. The French had already been pushed out of the south by the English, so they didn't want to lose what they had left. If you tour the north of the island, you'll come across a lot of communities with French names, like La Scie, Baie Verte, Pacquet, Fleur de Lys."

"In the end, the French only managed to hang on to Saint-Pierre and Miquelon," I said.

"That's right, the last trace of their Canadian colonial holdings. Though if you ever get a chance to visit old Quebec City, you'll think you're in France, or that you've stepped back in time."

"Is French still spoken anywhere here in Newfoundland?"

"I read recently that there are about fifteen thousand descendants of the French colonists still living there, and that there is a movement to preserve French as a regional language. However, it's probably impossible to preserve the unique brand of French that was spoken here, simply because the French speakers are no longer isolated, and there is what you might call a cross-pollination of the language between the influence of

Quebec, the Acadians of the Maritimes, and the French nationals of Saint-Pierre and Miquelon."

"That's fascinating," I said.

"I was worried your eyes might glaze over."

"Not at all, I find this all very interesting."

"What else would you like to know?"

"What was Robert's Arm like back in the eighties?"

He furrowed his brow. "Robert's Arm was a very different place back then. The young people weren't moving out west the way they are now. There was a feeling of hope, a feeling that this was the frontier, where you could come and make a life for yourself if you were willing to work hard. It would be a simple life but a rich one." He tapped on his chest. "Fulfilling, you know what I mean?"

"I think so."

"But you didn't come all this way for nostalgia. Is there something specific I can help you find?"

"I'm looking for the newspaper archives. Specifically, articles about a pair of snowmobilers who fell through the ice in the late eighties."

His mouth relaxed and his smile faded. A look of curiosity appeared in his eyes. "I thought you were researching Cressie."

"This might be related. According to the legend, RCMP divers are said to have encountered eels as thick as a man's thigh while trying to recover the snowmobilers."

"I've heard that part of it," John said. "Isn't it funny how these stories seem to snowball?"

"So much of what I've heard is just based on rumours. If I can confirm the accident happened, I'll have something tangible to really sink my teeth into."

"Sure," he said. "But we've had quite a few such accidents here."

"This one involves a man named Lou Fenton and a woman named Sarah Tindall. It happened February twenty-ninth, 1988."

His eyes flared wide for a split second. "Yes, I remember that," he said. "That was a sad night."

"What can you tell me about it?"

"Nothing more than the talk I heard around town. Lou was a local boy. I played hockey with him. The girl, she wasn't from around here."

He led the way to a black metal door, opened it, and turned on the light. The fluorescent tubes buzzed like a housefly before casting their glow on every corner of the dusty little room. Inside was shelf after shelf of sleeves holding old newspapers, as well as a microfiche reader. To my right was a pair of steel cabinets, the labels indicating their contents yellowed with age.

"This is what we call the archives. We keep our old newspapers in here, as well as all the documentation we have on the young men from these parts who served in the military."

The newspapers were stored in long black folders to keep them flat and protected. John pulled out the folder for 1988 and opened the cover. Immediately, the smell of dust and old paper filled the room like dark magic from a mummy's tomb.

"The paper was still a broadsheet back then. It's in tabloid format now," he said. He flipped through the newspapers slowly and carefully. "Here we are." He hovered over the newspaper carefully, bending at the waist to see it more clearly. "This is it. But as I suspected, no mention of any giant eels." He stepped aside and gestured at the faded sepia paper.

"Thank you, John," I said. "You've been very helpful."

I took my phone out and held it over the newspaper until the camera focused and the blurry image became clear. There were black-and-white photos of both Lou Fenton and Sarah Tindall. She was standing on a picnic blanket on the lawn of a church, looking beautiful in jeans and a T-shirt. She had the look of a Hollywood starlet.

"She looks like Frances Farmer," I said.

John leaned over my shoulder, squinting at the picture. "You're right, the resemblance is uncanny." He straightened up and smiled. "I wouldn't have expected someone your age to know who Frances Farmer was."

"I'm a movie buff, from a long line of movie buffs."

The article itself didn't provide much information that I didn't know already — the date, the names of the victims. It mentioned the RCMP diving operation that happened the day following the accident, but didn't name the divers. There was some speculation that the movement of the water beneath the ice would make the bodies impossible to find. The only new piece of information I got was about the supposed eyewitness to the accident, Pop Fitzcairn. Apparently, his real name was Samuel. He was quoted three times in the article.

"It was a shame what happened to Lou and Sarah, an awful shame." John tapped the photo with his index finger. "I remember now, the town held a memorial at that same church." He turned to me. "Do you think it was her who you pulled out of the water yesterday?"

"I have no reason to suspect it is or isn't," I said. "I'm just trying to catch a lake monster."

"They never recovered the bodies, so we weren't ever able to lay them to rest properly."

"I'm sorry," I said.

"Such is life, my dear. These waters have claimed more than their share of lives. It's the story of Newfoundland."

At that moment, a woman — presumably Fern, the librarian — appeared in the doorway. Grey hair was overtaking the blond on her head.

"Oh! Mr. O'Donahue," she said, a hint of surprise in her voice.

What was with this *Mr. O'Donahue* business? Robert's Arm was the epitome of casual and friendly, yet Fern said *Mr. O'Donahue* the way one would say *Your majesty*.

"Good afternoon, Fern dear," he said.

"Do you need something? Is there anything I can help with?"

"Oh no," he said. "I was just showing Laura here where we keep the old newspapers. She's interested in our history."

"I can help with that. You shouldn't bother yourself with it, Mr. O'Donahue."

"It's no bother at all," he said, smiling at her and bowing his head a little. Then his smile faded, and I glimpsed a hint of sadness in his face. Then it was gone, his poise cloaking whatever was lingering beneath the surface.

We stepped out of the claustrophobic archives and back into the main room of the library.

"Fern Devonshire is our librarian," he said, by way of introduction.

"Hi, how are you?" I said.

"Fine, just fine," she said, smiling. "And you?"

"Can't complain," I said. I turned to John, feeling the librarian's eyes probing my face. "Thank you again for all your help."

Fern looked at me with what seemed like disapproval. It wasn't a nasty look, just a glance you give something that doesn't belong. I politely ignored it.

"It was my pleasure," John said. "I spend hours in here, looking for evidence of better times, you might say. I'm happy to have someone to share my town with."

"Then I'm sorry to dig up only unpleasantness."

"The best things in life would have no meaning without it," he said. I noticed again a flicker, like something banging against the inside of his brown eyes, trying to get out.

I excused myself to find Lindsay and Saad, quite satisfied overall with the headway I'd made. I had confirmed the names of the two people who'd died in the snowmobile accident and when it took place. And it seemed more and more likely that the eel part of the story had been tacked on later.

Back outside, Saad tugged at the cuff of his jacket and looked at his watch. "We have just over an hour before we have to meet Willoughby at the boat launch."

The three of us ambled toward Cressie's Gas Bar with no real momentum. A motorcycle tore down the highway, its four-stroke engine sounding like a rotary de-barker in a sawmill. As we approached the edge of the parking lot, I stopped suddenly. Saad was keenly attuned to my movement and slowed immediately. Lindsay took two more steps before turning to face me.

"I want to pay a quick visit to Pop Fitzcairn, the guy who claims to have seen the snowmobile fall into the water that night," I said. "Get the story from the horse's mouth."

Lindsay looked over to Saad, then back to me. "Maybe we should talk to Beave first — have him set it up, like he did the other interviews."

"He's not a Cressie eyewitness," I said. "I just want to see if he remembers anything about that night that might help us."

"Like what?"

"I don't know yet."

"Lindsay has a point," Saad said. "It might be seen as … indelicate, showing up on someone's doorstep unannounced to ask about a tragedy they witnessed."

"News of the skeleton we found in the lake must have spread through the town by now," Lindsay said. "It might not be the right time."

"You're both making valid points," I said. "I will try not to be *indelicate*. Why don't you guys go back to the inn and I'll join you before we have to leave to meet Dr. Willoughby?"

Lindsay was an easy sell. Saad, on the other hand, had a habit of backing me up even when he disagreed. It was one of my favourite things about him. But that left all the prep work for Lindsay, and me feeling guilty.

Saad and I backtracked to the mouth of Crescent Avenue, passing Burton's Freshmart and the hardware store behind it. A man who was loading lumber into the back of a blue pickup with dolphin decals on the back took no notice of us as we walked past. The houses on either side of the street looked fairly modern, with sedans or trucks in the driveways, trailers and boats waiting to be hitched. The farther we walked, the more the road veered toward the lake, so that glimpses of the water soon became visible between the houses and sheds.

When we reached a fork in the road, we stayed on the one closest to the lake, just as Captain Phil had directed, Tommy's Arm River Bridge in the distance, its gazebo in the centre. The bridge was the jewel in the crown of the Hazelnut Hill Hiking and Adventure Trail, built in an attempt to boost tourism in the region.

The gravel road split again, and we took the literal high road, which wound up the adjacent hill toward Hazelnut Mountain. Calling this a mountain seemed a bit grandiose to me, given my Washington State upbringing.

We navigated the switchbacks of the road, though the tracks of ATVs clearly ran straight up and down, to avoid missing our destination. We finally came to Pop's driveway and that of his neighbour, which split off from it. They were marked with crudely made signs nailed into the trunk of an old pine stained with ashen streaks of dried sap. The sign on top said *Fitzcairn*, the one beneath read *Flynn*.

"Alphabetical order," I said to Saad.

He smiled and we kept walking. Pop's driveway was scarred with tire ruts. As we approached the house, it appeared abandoned. The porch steps were rotting and the outhouse at the edge of the property leaned to one side like a drunk. There was a burnished wood sign to the left of the front door that read *Fitzcairn*. A trio of wooden monarch butterflies were fastened to the wall to the right of the door, each one larger than the last.

Before going any farther, Saad and I turned to survey the landscape from that vantage point, as though the scenic beauty compelled us. The lake below was a pristine basin of rippling blue. The speedboats cutting across its peaceful surface looked about as small as dominoes. A snowmobile would be about the size of a pip on that domino. There was no way Pop Fitzcairn could have identified Sarah and Lou on a snowmobile from this distance. He would have had to have known it was them beforehand.

I glanced over at the neighbouring cabin and noticed a figure standing in the front window. The figure was backlit, so I couldn't tell if the person was watching us or had their back to the window. The faint sound of scratchy big band music emanated from the dwelling.

"Looks like we have an audience," I said, nodding toward the nosy neighbour.

Saad looked over his shoulder.

Easing my weight onto the first step, I tested it before moving up to the next. Once I was on the porch, I watched Saad repeat the same procedure. I knocked gently on the door. There was no answer. I knocked again, louder this time, but it still failed to achieve the desired result.

Saad walked across the porch toward the picture window and looked inside. "I don't see any lights on," he said

I knocked one more time.

"You won't find him in there," a voice said from behind us.

We turned to see the stooped-over figure of an elderly woman wearing a green housecoat standing at the foot of the path leading to the cabin next door.

"Pop's at hospital, in Corner Brook."

"Do you know when he'll be back?" I asked.

"He's never coming back," she said. "He's gone to die."

"I'm sorry," Saad said perfunctorily.

"Are you Mrs. Flynn?" I asked.

"That's me," she said. "Why are you folks lookin' for Pop?"

Saad glanced at me.

"We'd like to ask him about a snowmobile accident he witnessed," I said. "My name is Laura Reagan, this is Saad Javed."

"What business is that of yours?" she asked, narrowing her eyes.

"It's kind of a long story," I said.

"It is, is it?" Mrs. Flynn turned and started walking back toward the door of her cabin. She paused about halfway and looked as far back over her shoulder as her head would go, then waved us to come along. I followed first, Saad lagging behind as though we were Hansel and Gretel being lured into the witch's house.

NINE

Then there is the Great Horned Serpent, who is believed to inhabit the lakes here in Keji. Legends tell how the Horned Serpent would take young Mi'kmaq men, marry them, and take them back to their underwater world. In the same way, every year as the water levels rise toward the winter, the petroglyph of the Serpent returns to her home beneath the waves.

— Muin'iskw (Jean Labrador),
"The Legacy of Muin'iskw"

MRS. FLYNN'S HOME WAS A TINY A-FRAME nestled between two tall black spruce. The tiny gravel driveway out front was empty. A stone walkway led to the front door, and a wooden sign nailed to one of the trees read *Hanlan's Hideaway*.

Saad took a few quick steps around me and took hold of the tarnished brass handle on the old screen door, pulling it open for Mrs. Flynn. She ambled inside like a raccoon, no word of thanks or even an acknowledgement that the door was anything more than automatic. She kept her slippers on and walked through a doorway that opened into the kitchen, bracing herself on the frame as she turned to face us. There was a mole on her chin, with long hairs growing out of it. Past her, on her kitchen counter, was a bottle of Alberta Premium rye whisky.

"Would youse like a drink?" she asked me, her free hand reaching toward the bottle.

There was the air of an aging country singer about Mrs. Flynn — the weight of a hard life bending her shoulders, a lifetime of smooth cigarettes and hard liquor giving her a voice that Stevie Nicks, Kim Carnes, or even Tom Waits would be jealous of. She spoke loudly, as though she was hard of hearing, and I raised my voice to match.

"No, thank you," I said.

"You?" she asked Saad.

He raised a hand and shook his head.

She pointed the neck of the bottle at me again. "You sure?"

"Yes, ma'am."

"Now, what was it you wanted to ask Pop about? That snowmobile accident with Lou Fenton?"

I nodded. "Did you happen to see it?"

"Can't says I did," she said, her answer leaving her out of breath. "I was asleep. My husband was still with us then, and believe me, I couldn't hear nothin' outside of his snoring." She looked over my shoulder to Saad, who was framed perfectly by the front door. "You'd think it was a chainsaw when Carl really got going. I'd poke him sometimes with my knitting needle just to wake him up so I could get some peace and quiet."

"It seems like Pop was the only one who saw anything," I said.

"He was one to stay out on his bridge 'til all hours," Mrs. Flynn said.

"Now that I've seen his home, I wonder how it was he could even see a snowmobile on the lake from all the way up here, at night, let alone identify the riders."

"Oh, that's an easy one," she said, coughing a little. "Lou and that girl of his was living with Pop. He'd have seen them taking off all the way down the hill toward the lake."

"Were Lou and Pop related?"

Mrs. Flynn shook her head. "Oh no, but Pop was like a father figure to a lot of the lads in town. He'd no wife or kin of his own, but he coached hockey. Plus, he hired a lot of the local boys to help him in his business."

"What did he do?"

"He did whatever he could to earn a buck, like everyone else. Worked on fishing boats part of the year, but also cleared land."

"Like construction?" I asked.

Mrs. Flynn slid a glass along the counter closer to the bottle of Alberta Premium. There was an amber resin in the glass that proved that she'd already finished her first drink of the day. She poured another, sloppily tilting the neck of the bottle into the glass, letting the whisky flow wildly, then wrestling with the bottle until she got it upright again. "More like *de*struction. He had himself a digger, some saws, even some dynamite. He'd get contracts to clear lots for houses and other buildings. He was always hiring boys like Lou, Beave, Fred, and John to help him, and they was thankful for the work."

"He also gave them a place to live?" I asked.

"Only Lou," she said. "There was a fire at Lou's place sometime earlier, so he had nowhere else to go."

"Did you know Sarah well?"

Mrs. Flynn squinted at me, adjusting her cheater lenses to see me better. Her eyes scanned my face like an old typewriter, smoothly going from left to right then slamming back again. "No, not well. She was a runaway. We get one around here every few years." Abruptly, she stepped out of the kitchen and waddled back inside the living room, whisky sloshing around in her glass.

We followed.

Only when she was about halfway to an old rocking chair did she turn and give us another impatient wave.

Saad and I kicked off our boots in the hall and sat on a ratty old sofa with a ratty old quilt draped over the back.

"What do you mean by runaway, Mrs. Flynn?" I asked.

"Some from the big cities come out here tryin' to escape their lives. They think it's easy just to come out here and make a go of it. Think they can live off the land, live like us. Most of them don't last. They go right on back where they came from. Just last summer we had a lawyer come through — a Yank like you. He was a real hotshot, but he couldn't take the pressure."

"What was Sarah Tindall running from?" I asked.

Mrs. Flynn cocked her head back. Her face scrunched up as she recollected, looking like a ball of dough. "Let me think now. Was she the one that had a husband? Got married at seventeen and regretted the whole thing? No, I don't think that was her." She tapped her fingers slowly on the carved wooden armrest of the chair. "Ah, yes, I do remember her. Nice girl. A skinny thing with long straw-coloured hair. A bit of a dreamer, that one was. Very low-minded when she came here, but we raised her spirits." She laughed, then began to cough.

I leaned forward to help, but she waved me off and reached for her glass. She took a long pull of her drink, then seemed to cough and burp at the same time as though she'd swallowed as much air as whisky.

"Can you tell me when Sarah came to town? How long she lived here?"

"I don't remember the year. But the time of year, well, it was sometime between the Paddy scad and the piss-a-beds, as I recall," she said. "Now don't go looking at me like I'm some kind of omaloor."

"I'm sorry, I —"

Mrs. Flynn erupted in laughter that caused her to wheeze.

"I'm just kiddin' ya. It was the late spring when she came. Still a little cooler than when the visitors show up."

"So, she just showed up in town without knowing someone in advance? Or having a job?"

"We Newfies make it easy to fit in. And the boys were lining up to introduce themselves to a good-lookin' thing like her. Men in this town only want two things: t'work, and for someone t'help them melt the snow!" Mrs. Flynn broke into a fit of laughter so severe I thought she really might be dying this time.

I shifted to the edge of the sofa, ready to leap to her rescue.

"I just dies at m'self!" she said, smacking the arms of her chair and laughing some more. "She fell in pretty quick with the boys. But she stuck with Lou Fenton. Maybe 'cause he always had one eye on the batty. Girls a that sort don't want someone dotin' on them. They likes a challenge."

I wished I had a native speaker on hand to translate Mrs. Flynn's regional dialect for me, to make sure there wasn't some little nuance that I was missing. Nonetheless, a blurry image of Sarah Tindall was forming in my head.

"How long did she live here?" I asked.

"A year, maybe two. She settled in quick like a summer rain. You start seein' a new face 'round town, then you see it everywhere. Then, well, the snowmobile accident."

"Did anyone ever come looking for her? Family or some old friend?"

"No, not a soul. Makes ya wonder if she had anyone outside a this town."

"But she fit in well here? She had friends? She made a life for herself?"

"She fit in a little too well, if youse know what I mean."

"I'm not sure that I do."

Mrs. Flynn shook her head. "I'm not some old gossip, so get that idea out of yer head this instant, but let me just say she was a girl smart enough to test drive before she'd buy, if yas catch my drift."

I could feel Saad's puzzled glance on the side of my face.

"It was hard for her to make friends with some of the younger women. They didn't like this flighty beauty queen showin' up and batting her eyelashes at all the boys, you know. But she was an easygoing sort. Her and Fern Devonshire was thick as thieves, though."

Finally, someone who was actually close to Sarah. Fern Devonshire, the librarian. She wouldn't be hard to track down. I stifled a smile, as it seemed inappropriate, but I couldn't help feeling a sense of satisfaction.

Saad and I walked back down the limestone plain toward the inn. The moss under my feet felt like sponge, but with a finite give as the hard limestone below made its presence felt.

"What was that last part?" Saad asked.

"Nothing," I said.

I listened to the sounds of our boots crunching the gravel, of outboard motors tearing through the water, of someone nearby chopping wood.

"You think Pop made the whole thing up," he said, more a statement than a question.

"I do."

"And your theory is that it was Sarah Tindall that we pulled out of the lake."

"Nope. That's my *hypothesis*," I said. If there was one thing I could not stand, it was the incorrect use of the term *theory* to invalidate science — *Evolution is just a theory*. "It'll be my theory, assuming I find data to substantiate it. So far, we know that two people are missing, supposedly having fallen through the ice in Lake Crescent. We only have one source to corroborate that. We found the remains of a woman roughly the same age as the missing woman, but the circumstances in which we found her don't support Pop Fitzcairn's account of the event. From what Mrs. Flynn told us, Pop and Lou were close, so we can't rule out the possibility that Pop would lie on Lou's behalf."

"So, you think Lou killed Sarah, dumped her body in the water, then took off?"

"I'm not sure," I said. "Fred told me that Lou owed money around town, and Mrs. Flynn sure made it sound like Sarah had her pick of the men around here. What if

Lou thought he was losing her to someone else? What if he killed her in a fit of rage, cracking her skull open, then needed a way out? He gets Pop to tell this story and then the world thinks they're both dead, so neither the police nor Lou's creditors are looking for him."

Saad was quiet, looking down at his feet as we walked.

"Why wrap the body in a tarp?" he finally asked.

"I can't figure that part out," I said. "If it were me —"

"If you were a deranged murderer?" Saad asked.

"If I were a deranged murderer, I'd dump a snowmobile at the hole in the ice for the police to find. I'd hide the body, sealing it in plastic, maybe bury it. When the ice thawed, I'd dump it in the lake, in winter clothing, to further corroborate Pop's account if the body was ever recovered."

"What about the skull fracture?" I asked.

"That's a good point, I'm not a very good murderer. Also, that would put the bulk of the work, and the risk, on Pop, which is probably too much to ask, no matter how close they were."

"If either Pop or Lou had to store the body on land, waiting for the lake to thaw, they might have put the body in lye, or something to dissolve the flesh from the bones, then dressed the skeleton and wrapped it in the tarp. Maybe the whole idea was to have the clothes rot and the bones fall out and get moved around by the current."

"Like it was meant to be time-released, scattered by the current?"

Saad shrugged. "If a pile of bones was discovered, it might have been assumed that the skull fracture was a result of the skull slamming about against a rock underwater. That's why they didn't dump the body too close to the site of the accident. They had a body to dispose of, and the official story calls for it to be found in the lake, so they dump it in the lake, hoping the bones will scatter and they'll be no trace evidence leading back to them."

"That's possible, but seems too elaborate. But this whole thing is too elaborate, isn't it? The Atlantic Ocean is just a few minutes from here, not to mention that there are fissures in the limestone fifty, even a hundred feet deep in some areas around town. Why not just dump the body down one of them? It would get so smashed up it would completely cover up the skull fracture, and that's assuming anybody ever found it. No, somebody had a specific reason for wrapping the body that way and leaving it there."

"Then there's the coin …"

"That's right. The coin. But we'll have to table the speculation for now and get back to the inn to meet Lindsay. Dr. Willoughby is expecting us shortly."

T E N

According to local folklore, in the 1950s two men said they spotted an overturned boat in Crescent Lake as they walked the shore, concerned they started to help but the "monster" turned and slipped into the water.

— *Telegram* (St. John's),
March 2, 2010

THE NEXT MORNING, THE SUN WAS OUT AND the boughs outside the window were alive with birds flitting around among the pine needles. As we set out in the van, it struck me how much of a difference sunlight can make. Even the rocks had some colour to them.

According to Beave, Frank Marsh was one of the few and best eyewitnesses to Cressie, and he'd set the whole thing up for us.

Danny, Chris, and I waited for Beave out front of Marsh's house, a house with sky-blue siding at the end of a row of houses with sky-blue siding on Berg Street, opposite an outcropping of trees bordered by a wall of rocks. A detached two-car garage was half-built around the back.

Maybe Beave was confused? Maybe he expected us to pick him up in the van? Chris drummed on the steering wheel; Danny stared at his phone, typed, and stared some more. When he looked up, he prolonged his gaze out the windshield, then across the van out Chris's window, before looking over at me. He wouldn't say anything, or look at me for more than a millisecond before dropping his eyes back down to his phone. It was only after the third performance of the routine that I called him out. "Okay, I'll phone Beave."

Beave's number was saved in my new phone that the network had supplied me, so after a few taps on the screen I was holding the phone to my ear and listening to it ring. I got his answering machine. Not voice mail, but an old-fashioned machine with the mini-cassette in it and the pops, clicks, and feedback that go along with it.

"Good morning, Beave, it's Laura. We're at Frank Marsh's house. I hope you're on your way here. Call me if you get this."

Eventually, Frank himself came out on his bridge and waved us in. "No sense in you waiting out there," he said.

We — meaning Danny, who lived his life by the motto *the show must go on* — decided to start without

Beave. He jumped out of the van and followed on Frank Marsh's heels. Chris and I lumbered slowly after them. We had lost some momentum after finding that skeleton in the brackish water of Lake Crescent.

Frank paused on the sill of his open front door, gesturing for us to enter. Danny waited on the porch steps for Chris and I to catch up. Chris went up the steps first. As I followed, Danny leaned toward me.

"We should cut that runt from the program," Danny whispered "I don't get dicked around. Ever."

Frank led us into his dining room, a terracotta-coloured room with an oak table in the centre surrounded by oak chairs. An oak cabinet sat in the back corner. Frank took a seat at the head of the table, facing a window that looked out onto the backyard. Outside I could see three birdfeeders atop poles buried in the lawn. A blue jay appeared and chased away some chickadees, only to be sent on its way by a black squirrel jumping onto the feeder, rocking it violently.

There was a chemical stink in the air of the dining room, like Frank had tried to mask the odour of cigarettes with a cheap deodorizing aerosol spray. I could hear footsteps upstairs, but whoever it was didn't come down.

Chris set the camera up in the farthest corner from Frank, and I sat opposite him. I didn't need to be in the shot. In fact, the less of my coaching the better.

"It was a real duckish evening," he started.

"I'm sorry, what do you mean by *duckish*?"

"Kinda gloomy like," he said.

"Okay, go on."

"I was just sitting out back," he said. "Watching the water. It helps me think."

He paused. I nodded at him.

"So then I see something moving. Not swimming really, it didn't leave a wake or anything like that. It was more like churning in the water. It created more of a swell, a deep swell. Then a head came out of the water. It had long features, it was long, and pointed."

"How far out was it?" I asked.

"Not more than fifty feet away from me, I'd say."

"And you say the creature wasn't swimming?"

"No, it was just out on the water there, shivering, if you like. Just floating there."

"What can you tell me about its features?" I asked.

"It had a little round snout. The whole thing was about fifteen, twenty feet long."

"What did it do next?"

"It just sorta ducked under the water," he said. "I was fit to be tied. I'd heard of Cressie me whole life, but I never thought I'd see it."

Frank insisted we stay for tea or coffee, but we passed. Beave was still on my mind. I double-checked my phone to make sure I had no missed calls. We had a few more interviews to conduct, and I was concerned that the other subjects wouldn't be as agreeable as Frank with letting strangers into their homes, without Beave as a go-between.

"We should have brought the sketch artist," Danny said, pulling his door closed as he got in the van.

"What good would that have done?"

"It would've made better TV," he said. "And having someone who has worked in law enforcement goes over big with the older male segment of our audience."

Frank waved to us from his porch, and continued waving as we began to drive away. The small window just below the apex of his roof was dark except for white curtains. I swear I saw the curtains move a little as we were leaving.

As we drove by the harbour, I saw Captain Phil standing on the dock.

"Chris, pull over here, please. I'll just be a second."

We slowed down and Chris let me out at the dock. The waters were still, as there was no wind to speak of.

"You haven't seen Beave today, have you?" I asked the captain.

"Nope, I haven't seen him."

"Does he live close by?"

"Down the road a ways." He raised his arm and pointed with all five fingers. "Follow Main Street to Middle Road, follow Middle until it turns into Orlando Road, then take Parsons Avenue to Anthonys Avenue, then down Water Pond Road."

"Do you remember his address? I have it on my laptop, but not on my phone."

"It's the red cabin," he said. "I can walk you there."

Captain Phil moved toward me up the dock, hobbling again like he had arthritis in his knees, maybe his hips, too. I could just imagine Chris and Danny watching me, framed in the van's rear-view and side mirrors.

"How long is the walk?" I asked.

"Oh, we'll be there in a jiffy," he replied.

I watched Captain Phil take a few more feeble steps before suggesting we just take the van.

"What's this?" Danny asked, as the captain and I got in the van.

"Captain Phil is going to take us to Beave's house. It's not far."

"Time is money," Danny said.

"Then this is a wise investment," I said.

A few minutes later we pulled up to Beave's house, which looked dark and empty, even on such a bright day. Chris and Danny stayed in the van while Captain Phil and I got out and walked up the gravel driveway. Chris leaned out the open window, his boa-constrictor-thick arm resting against the side of the door. He was watching our backs, which was habit after a career of following people into unpredictable situations with a camera. Danny, on the other hand, disappeared into his phone like a moody teenager.

We walked up the moss-covered stone steps to the screen door and knocked. There was no answer. Captain Phil leaned against the side of the house as though we'd just summited Everest. As we stood there, blue jays squawked loudly in the trees beside the house.

"Try the door," Captain Phil suggested, nodding toward it.

"I don't want to barge in on him."

"Could be he's had a heart attack," he said. "Lord knows he ain't no spring chicken."

The weathered screen on the outer door was a faded grey. When I pulled it open, it screeched like a bird of prey and the blue jays grew silent. I peered through the rectangular windows on the upper half of the front door, but didn't see anyone stirring. When I took hold of the handle and squeezed, putting some weight into it, the door didn't move. It was locked.

"There's a funny thing," Captain Phil said. "I've never known Beave to lock his door. No one does around here."

"Maybe he doesn't feel safe with a gang of Americans around," I said, hoping to get a smile out of the captain.

A dirt path led along the side of the house. I left the captain at the front door and followed the path back to a tiny red garage with a white door. There was a window at the back of the garage. Peering in, all I could see was a garbage can, rakes, shovels, and a lawn mower.

"There's no car inside," I called.

"Beave drives a pickup," he called back.

"It's not there."

When I came back around the front, Captain Phil was leaning against the front window, his hands cupped over his eyes as he stared inside.

"This is all very strange," he said.

"What?"

"This Cressie business is more than just a hobby, it's his life. It's about the only thing he ever gets excited about. Once you get him started, it's hard to get him to

stop. He'd give his right arm to be part of your movie."
He looked down at the dirt caked on his boots and let
out a long sigh.

"Guess there's nothing much we can do," I said.
"Is there some place we can drop you? Back at the
harbour?"

"That'll be just fine," he said.

"Beave's left his den?" Chris asked when we got back
to the van.

I nodded.

The harbour was like a postcard through the windshield. I'd missed its beauty when I'd approached before, having had a particular target in mind. For the
first time, I was able to see the big picture, to take it
all in. There was a small peninsula jutting out, known
locally as Harbour Island, a mound of rocky hills and
pine trees like a crown; the boathouses built around the
circumference were like its jewels. The land around the
harbour rose up around the water, the trees like spectators at a coliseum.

Across the harbour, moored in front of Showalter
House, the *Tide Queen* looked lonely and neglected,
listing when the mountains funnelled the strong wind
from the Atlantic into the harbour. I realized I hadn't
seen Jimmy O'Donahue since the conger eel incident.
Perhaps he was under house arrest, imposed not by
Sergeant Deloitte and the RCMP but by a higher power
in Robert's Arm — his father.

Our next interviewees were a husband and wife, Bert and Donna Cornell. They lived just off Paddocks Road on a private lane they shared with a large house with a barn-style two-car garage beside it. The Cornells' lived in a yellow bungalow with a white porch on the left side of the private lane.

"Where's Beave?" was the first question out of Bert's mouth after opening his front door and surveying Chris, Danny, and me.

Bert was a tall, wide-set man with a very round head covered in light brown hair that was going white at the sideburns. He was wearing glasses and was dressed in an old T-shirt and blue jeans. He certainly hadn't gussied up to be on TV.

"He's —" Danny started.

"We don't know," I said, before Danny had a chance to spin the situation. "I take it you haven't heard from him.

"Not since he telephoned us two days ago."

"Ask them about the body they pulled out of the lake," a woman's voice said from inside the house.

"May we come in?" I asked.

Without Beave to make the introductions and lend credibility to the idea that we weren't out to make the locals look foolish, I realized we had to start from scratch. Growing up in my father's house normalized his eccentric passion, and people like Beave, to me. But not everyone wanted to open their homes to strangers and talk on camera about seeing a monster.

"We'd just like to ask you and your wife a few questions about what you saw," I said. "We'll be out of your hair in no time."

Bert stepped back and pulled the door open wide, gesturing with his other hand. Chris and Danny waited for me to go in first. The walls of the house were covered in fake wood panelling, pictures of their now-adult children in graduation gowns hung in gold and silver frames. Bert ushered us into the living room, which had a fireplace and a torsion pendulum clock on the mantle encased in a glass dome. Beside it was a wooden sign resting against the brick of the chimney that read, *Thankful, Grateful, and Truly Blessed.* A paperback lay open on the cushion of an armchair.

As Chris set up his camera and tripod in the corner beside a log holder and tool set, Donna came in with a tray of teacups, a teapot, and some cookies, setting it down on the coffee table beside a newspaper. To my surprise, the headline read *Body Found in Lake Crescent.* For some reason, I'd assumed news didn't travel quite so fast in Robert's Arm.

"Molasses cookies are Beave's favourite," Donna said.

Unlike her husband, Donna was dressed for TV. She wore black slacks and a blue blouse with white buttons. She had on a touch more foundation and eyeshadow than might be normal for around the house. Her dye job was recent, too, and not a millimetre of white was exposed at her roots. She wore flower earrings with the petals made of gold and the stamen a navy-blue polished stone.

"Is Beave a close friend of yours?" I asked, looking first to Bert, then Donna.

"I wouldn't say close," Bert said. "He's not what you'd consider a social butterfly."

"He'll come out to some of the community events, you know, around the holidays," Donna said. "I always keep an eye out for who eats my goodies and what they prefer. Mayor Dunlop loves my cherry tarts; John O'Donahue, who was mayor before her, loves my peach cobbler, but I don't get the chance to make it too much. Peaches are imported from the mainland, so they don't stay fresh long by the time they get up here."

Donna poured me a cup of Earl Grey tea. I took it black. Danny had her add two teaspoons of sugar and a splash of milk; Chris declined the milk but copied Danny's serving of sugar. Bert took the teapot from his wife to pour his own. She sat down and leaned back on the floral-patterned sofa with her cup and saucer in her hands, taking that first sip and closing her eyes while it warmed her. I glanced down at the newspaper to see what the article said about the human remains found in the lake.

"Beave seems a little shy, but he doesn't seem like the reclusive type," I said. "He seems very kind and well mannered."

"Oh, he is, love, he is," Donna said, taking another sip of tea.

"He certainly is now," Bert said, flashing an energetic smile. "There was a time when he and the other boys — Lou, Johnny, Fred — were raising all kinds of hell around here."

Donna turned and looked at her husband soberly. He seemed to pick up the signal loud and clear.

"Those were different times," Bert said. "In them days we all thought the world was our oyster. Carefree, I guess the word is."

"We're all set," Chris said. "Good to go." He gave me the thumbs-up.

Eyewitness interviews have always been the bread and butter of documentary series about the paranormal, supernatural, and unexplained. Since humans are notoriously unreliable witnesses, I always viewed eyewitness testimony with extreme skepticism when there was no physical evidence to corroborate an account. However, the interviews made good TV, because above anything else, we experience the world and learn about it through stories. Details and data don't carry the same weight as a good emotional narrative. For Danny, eyewitnesses were the most valuable asset for *Creature X*.

"Just tell us what you saw," I said. "Maybe set the stage for us. Where were you when you saw Cressie? What kind of day was it?"

"We were driving to our cabin, by the turnoff to Port Anson, you know, the Horse Feeder on one side and the lake on the other," Bert said.

I pictured it as he spoke, the stretch of highway just before Robert's Arm, the road sandwiched between a long narrow pond and Lake Crescent. There was some brush between the pond and the road, and nothing but a guardrail and two feet of cement between the road and the lake.

"It was a real dull evening. The water was like glass, not a ripple on it."

"Around what time?"

"Six thirty, maybe seven," Bert said.

"Heaven knows why," Donna said, "but I just suddenly turned and looked out to my right —"

"We both did," Bert added.

"And there it was," Donna said. "Ripples coming out of nowhere, then a head coming out of the water."

She set the cup and saucer in her lap, holding it steady with her left hand and making the shape of Cressie's head with her right.

"It was huge," Bert said. "Ten, twelve, maybe fifteen feet long."

"Any reason you both looked up and over at the lake at that moment?"

Bert looked over at Donna, who shrugged her shoulders. He followed suit.

"What were your first reactions?"

"I said, 'Oh my god, Bert, that's Cressie!'"

"I was almost doubting my own eyes," Bert said.

"What was Cressie doing? Was it swimming, or staying in one spot? Did its body undulate like an eel's?"

Bert looked over at his wife, who was raising her teacup toward her painted lips. Seeing that she wouldn't be fielding that question, he looked back at me.

"She seemed to be just floating there. Before you knew it, there were shrubs on the side of the road blocking our view. I said to Donna, 'We need to go back and take another look.' There was some traffic on the road so I drove a little farther to a driveway so that I could turn around safely. As you might know, there's no shoulder on that stretch of road so it's difficult to make a U-turn. When we got back to the same spot, albeit on the other side of the road, Cressie was gone. The water was so still again, it was like nothing was ever there."

No real details, no *actionable intelligence* as they say in espionage films. Aside from *dark*, there were no details as to Cressie's colour or features. Nothing they described about Cressie's behaviour could be tested against that of animals known to reside in Lake Crescent. I wasn't sure that we could perform any meaningful investigation of that section of the lake either, although it wouldn't hurt to send the ROV down to have a look. The footage overlaid with the audio of the interview may make for better television than the clichéd dramatic re-enactment.

"What can you tell us about the body you pulled out of the lake?" Donna asked quietly.

"We've been asked by the police not to discuss it, I'm afraid."

"It's already in the news," Bert said.

The newspaper article, like the interview we had just conducted, was light on concrete facts. A body had been found in Lake Crescent by an American TV crew filming a documentary about Cressie. Thankfully, my name was not mentioned. Sergeant Deloitte apparently chose not to divulge any of the observations Lindsay had made when examining the skeleton. No details about the way the remains were bound in a tarp, or the gold coin, were in the article. The final paragraph made mention of Jimmy O'Donahue, described as a local fisherman, who had caught a large eel in that part of the lake just the day before. I imagined how unhappy his father must be.

"We don't know any more than what's in the news," I said.

Husband and wife both turned and nodded at each other.

By the time we left the Cornell home, it felt more like we'd been visiting distant relations than conducting a TV interview. Donna even sent us off with a freezer bag filled with cookies she'd baked that morning.

The way back to the inn took us past the ambulance station, where two RCMP cruisers and an ambulance sat outside. Sergeant Deloitte stood next to it.

"Could you let me out here, please," I said to Chris. "I'll walk back to the inn. It's only a couple minutes away."

"I'm starting to feel like a cabbie," Chris said, smiling at me in the rear-view mirror.

"On your salary? You're more like my chauffeur," I said, smiling back.

"We still have work to do," Danny said, turning around to face me.

"I know," I said. "I won't be long."

They dropped me off in the parking lot, the van crunching over the gravel as it left. As I drew closer, I saw that Sergeant Deloitte stood with his hat in his hand. The skeleton was being loaded into the back of the ambulance.

He nodded at me as I approached.

"We're taking her to a funeral home in Springdale," he said, his eyes fixed to the gurney and the body bag mounted on it. "The medical examiner was recalled from his holiday, it's —"

"St. George's Day weekend, I know."

"I believe he'd booked the whole week off, but that's sunk now. He's being flown in from St. John's. I don't think he's too happy about it, but I'm sure he'll confirm your friend's findings for the record."

"I see," I said, not knowing what I should or could say.

I felt eyes on my back. I looked over my shoulder and saw the silhouette of a tall lean figure in a window of the nearby library. He — the figure looked male — backed away from the glass.

"When you join the Mounties," Sergeant Deloitte began, "you don't get to choose your post. It took me a long time to get stationed in my home province. Which is all well and good until a time like this. I like being detached from death. When I was in Saskatchewan, I knew I'd never come across the body of someone I knew. I could very well have known that lady."

We stood beside each other in funereal silence, watching as the remains were loaded into the ambulance.

"You haven't seen Beave Cannings around, have you?" I asked.

Sergeant Deloitte, squinting, looked over at me.

"He was supposed to take us around to visit a couple of Cressie eyewitnesses this morning, but he never showed. I checked his house. He wasn't there, and the place was locked up."

"A body turns up in a small town and everybody gets suspicious," Deloitte said. "Everything becomes mysterious."

He turned to face me. "I appreciate your help on this, but try not to get carried away."

"That doesn't seem weird to you?"

"I've known Beave since I was a boy. He and the other lads here used to beat my school's hockey team every single game. I don't know that he's ever left the island his whole life. Just give it a few hours, he'll pull up red-faced and ashamed that the whole thing slipped his mind."

"Phil Parsons, whose boat we chartered —"

"I know Phil," Deloitte said.

"He seemed concerned about Beave's disappearance," I said.

"I'm concerned, too," he said. "I'll keep an eye out. But in the meantime, I have to worry about this." He gestured toward the wide garage door of the ambulance station, then said goodbye and walked back inside.

As I stood there, a light mist began to gently fall. I almost didn't notice it.

The librarian stepped outside and started locking up. "Library's closed, I'm afraid," she said, noticing me.

"I was actually hoping to talk to you."

"Me? About what?"

"Sarah Tindall. Did you know her?"

"Sarah Tindall. You know, I hadn't heard that name in years, and now I must have heard it a dozen times today. Is that who you think that body was?"

"That doesn't seem likely to me. I mean, what are the odds that I happen upon the skeleton of a woman I'm researching for a documentary?" Not to mention the fact that the body didn't wrap itself in that tarp. Even if the cause of death was an accident, someone went to the trouble of concealing the death from authorities. Someone in town must know more than they were telling.

"I suppose you're right," Fern said.

"What can you tell me about Sarah?"

"I think she came with all sorts of notions of what life out here was like. She was disappointed when she saw how it really was. That poor thing was haunted, you know? Wandering the shore of the lake at all hours of the night like something out of a ghost story."

"Were the two of you close?"

"As close as anyone around here. We used to sit down by the lake, our legs in the water, talking for hours, watching the sun set and the stars come out. But do you think I could tell you anything about her? I didn't know her age, or where she was born. I got the impression that she had a husband somewhere, but I don't remember why. She was American — I picked up on that."

"Why would you say she was American?"

"Her spelling, on notes she'd leave me. *Centre* spelled *e-r* not *r-e*. *Neighbour* without the *u*." She smiled, almost apologetically.

"How did the rest of the town treat her?"

"She turned this town on its ear, I'll say."

"How so?"

"In a place like this, you get to feeling like your entire life is mapped out for you from the day you were born. Your school, your job, even your spouse. There are very few options if you stay in a town this size. People either leave, or they settle in. Lou Fenton settled in. He was going to work in the pulpwood industry, just like his father, and he was going to marry a nice local girl he'd known since grade school. Then Sarah rushed into town like a flood, and nothing was the same. Sarah wasn't exactly taken with him at first. She tried a few of the boys on for size, but Lou was the best fit. He wasn't so set in his ways; he didn't expect her to play to role of the little woman."

"The little woman around here is different than where I come from."

"Just 'cause we know how to gut, scale, and salt a cod doesn't mean we don't have expectations on us," she said, smiling. "But Lou always did have one foot off the ground, like he might take off any minute. You just needed to make him an offer."

"And Sarah offered?"

"She made him feel like he wasn't stuck here like the rest of us. I think he started seeing things through her eyes."

"How did that 'nice local girl' take it?"

"She got over it," Fern said. "She even became the mayor."

"Mayor Dunlop?"

"Certainly. She's the only lady mayor we've had. Before her, it was Mr. O'Donahue going well back into the nineties."

"Where did Sarah live when she came out here?"

"She lived with Lou most of the time I knew her," Fern said, pausing mid-step and looking up at the overcast sky. "Must have been the motel before that."

"One more thing," I said. "You said she was haunted. Was she ever really happy?"

"Sure, she had happy times out here. When I say haunted, I don't mean she was troubled or scared. Just, I don't know, lost."

"But her life here was a happy one overall?"

"You know," Fern said, "I can remember one time she came over to my house, unannounced, just after supper. She looked upset but didn't say a word about it, just asked all sorts of questions and carried on like everything was normal."

"What kind of questions?"

"Just chit-chat. How old was the house, and how long had my family been here, stuff like that. It was like she just didn't want to leave."

"Was she scared?" I asked. "Did Lou ever get rough with her?"

"By Jesus, no, nothing like that. He was one of the good ones."

I couldn't tell if that meant there had been bad ones, but I hesitated about asking too much.

"After the … accident, did her strange behaviour make any more sense?"

Fern looked down at her shoes and shook her head like she was trying to get an idea out.

"Maybe, I mean, yes. I got to thinking all sorts of things. There was a bit of a romantic mystery about her, so naturally I thought a few things might have happened. When a body doesn't turn up, it leaves many possibilities open. But then I got a hold of myself. These accidents, tragic as they might be, happen all over this island. Hunters fall down snow-covered crevasses, fisherman tumble overboard in rough waters, people drive into moose, and snowmobilers fall down steep hills or through the ice. A person takes so many risks out here that they forget that they're taking risks at all. What happened to Lou and Sarah still breaks my heart when I think on it, but these things happen. Can't go around making more of it then there was just because I knew them."

"Thank you, Fern."

ELEVEN

For strange and gigantic creatures have been seen right on our own doorstep. Either a variety of colossal eel, or the more spectacular hump-back beast with a long neck, has been sighted in every Atlantic province.

— John Braddock, "Monsters of the Maritimes," *Atlantic Advocate*, January 1968

THE INN WAS WARM, AND THE SMELL OF A fire competed with that of wet wool. In the living room, Duncan, Saad, and Lindsay sat on the floor, a laptop on the coffee table in front of them. They held steaming cups in their hands. It seemed as perfect a way to take shelter from the rain as any.

Saad was the first to spot me. Lindsay smiled without flashing teeth, and Duncan gave a little salute. They were watching John Carpenter's *The Thing*.

"My HDMI cable wouldn't hook up to the telly," Duncan said.

Despite his Ph.D., Duncan was still a relatively young man, relaxed and casual, and not above crouching on the floor to watch a space alien terrorize an Antarctic research team.

"So, is the game afoot then?" he asked as I crossed the threshold into the next room.

"Excuse me?" I said, taking a step back.

"Is your nose twitching, or whatever happens when there's a mystery about?"

I scanned the paleontologist's face and found no signs of mockery. "The only mystery I care about is whether or not a giant eel lives in this lake," I said.

Saad looked down at the phone in his lap. He knew I was lying.

"I was sort of hoping to be part of the sleuthing this time," Duncan said. "I missed all the action in Oregon."

"You didn't miss much," I said.

"I sincerely doubt that."

According to its website, the biggest selling point that Lake Crescent Inn had going for it was the Wi-Fi, described as "high-speed internet." That may have been an exaggeration. We'd moved to the dining room, where the table and the lighting suited our purpose better than the cozy living room. The Q&A that Lindsay, Duncan, and I did over Skype with the *Creature X* online community didn't quite flow as I would have hoped. The lag, which made it difficult to understand the questions and to manage the answers, caused the whole thing to be a hot mess.

We decided afterward to reconvene at Skipper's Pub and Eatery in the nearby town of Badger. Duncan borrowed one of the vans to go back to his motel and pick up Clyde and Dr. Willoughby. Lindsay went up to our room to change. After checking my email, I decided to google the Portuguese coin.

It took a while to locate any useful information. Many collectors' websites offered low-res images and no pricing information. Luckily, I found a PDF of a catalogue from Sotheby's containing a collection of antique Portuguese coins that had gone up for auction four years ago. The images were large and clear, with exceptional detail. More importantly, it had estimates of the value of each coin: twelve thousand British pounds each.

"Holy shit!" I said.

"What's up?" Chris said, poking his head in.

"Nothing, never mind."

"Cool," he said and disappeared.

I carried my laptop upstairs, where I could snoop unnoticed. Chris was dependable and loyal to his employer. I didn't want him seeing anything he might mention to Danny.

The coins up for auction were shiny, in mint condition. Reading more about coins, I was surprised to learn that coins with patina may be more valuable.

But the way our coin was bent would certainly have devalued it. I spent a while on Google reading articles about bent coins. As it turns out, coin bending is a fairly popular trick among novice magicians. But I wasn't about to call up Sergeant Deloitte and ask him to put out an APB on a man in a black top hat and cape just yet. Further reading brought me to the term *crooked coin*. A crooked coin was a love token popular in the latter half of the seventeenth century. A young man would bend a coin and give it to his intended; if she kept the coin, it meant that she consented to being courted by him. For a moment, I thought that maybe the remains were that old, perhaps found on someone's property. Maybe the person who found them had to move them and didn't want to go through the proper government channels, as an archaeological site assessment would need to be conducted. So, they bound the remains in a tarp, securing the love token around the skeleton's neck, and lowered it into the water, not far from its original burial site but on no one's property. Then I remembered her teeth and the fillings that were definitely from much later than the seventeenth century.

Lindsay came out of the bathroom, walked straight toward her bed, spun around, and fell onto the creaky mattress like a tree in the woods. She flung her arms out to the side on impact; her feet, clad in fluffy white thermal socks, stayed planted on the floorboards.

"I was thinking about the woman in the tarp," I said to her. "The angle of the wound would seem to suggest that the murderer was much taller, the force behind such a blow would point to a man. Probably a man she knew."

"Statistically speaking, one-third of murdered American women are killed by men they are in a relationship with," Lindsay said. "If the coin was bent that way for the victim, that might explain the spot where we found the body. Newfoundland has six thousand miles of coastline, not to mention the vastness of the Atlantic. How hard can it be to make five square feet of body disappear? But the killer chose to deposit the body close to land, close to a town, in a spot that would both conceal the act of hiding the body and forever mark its final resting place." She looked down at her socks, grey kitten faces on a blue background. "It's possible that the current moved the body, or something else, and it ended up getting wedged into those rocks just by happenstance."

"I suppose," I said. "Anything's possible. But I suspect that the killer was in love with his victim."

"He loved her so much he killed her?"

"Love makes people crazy."

She began bouncing her left heel off the floor. I never figured her the type for a nervous tic. When she caught me staring at her bouncing foot, she turned, lifted her feet onto the bed, and lay back, crossing her ankles on top of the folded quilt at the end of the bed.

"You can talk to me if you want," I said.

"No, I'm fine."

A strong breeze hit the side of the inn and the air whistled through the gaps in the weatherstripping. I heard footsteps in the hallway.

Lindsay cleared her throat. "It was just an email. That's how it started. One single email. I actually thought it was spam. The subject line was *I really need to tell you something...*"

She paused for a second, as though something in the corner of the room had caught her eye. I sat quietly, waiting. She took a deep breath and looked down into her lap. "He said he thought he was falling in love with me. What do you say to that? So, I told him I didn't feel the same way. I never thought for a second that he'd try anything."

"That's the scariest part," I said.

"The worst part wasn't the backlash, the people blaming me, viewing me as a troublemaker. The worst part of it was questioning myself. I'd stare at my reflection in the window on the bus and ask myself, *Did I really have to go on an expedition with him? Did I have to?*"

"It wasn't your fault."

"I know that. In my conscious mind, I know that. But I can't help but think ... It's like locking your door. If you don't lock your door and somebody steals all your things, yes, the burglar is in the wrong, but you could have still prevented it."

"You were not responsible for his actions. He was."

"I think of things in terms of cause and effect. The warning signs were there."

At the Muay Thai gym where I train, there is a once-a-week women's self-defence class. The doors are locked, and no men are allowed in except the instructor. We learn all the illegal techniques that have been weeded out of the sport, all the dirty fighting that keeps you alive on the street. But we also get tips on how not to be a victim. Not travelling alone at night, always knowing the route you're taking ahead of time.

It's easy to see how people take it one step further and assume that if you haven't predicted and prevented every threat, then you are somehow complicit. Humans seem to almost naturally want to blame victims, to make themselves feel better about the world. My dad called that Monday-morning quarterbacking.

"I wouldn't have done anything different in your position," I said. "That might be cold comfort, but it's the truth. When you say 'the warning signs were there,' you mean the one email, right? I think if you went to the harassment committee with that alone, you'd be even more of a pariah. The haters would have had a field day with that. They would have accused you of dragging a professor's name through the mud just because he had a 'crush' on you. What else were you supposed to do? Avoid fieldwork because of his feelings? No. You shouldn't have to change the course of your academic career because of this guy."

"I've been over all these points a thousand times in my head, Laura," she said. "But still. People don't understand how important it is to finish your research, to publish. They don't understand how important strong letters of recommendation are." She let out a long sigh that seemed to roll over the floor like a fog, filling every corner of the room.

My gut told me not to talk but to listen, so I waited. There was very little I could say, anyway.

"I will do my Ph.D. I will. This won't stop me. I just need a little time."

"I'm glad to hear that," I said. "And I'm happy to have you here in the meantime."

"Thank you, Laura. This has been … I don't know … cathartic, maybe?"

"I just want to be clear that if you ever, even for a moment, feel uncomfortable while working on this show, you can tell me. I have a zero-tolerance policy for harassment."

"If the stories Saad told me about what you did in Oregon are true, I believe you."

"What did he tell you?"

She smiled. "That you're a bit of a badass."

My phone was vibrating, making a grinding sound against the nightstand. I found it by feel, my eyes not yet ready to open and adjust to the dim light of the room. Lindsay made a sound and rolled over, the bed-springs creaking beneath her.

The time on my phone read three fifteen.

"Hello?"

"Hello? Ms. Reagan?"

"Yes."

"I'm sorry to disturb you so late at night. My name is Constable Vance, I'm calling from the Corner

Brook regional office of the Royal Newfoundland Constabulary. There was a car accident just off the Trans-Canada Highway, near Humber Village. The driver is unconscious. He's been taken to Western Memorial Regional Hospital in Corner Brook."

"Who?" I asked, sitting up.

"That's why I'm calling," he said. "He has no ID on him, and there are no ownership papers in the car and no licence plates. Only thing with a name on it in the vehicle was your business card."

"Where did you say you were calling from again, Constable?" I asked as I reached for my laptop. I crept out of the room as quickly as I could in the dark.

"Corner Brook," he said. "On the west side of Newfoundland."

I slipped downstairs to the living room.

"Is he about five foot eight, in his late fifties but sort of boyish-looking? Dark-brown hair? Wide sideburns? Missing several teeth?"

A quilt was draped over the back of the armchair facing the TV. In the glow of my laptop's start-up screen, I saw that every other square of the quilt had a mallard drake at the centre. I wrapped it around my shoulders like a shawl.

Pulling up a map online, I searched for the town of Corner Brook, scrolling out to get an idea of where it was on the island and where it was relative to my position. Corner Brook wasn't directly on the west coast of Newfoundland, but toward the end of an inlet. It was on a central latitude, past Deer Lake where we'd flown in. There was only one Newfoundlander with my business card who I had reason to suspect might be all the way up there.

"I can't confirm the teeth or any facial details, as he's suffered a lot of injuries. But the height and the hair fit your description."

"I think the man's name is Beave Cannings," I said. "Sorry, Theodore Cannings. People call him Beave."

"Once we get him stabilized, could I send you a picture for confirmation?"

"You can," I said. "Could you also contact Sergeant Roy Deloitte from the Springdale RCMP detachment? He's been looking for Mr. Cannings."

"I can certainly do that, ma'am," he said.

"If you need anything from me, feel free to call," I said.

TWELVE

Whatever it is that lurks beneath the waves in Crescent Lake — be it giant carnivorous eels or creatures as yet unknown — there can be no doubt that it is large, it is ... vicious, and it remains one of the most credible North American lake cryptids.
— Rob Morphy Cressie (Newfoundland), February 4, 2010, cryptopia.us

WHEN I AWOKE, I WAS STILL WRAPPED IN the mallard quilt, the sun high enough that its rays poured through the pointed peaks of the evergreen trees outside and right through the living room window. I couldn't be sure if the events from the night prior had actually taken place, but when I checked my phone, I saw that a number I didn't recognize had indeed called at quarter past three.

Lindsay came down the stairs in a cat-like silence. She had changed into flannel pants, a hoodie, and white wool socks that made it look as if she had rabbits on her feet. "I was worried when I didn't hear any snoring," she said. She hunched over and looked me in the face like a doctor might. I couldn't tell if she was kidding. Then the corners of her mouth turned up into a smile. "Is everything okay?"

"As good as can be expected," I said, massaging the back of my neck. The stiffness of a few hours' sleep in that chair would take some time to work out. From my mid-back down, I felt frozen in place.

Lindsay walked around the coffee table and fell back on the couch. I debated telling her about the call, the car accident, Beave, rolling it around my tired skull. It didn't seem prudent, at least not until the accident victim was positively identified.

Lindsay seemed to be reading my face as she slouched on the couch. Thankfully, the rest of the inn was waking up and soon there would be enough distractions to rescue me from her scrutiny.

Chris came down the stairs and looked surprised to see the two of us up already.

"Have you been down here since that phone call?" Lindsay finally asked.

"Yes," I said. "Sorry to have woken you."

"I wasn't really asleep," she said.

"Oh."

Chris glanced over at me with a raised eyebrow.

I could have lied. I could have said it was my mom and she'd forgotten about the four-and-a-half-hour time difference between her place and Newfoundland. That wouldn't have worked on Saad, but Lindsay didn't know me well enough to understand the complexity of my relationship with my mother. Instead, I decided to just let the matter drop completely, betting that Lindsay wouldn't push. And though she did look at me awhile longer, her gaze eventually settled on the floor. The smell of freshly brewed coffee soon permeated the room. The matter seemed closed.

Then my phone rang again.

"Hello?" I answered.

"Laura, it's Sergeant Deloitte. I wanted to thank you for putting Constable Vance in touch with me about Beave."

"So, it was Beave? How's he doing?"

"He hasn't regained consciousness."

"I'm sorry to hear that. Do you know what he was doing up there?"

"I was hoping you might know. The car he was found in didn't belong to him. I'd never seen him drive it. And it looks like he may have been in a fight before he had the car accident."

"What makes you say that?"

There were a few seconds of silence. "His right hand was bruised and the skin on the knuckles was scraped, like he'd punched someone. Not what you'd expect from a collision."

The name Corner Brook had sounded familiar when Constable Vance first said it. I'd been staring at maps of the island preparing for this little expedition, so maybe that was it. Then I remembered Mrs. Flynn. She'd mentioned that Pop Fitzcairn was in the hospital there.

"I'll be around later today with the file you asked for," he said in answer to my silence.

"Sergeant, this might be a shot in the dark, but maybe Beave was on his way to, or on his way back from, seeing Pop Fitzcairn. I'm told he's in the hospital in Corner Brook and not expected to make it out."

"That's as good a guess as any," he said.

"If he got word that Pop had taken a bad turn, it might explain why he'd take off without telling me."

"Better we don't get carried away with wild speculation."

"You're right."

"Please keep me in the loop on this, Sergeant," I said. "The team and I are worried about Beave. He's an important part of our program."

Pouring myself a cup of coffee, I sat down at the dining room table with Lindsay and Chris.

Lindsay looked inquiringly at me over top of the dark-brown frames of her glasses. "For someone who is not a cop, or a criminal, or a lawyer, you have a lot of contact with the police," she said.

"Beave was in a car accident," I said. "He had no ID, but had my card on him, so the provincial police called me. I put them in touch with Sergeant Deloitte."

"Oh my god, is he okay?" she asked.

"He's unconscious but stable," I said. "The circumstances surrounding the accident are a little strange."

"Strange how?"

"Strange in the none-of-our-business kind of way," Danny said as he walked through the doorway, moving straight toward the coffee. "Our business is out on the water today, right?"

"Right," I said. "We'll visit the locations where our eyewitnesses spotted Cressie, then check the traps."

"Sure," he said before taking his first sip.

Our morning on the water became tedious as the boat careened over the same course, the herring in the traps still untouched and decaying. If it was possible to wear a rut into water, we'd have done so. The skeleton we'd brought up from the lake bottom now made our job there seem frivolous. My crew's enthusiasm, and my own, had waned.

As I stepped off the *Darling Mae*, I noticed an RCMP car driving toward the dock. The white cruiser stood out in the sombre, overcast surroundings.

I carried my share of the equipment toward the van, handing it to Chris, who squatted in the back and stowed every tote and container with surgical precision. Then I stepped around the open van doors as the cruiser came to a stop, with Sergeant Deloitte behind the wheel.

Without a word to the others, I approached the vehicle. The passenger side window hummed as it lowered. There was a large brown string-and-button envelope sitting on the passenger seat.

"Good day," Deloitte said as he scooped up the envelope and handed it to me. "Here's the file you wanted. I haven't had a chance to go over it, so I'm not sure how much use it'll be to you."

"That's fine," I said. "Just having it is very helpful."

The envelope had the RCMP insignia at the top: a crown sitting atop an oval, the RCMP motto in French encircling the head of a bison, a laurel of maple leaves starting at the bottom and curving around the oval. There were lines printed below, on them handwritten words, maybe dates or names, which had been crossed out with ballpoint pen or magic marker.

"I'm going over to Beave's cabin right now. The lady he hired to clean his place hasn't heard from him, so she called in. Constable Hodges is there with her now."

"You didn't break the news about Beave's car accident?" I asked.

"I've had no reason to," he said. "I'll tell her when I get over there, but —"

"But you want to take a quick look around, given the strange circumstances surrounding the accident?"

Deloitte's mouth tightened and he nodded. "Now I don't want you making more out of this than there is," he said, raising a finger at me. "But you've said a few things that got me thinking."

"Mind if I come with you?" I asked.

Deloitte looked out through the windshield, his mouth hanging open a little. He closed it, took a deep breath, and tightened his grip on the wheel. He turned back to me and smiled. "Hop in!"

Maybe it was because I'd done him a good turn, or maybe he was hoping for good publicity, it didn't really matter. The moment I sat down, the envelope resting on my knees, and buckled my safety belt, I started to question my own actions. What did I hope to find at Beave's?

We drove in silence, Deloitte waving at locals as they walked along the edge of the road. As we approached Beave's house, Deloitte looked over at me. "Now I don't want you volunteering any information or asking too many questions, okay?"

"I'll follow your lead," I said.

"We don't want to stir anything up. Claire Dooley gets worked up easily."

I got out of the car first but waited for Deloitte, following him up the stone path. He paused at the steps and made a *ladies first* gesture. I went up the stairs, taking the two steps that put me in line with the front door. I waited for the sergeant to lead the way.

Beave's front door was open when we got there. The house was dark, but inside I heard the voices of two women talking. Deloitte walked inside, stepping out of the hallway into the living room to make space for me.

Footsteps echoed through the house, and then a figure appeared in the hall. It was the constable from the RCMP detachment in Springdale, the one who was working the front desk when we visited, which explained why Deloitte had said her name as though I would know who Hodges was.

"Yes?" she asked, her tone flat and disinterested.

Deloitte poked his head around the corner. "She's with me, Constable," Deloitte said. "Anything?"

"It's not like I'm searching the place," Hodges said. "Just a friendly pop-in to make sure there are no signs of distress."

"And how are you today, Ms. Claire?" he asked.

Standing behind Constable Hodges was a slightly overweight woman wearing a white sweater and pink sweatpants. The constable made way for her and I got a better look at her face. Glasses rested on her bulbous nose.

She tilted her head down, peering over her glasses at me. "Well, I'm a little concerned, to be honest," she said.

"Claire, this is Laura Reagan," Deloitte said. "Beave was helping her with a TV program she's making about Cressie."

She nodded. "He told me about it. That's all he talked about lately. I've never seen him so excited."

I followed Deloitte into the living room, and the constable and Claire joined us.

"Claire picks up after Beave," Deloitte told me, to complete the introduction.

"That must keep you busy," I said with a smile.

"The old boy's no slawmeen, but he a man, ain't he?"

Sergeant Deloitte leaned in close, his hat in his hands. "An untidy person," he whispered.

"Thanks," I whispered back.

I took a few minutes to look around. Beave's home could have been a beautiful old cabin. It smelled of wood, and the beams stretching across the ceiling were hewn by hand. But it had fallen on hard times. Aside from the mess that thrived in Claire's absence, the cabin needed a new roof, a thousand gallons of paint, and new flooring in both the kitchen and bathroom. However, the stone fireplace that dominated the living room added a rustic charm to the whole place. The smell brought me back to the cabins and lodges Dad took me to when we were exploring the mountains and river valleys of Washington, Oregon, even Northern California.

Claire stood still behind me while the two Mounties poked around. Her work was evident, as there was no dust on the fireplace mantle, nor on the picture frames and knickknacks crowding it: stones, fossils, figurines, matchbox race cars, a baseball with an illegible autograph, even the spent shell casing, which looked more for war than for hunting. Most of the pictures were of Beave holding an impressive catch or standing above a regal bull moose that he'd brought down, the butt of his rifle resting on his hip.

My eye was drawn to one photograph of him and two other men, each holding large fish, the lake in the background and behind it a mountain collared in evergreen trees. The youngest of the three men looked university age, with a shock of blond hair that caught the sunlight. The other man was older, tall and thin, with a scarred and lined face. Picking up the picture, I could see that it had no stand and was just leaning against the stone. A length of wire was draped across the back of it.

In fact, all the pictures at the back of the mantle looked like they were meant to be hung.

"Claire," I said, "can you tell me who this is?"

"That's Beave, Lou Fenton, and Pop Fitzcairn," she said.

Lou Fenton, one half of the tragic pair of lovers who supposedly fell through the ice of Lake Crescent. So, there was a connection between Beave and Lou, beyond being just "a lad he grew up with" — which also meant a connection between Beave and Sarah. Beave's mysterious disappearance after the discovery of the body — whoever it was — suddenly didn't sit well with me.

Claire started breathing heavily, narrowing her eyes. She took her glasses off and wiped her eyes with her thumb. "I hope Beave is okay," she said.

I looked at Sergeant Deloitte, wondering when he planned on telling Claire about Beave's accident, but he had his back to me as he moved deeper into the house. It seemed like he might never tell her, or at least not until he found whatever he seemed to be looking for.

Claire was watching me, as if the house and its contents were her responsibility and she wasn't about to let a stranger upset the balance she had worked so hard to strike. I set the frame back down on the mantle, exactly as I had found it.

Deloitte walked through the kitchen, which was adjacent to the living room, and I watched through the doorway as he peaked over the edge of the sink and even opening the fridge door. It seemed he was looking for clues to Beave's behaviour prior to his sudden departure. Was the fridge well stocked? Were there dirty dishes in the sink? Was there anything that indicated either a planned absence or a quick getaway? He shot me a glance, and I directed my gaze to the phone that sat on an end table beside the couch in the living room, just around the corner from where Deloitte stood. It was an ugly large-buttoned white telephone with a thin green display screen and a built-in mini-cassette answering machine. I hadn't seen anything like it in two decades.

The sergeant walked around the corner and looked down at the phone. A red light flashed, indicating that Beave had a message. He didn't play the messages. Instead he scrolled down the list of callers.

"Claire, your number ends with 5872?"

"That's right," she said.

"The only other number that called in was long distance, which I've seen enough in the last few days to recognize as yours," he said, looking at me.

"And outgoing calls?" I asked.

"Don't know if this old thing can tell me that," he said.

I walked over. "I think that will do it," I said, pointing to an arrow-shaped button.

As he scrolled through the outgoing calls, I took out my phone to see if the numbers matched any Beave had given me of our interviewees. They did. In fact, it seemed Beave hadn't made any calls outside of those related to either having his house cleaned or the Cressie interviews. In a community so small and so friendly, that seemed odd, unless they just knocked on each other's doors and skipped the phone altogether.

"Does Beave have a mobile phone?" Deloitte asked. It was clear who the question was intended for.

"Not as far as I know," Claire said.

"Well," he said, "I guess we'll just have to wait and see for now. Just to be cautious, I'll contact the traffic division and see if there've been any car accidents involving a man matching Beave's description. I'll contact the local hospitals."

He walked one last circle around the living room, pausing in front of the mantle and pointing at the photograph I'd picked up minutes earlier. "Were Beave and Pop still in touch?"

"Can't says that I know for sure," Claire said. "They never talked when I was around. Don't think Beave ever mentioned him, and I been working for him for years."

"Thank you, Ms. Claire," he said, a friendly smile on his lips.

Deloitte walked over to the screen door and pushed it open. Claire went through first, then me, then he let it go. Constable Hodges held her own door. It didn't seem rude of Deloitte, just a choreographed routine they'd practised a hundred times. We formed a circle on the porch.

"I'll have someone drive by tonight, and again tomorrow morning," Deloitte told Claire. "Just to check up."

"This just isn't like him," she said, worry creeping into her voice.

"I know, dear, but you know how us older men get, eccentric and everything. He's probably down by Cressie's Castle on the trail there, pointing a camera at the lake just waiting to bring a Cressie photo to Ms. Reagan here." He pointed his nose in my direction without taking his eyes off Claire. "But we'll keep an eye out," he said. "Thank you for bringing this to our attention. Have yourself a good day now, and we'll see you soon."

Claire took the front steps slowly, leaning heavily on the railing, which creaked under her weight, its peeling paint exposing the bare wood underneath. She made her way to a rust-bottomed green Plymouth Voyager parked on the street. She lingered a moment, looking back at us, before sitting down inside.

Deloitte waited until she closed the door, turned the engine, and pulled away. "Hodges," he said, "a Constable Vance got in touch with Laura here at three in the morning. The constabulary had found a car in a ditch by the side of the Trans-Canada near Corner Brook. The victim had no ID, only Laura's business card. The description of the man matched Beave, but he was pretty badly beaten up, and not only from the car wreck. Laura put Vance in touch with me and I was able to confirm that it's Beave. He's in the hospital in Corner Brook now, unconscious but expected to make a full recovery."

Constable Hodges stood there a moment with her thumbs hooked into her belt, processing the new information. "Okay, so why not tell Claire? The poor thing's going to worry herself sick."

"I wanted the chance to take a look around Beave's place, get an idea if something spooked him or if he planned on going somewhere. By all accounts, he was due to stick around town and help Laura with her program. Something's wrong here."

She turned to me and sized me up with her cop gaze. "I guess finding a body isn't enough for some people," she said.

"Seems like it's two-for-one mystery day," I said. "But you're right, this is enough for me, I'm going to head back. Thank you again for the file, Sergeant."

"Want me to take you back to —"

"That's all right, Sergeant. The walk will give me time to think."

It felt like I'd just broken even. I'd established that it was unlikely that Beave planned to leave, so his departure was abrupt and therefore suspicious. But I'd also established that he treasured his friendship with Pop Fitzcairn. Even though they didn't seem to speak with any frequency, Beave still kept that picture on his mantle, in plain view, to be dusted off by Claire Dooley. It still meant something to him. Could some late-night, maudlin moment of regret have compelled his flight out of Robert's Arm?

But I was looking at things all wrong. I had the file, which would offer some background to use in the show and hopefully more leads to pursue. My problem was Cressie, not a body found in a remote Canadian lake. Beave was an acquaintance to be concerned about, not a mystery for me to solve.

The sun had already reached its apex and had begun its westward descent. When I crossed over the land bridge on Orlando Road, a valley on either side of me, I weighed my options. Instead of taking Middle Road and going back toward the harbour, I decided to turn right at the split and follow the sun. I knew the lay of the land just well enough to know that the inn was west of my position and that not many roads led in that direction. Any that did would take me close to my destination.

The terrain rose slightly as I headed west; yellow, white, and light blue houses lined the road. To the right, the land rose up behind them, forming a tree-covered hump of earth like a sleeping giant. A car came up behind me, slowly, quietly.

I saw it was a minivan as it passed me. The driver turned to me, then slowed down. He rolled down the window. "Need a lift?"

It was John O'Donahue.

"I can manage, thank you," I said. "It's not far."

"If it's all the same to you, I'd feel better about it."

When I reached for the door handle and got in, he smiled. He turned and put both hands on the wheel, looking intently through the windshield. A pine-tree-shaped air freshener dangled from the rear-view mirror.

"You're going back to the inn?"

"Yes, please."

He put the minivan in drive and made a three-point-turn, pulling into a driveway with a pickup and two ATVs in it.

"Does this road not lead back to the inn?" I asked, pointing my thumb over my shoulder.

"Trust me, I know where I'm going," he said, a faintest hint of impatience in his usually placid voice.

We drove along Main Street toward Church Road, along the route the team and I usually took from the inn to the harbour.

"Any trouble finding things?" he asked.

"So far so good."

"Just let me know if you need any help," John said. "I may not be able to point you in the direction of a giant eel, but few folks know as much about this area as I do."

When we got to the harbour, he stopped the minivan abruptly, before the trees began to block the view. He pointed out my window, reaching across the car to do so. "You see there? Right there is the final resting place of the *Pine Lake*. The *Pine Lake* was originally a troop transport in World War One. After that, she was used as a pulp carrier. She used to carry two thousand cords of pulpwood at a time until the late fifties, when she was determined to be a safety risk. So, the people of the town set her aflame and watched her drift, like the funeral of a Viking nobleman. The smoke was thick, black, and rose so high that neighbouring towns like Springdale thought all of Robert's Arm had caught fire."

"That's crazy," I said.

"When the water's clear, you can still see what's left of the hull. And just beyond the harbour lies the *Grayhound*, an old iron ship that used to carry the mail up and down the coast. You can see her propellers through the water. There's so much history here. Sometimes it feels like everyone will go away and forget it." He sat quietly, as if staring after his words as they floated away.

The pine scent of the air freshener mixed with John's aftershave. The smell reminded me of my father.

"Would you like to have dinner with me?" John asked. "Nothing fancy, but I've learned to be a pretty decent cook."

There are guys who are perfectly transparent, then there are the guys who are opaque. Was it an innocent invite from a cordial host who saw himself as the ambassador of this little fishing town? Was it something more? Though he didn't look all that much older than me, I figured I was half John's age. It seemed wise to cut this potential advance short, though part of me was curious.

"Not tonight, I'm afraid," I said. "I still have lots of work to do. We're doing a live chat thing for the show, giving our audience a chance to discuss the expedition with us."

"But the show hasn't even finished filming," he said.

"The final product won't be on television for a while, but the online component starts before we even arrive."

"Oh, well, I see," John said, clearing his throat. "You let me know if you need anything then, anything at all."

"Thank you," I said. A thought suddenly occurred to me. "John, do you know anything about pirate treasure here on the island?"

He looked surprised.

"I know how that sounds," I said, smiling despite myself.

"Some old coins are found every so often. And the remains of pirate hideouts are sometimes found in quiet coves, away from where the larger settlements were located. But as far as chests filled with gold, none were ever found when I was working for the Provincial Archaeology Office. Haven't heard of any since either. Not that we didn't have our share of pirates. The most famous was Peter Easton. He was a privateer, raiding and capturing vessels off the coast of Newfoundland in the name of Elizabeth the First. When King James came to power, he put an end to all privateering, but that didn't stop Peter."

I nodded for him to continue.

"Then there's the legend of Jack Brill. He was another pirate, Irish or Scottish, maybe Welsh. The legend changes so often. He was captain of a ship called the *Quarter Horse*, so named because it was fast and compact like the breed of race horses. Legend has it he was stabbed to death in a knife fight with an English soldier over a beautiful chambermaid. He's said to have hidden his stash somewhere around this part of the island. We've had treasure hunters digging around as long as I've been alive, hoping they could find Brill's treasure."

"Do you think there's anything to the legend?"

John shrugged. "I've never seen any historical record that convinced me there was a Jack Brill."

"What did you do for the archaeology office?" I asked.

"Mostly paperwork," he said, smiling. "I approved development permits. If anyone, either the government or a private business, wanted to develop on land with a potential historical value, I oversaw the site assessment. If we deemed a site as having historical value, we'd bring in a team of archaeologists to excavate it. If there were no signs of any archaeological importance, we'd grant development permits."

The deep sadness returned to his eyes, more vibrant than before, like it was somehow in high definition. It seemed like the time to push him a little further. Not too hard, but just enough.

"Could you take a look at something for me?" I asked, pulling out my phone.

"Certainly."

"I know you know a lot about the area," I said, opening up the picture of a coin I found online, similar to the one found on the skeleton. "Do you know what this is, and where I might find one here on the island?"

He leaned in close and squinted at the picture. There was a tremor across his face, a slight twitching of the muscles that betrayed his poker face. His mouth opened a little then closed again. "Uh, that's a Portuguese gold coin, a few hundred years old, I'd say."

"Where might I find coins like these?"

"That's difficult to say outside of private collections. Newfoundland has had its share of settlers, including villages made up of Portuguese fisherman. Since they traded with the other colonies, you might find their coins at any of a dozen archaeological sites."

"Any idea how much a coin like this might be worth?"

John was silent for a beat or two. "No, I'm afraid not."

"Thanks again, John."

"The pleasure was mine."

The van slowed halfway down the driveway that led to the inn. There were trees on either side of us. John parked just ahead of the inn's front door. Slipping my fingers over the latch, I started to open the door. John rested his hand gently on my shoulder and cleared his throat. "I hope you haven't forgotten my offer," he said.

"The St. George's Day feast? Of course not," I said. "I'm sorry I haven't been able to give you a firm answer. Shooting on such a short schedule is hectic enough without the hiccups we've experienced."

"The skeleton in the lake and Beave's skedaddling."

"Exactly," I said.

"Well, there's no pressure," he said. "You can call five minutes before arriving if that suits you, or don't fret about calling at all. My home is always open to you."

The air felt thick, or maybe it was just the tension in my chest. I listened to the gentle hum of John's van as I walked up the steps. He was going to wait until I was inside before driving off. I turned and waved before I pulled the door open, saw his hand rise from off the steering wheel. I watched the headlights peel back, then he was gone.

THIRTEEN

There are sightings of a mysterious creature in Crescent Lake that date back for
centuries. Tales of massive eels; eels the
size of canoes with the strength to capsize
boats are plentiful.

— Denver Michaels, *People Are Seeing
Something: A Survey of Lake Monsters in
the United States and Canada*, 2016

I WALKED INTO THE INN LIKE IT WAS PAST
curfew at my mom's house. It wasn't quite sneaking but
pretty close to it. I had the file under my arm so it I
could feign that it was all business. Our misadventure
in Oregon had given me a reputation that I didn't ask
for and certainly didn't want. The last thing I wanted
was for the team to think I wasn't serious about the
show and was instead playing detective.

The television was on in the living room. Fred and Chris were watching a hockey game. Danny was in the dining room, which had become his ad hoc office. Their screens held their attention as I turned the corner and slipped upstairs to my room. A quick glance down the hallway gave me all the information I needed. The only light underneath a door came from Saad's room. Lindsay might have been napping, so I turned the doorknob slowly, opening enough of a gap to peer into the darkness. Her bed was empty, perfectly made.

I heard her voice, louder than a whisper but not by much. It was coming from down the hall, from Saad's room. His usual soft-spoken bass voice was inaudible from where I stood. Tossing the file onto my bed like a frisbee, I moved slowly down the hall.

The door to Saad's room was closed. No shadows moved beneath it. No sounds except low voices. I raised my hand to knock but hesitated. The old floorboards creaked beneath me as I shifted my weight. The low voices stopped. It forced my hand. I knocked and Saad opened the door just wide enough for his face to fill the gap.

"Laura," he said before pulling the door wider. "I was going to call you."

He stepped aside and ushered me inside. Once I was a half-step past him, he closed the door behind me. Lindsay sat on his bed, his laptop open beside her. What would his mother say?

"Saad found something you might find interesting," she said.

"We both picked up on it," he said, quick to share credit or at least shrug the spotlight.

Lindsay flashed a quick smile at Saad before turning the laptop screen toward me. "We were reviewing all the GoPro footage we've taken, obviously starting from the beginning. The footage from the *Darling Mae* at the moment we recovered that skeleton is especially significant."

Saad sat down on the bed, the laptop between them. It felt like I was watching two undergrads give a presentation they'd prepared at the last minute. Saad slid his index finger along the touchpad, enlarging one window to dominate the screen, then clicking the space bar.

"This is the footage from your camera," he said.

I re-watched that moment from a slightly higher perspective, hearing Danny's callous remarks about our bet and then him barking at me not to touch anything. Water spilled out of the tarp and onto the deck.

"This is the video captured on my camera," Saad said.

The clip began with his arms reaching over the gunwale as he assisted in bringing up the ROV and the tarp. It was like playing a first-person shooter, except I could hear Saad's hesitant breathing, and the whispers of the others, the "got it" and "oh shit" and "easy, easy, easy." I watched them set the tarp down, then saw myself, standing idly, Danny on one side and Beave on the other. Our faces were a trio of surprise and concern, with a slight eye-roll by Danny. Beave's shock dissipated quickly, his lined face hardening. My mouth hung open, my eyes wide — not the look of stoicism I would have preferred. It was a perspective that seemed entirely different from the way I experienced it.

"Well, I'm sorry I just stood there," I said.

"I wasn't much better," Lindsay said. "Play mine."

Saad swiped and clicked and Lindsay's perspective was on screen for us to see. Her lean arms clad in orange sleeves pawed at the tarp as she tried to reach around the others. For a moment, she had a decent grip with her left hand on the tarp's edge, then lost it as the others began to turn when they pulled the tarp aboard.

"A for effort," I said.

Lindsay took a step back on the deck, giving the others a wide berth as they lay the body down. She, too, looked over at Beave, Danny, and me, albeit from an angle that highlighted Beave and almost cut out Danny completely. The same looks: face-hardening, mouth-gaping, eye-rolling. I'm not sure what I was supposed to be seeing.

"So, we saw and heard the reactions of the crew after the remains were brought aboard, yes?" Lindsay asked.

I nodded.

"Now play the clips forward," she said to Saad.

I relived my examination of the skeleton, the leather pouch, my narration of the gold and speculation that it was a coin. Saad's clip was very much the same, him staring down at the tarp, the skeleton, my voice picked up by his camera's mic. When I came into frame, I looked more as I would like to see myself — acting, not reacting. Lindsay's clip was similar, taken from farther back on the port side, the wind sweeping over her microphone, making the audio hard to decipher. She didn't just have me in the frame but Danny and Beave as well.

"Now watch carefully," Lindsay said.

I didn't watch myself, as I knew from Saad's clip that I wasn't where the action was going to be. My eyes bounced between Beave and Danny like a game of Pong. I heard my own voice and struggled to make out each word. "It's round. Not like a ring, more like a coin." At the word *coin*, Beave's hard face crumbled, changing into an expression of wild-eyed fear. He fell back against the bulkhead of the bridge like he'd been hit by George Foreman.

"Whoa," I said. "He was taking it well, then I say 'coin' and he loses it. He knows something."

"Right?" Lindsay said.

I thought John's reaction to the coin had been a little weird, but Beave's was unmistakably strange. That coin meant something to him. Something that made him want to disappear.

"Then he takes a powder —" Saad said.

"And we can't even ask him about it, you're right," I said. "And no more old movies for you, Saad."

"So?" Lindsay asked, standing up and putting her hands on her hips. "I know it's nowhere near conclusive, but we know Beave knows something, and he's —"

"On the lam," Saad said, smiling at me.

"I'll bring this to Sergeant Deloitte," I said. "But that's it. We're trying to tape a show here, not get into trouble."

Lindsay folded her arms and looked at me as though I was pitching her a cure-all elixir from the back of a horse-drawn wagon.

"Seriously," I said.

She looked at Saad. He cocked an eyebrow at her, then they both looked at me. Footsteps caused the floorboards to creak again. Someone else knocked.

"Chow time!" Chris said through the door. "We're heading out for some pub grub."

The bar was empty, and it wasn't long before a round of pints and several baskets of fries landed at our table. Chris and Duncan, after boasting about their own prowess at darts, challenged each other to a game, all the while acting as though they had nothing to prove. Dr. Willoughby was content to watch them play, his pint warming in his hand. Clyde then challenged Danny to a game of pool, but Danny's phone was all-consuming, and he sat leaning away from the table, balanced on the two back legs of his chair, scrolling and texting. Lindsay, a pescatarian, debated over what kind of deep-fried seafood she was in the mood for. I ordered chicken fingers that were hard and dry, fresh from the freezer of the grocery store. After drowning them in the plum sauce that came in a little plastic tub, they became semi-edible. Classic rock blasted from the speakers mounted in the corners of the room.

"My goodness, I must be out of practice," Duncan said, returning to the table for a handful of fries. "Fancy a game?"

Lindsay and I looked at each other.

"No thanks," I said.

"Me, neither, upon reflection," he said, sitting down.

Dr. Willoughby took his place. I watched him hold a dart at eye-level for a long time, testing trajectories without ever letting go. When he finally did, the dart lodged into the black corkboard half a foot below the circular target. He shrugged at Chris.

"Are you staying on the wagon?" Duncan asked me.

"Excuse me?" I asked, pointing down at my beer, which was nearing empty.

"I mean, are you staying away from the mystery of the body in the lake?"

"You make it sound like a pulp novel," I said. "Yes, I am staying out of the investigation."

"I see," he said suspiciously. "I was just having a chat with Chris and he said you met with that RCMP sergeant."

"That was something else," I said. "Having to do with Beave Cannings. I'm a little concerned about his absence."

"He had his chance," Danny said without looking up. "When he shows up again he's not getting back on this show."

"And you don't think these two occurrences are related?" Duncan asked.

"The body and Beave's disappearance? We shouldn't assume they are related."

Lindsay's eyes lifted as she dipped a fish stick into tartar sauce and nibbled at the tip. They darted from me to Saad, who was dipping a French fry into the glob of ketchup he'd sprayed out onto the check-patterned paper that lined the plastic baskets that the food came in.

"I'm not so sure. After all, it was a rather sudden disappearance," he said.

"Sergeant Deloitte didn't indicate to me that he suspected Beave of any crimes, let alone murder."

"Maybe it's Sarah Tindall's skeleton," Lindsay said.

I shot her a look.

"That's as good a hypothesis as any," Duncan said. "Perhaps there was a love triangle. Beave couldn't stand Sarah and Lou being an item."

"We would have heard about it," I said, "given the size of the town. Also, Lindsay, you examined the body. Did that look like someone who went through the ice on a snowmobile?"

"Well, who else could it be?" Lindsay asked. "And why would Beave run?"

"It could be anyone," I said. "And we don't know that Beave *ran.*"

"We learned that Pop Fitzcairn is in the hospital and not expected to recover," Saad said. "Maybe Beave went to visit him? If his condition deteriorated, that might explain —"

"No, no, no," Duncan said. "You're ruining all the intrigue." He took a long sip of his pint. "It seems I'm fairing as well at this game as I did at darts. Let's have a proper mystery, guys." He clapped, then pointed at Lindsay. "Are you saying the body is Sarah Tindall?"

"Well, not with any certainty," she said.

"For the sake of the game, I'll take that as a yes. So, we have our victim. The story as we heard it must be wrong then. No snowmobile accident, no lovers falling together into the cold blackness of the water, no giant eels. Boo!"

"The accident story seems far-fetched," Saad said. "Laura and I saw the eyewitness's vantage point, and it's hard to believe he could have seen anything at night, from that distance. But that doesn't rule out the giant eels."

Duncan laughed. "True enough. If divers followed up on even a false report, they may have come across giant eels. Are you with us so far, Laura?"

"Well, Pop Fitzcairn's neighbour told us that Lou and Sarah were living with Pop at the time, so he would have known it was them leaving his place by snowmobile, therefore it's reasonable to assume he watched them as they took off into the night."

"Ah! That changes things, doesn't it? Where do you suppose they were going?"

"And why were they living with Pop?" Lindsay asked.

"Apparently, Lou's house caught fire," Saad said.

"That's certainly something, isn't it?" Duncan asked. "How did this fire happen?"

Saad shrugged, so Duncan looked at me.

"That part is not clear," I said.

"So, if there's anything to the story of the accident, then we can rule out the remains being those of Sarah Tindall."

He furrowed his brow while taking another long sip. He put the pint back on the cardboard coaster and chewed his lip. Saad and Lindsay got back to eating, fries and fish sticks respectively.

"Dash it all," Duncan said. "We'll say the remains are those of Sarah Tindall!"

Danny looked up from his phone, made eye contact with Duncan, and shook his head.

"Otherwise we have no game," he said. Then, putting on a bad Belgian accent, "'Ow elze to stimulate our litto grey cellz?"

"Okay, I'll play," Lindsay said. "So, that was Sarah Tindall in the lake, which means that there was no snow-mobile accident, which means Lou Fenton is still alive and his old friend Pop Fitzcairn helped him cover it up."

"Where does Beave fit in?" I asked casually, to give the impression I was playing along.

"And what of that gold coin?" Duncan added.

We ordered another round of drinks.

"The coin was bent in the fashion of a love token," Lindsay said, looking across the table at me.

"So, the love triangle hypothesis is back on the table," Duncan said. "We have two young lovers, Lou and Sarah, then Beave, the jealous third party. Maybe this fire at Lou's house was only the first attempt, yes? Brilliant. So, he tries again and succeeds, but he's heart-broken to have killed his lady love, so he ties a love token around her neck and gives her a burial at sea, or lake rather. Now he walks those shores, staring into the blue … well, I think I may be going off the rails here."

"Beave would have needed to recruit Pop Fitzcairn to claim to witness the snowmobile accident," I said. "And why not just dump a snowmobile and Lou's body in the lake, too, in order to corroborate the story?"

"We don't know that Lou isn't in the lake somewhere," Saad said.

"Whose side are you on?" I asked.

"So, Beave has left town upon discovery of the corpse and perhaps is attempting at this very moment to prevent Pop Fitzcairn from making a deathbed confession and ruining the decades-old scheme."

I didn't tell them that Beave was in the very same hospital as Pop Fitzcairn, badly injured and unconscious. Partly it was out of respect for Sergeant Deloitte, but mostly it was to stop the game from going any further. My team would have had a field day with what Deloitte said about the injuries on Beave resembling those of a fist fight, not a car accident.

"This is a documentary, not a crime drama," Danny said, setting his phone down on the table. "We don't need a writers' room."

"I've seen the quote-unquote documentaries that air on your network — *Prehistoric Paranormal* and *Hunt for Hitler's Hidden Hideaways*," said Duncan. "Their flights of fancy certainly have ... *imagination*, to say the least."

"We like to show multiple perspectives," Danny said. "I don't see you turning down NatureWorld's money."

"Certainly not," Duncan said, raising the fresh pint that was delivered to him. "To NatureWorld's money!

May it be deposited into our bank accounts and pay our mortgages." He turned and looked at us millennials. "Or rent," he added.

"Here, here," I said.

Lindsay fell asleep on the drive back to the inn, her head dangerously close to resting on my shoulder. She awoke only as we were partway up the inn's driveway, and only for long enough for us to say our goodnights to the rest of the team. When we got back to our room, she fell back on her bed, her forearm across her face, only her mouth and chin visible.

I lay in bed, trying to keep thoughts of the coin, the skeleton, and murder out of my mind. Although we had enough footage to put together an instructional video about surveying a lake's eel population, there was very little material gripping enough for a cable program. Unlike Bigfoot, giant eels don't come with their own brand power. I didn't want our first foray into something a bit different to be a ratings flop.

I got up, dug into my bag, and found my dad's journal, which had been stuffed underneath my clothes. It contained a loose narrative of anecdotes, Polaroid photos, and crude sketches. I flipped through the menagerie of mythic beasts all the way to the end, to Cressie. There was a weird doodle in the margin, like a half-crushed water bottle with electricity flowing from the top and the bottom. I wasn't sure what it was supposed to be. Maybe Dad just got bored staring at the white space.

As I read his notes rehashing the Cressie legend, I noticed that the sentence *Just like Old Ned?* appeared twice, in red pen. The first instance was in the paragraph describing mysterious holes in the ice. The second, however, took on a new significance to me. I flipped back to find Dad's notes on Old Ned.

"You should go to sleep," Lindsay said.

"Sorry to keep you up," I said.

"You're not," Lindsay said. "I have a difficult time sleeping in beds that aren't my own."

"That sucks."

"Tell me about it. What are you reading?"

"About lake monsters. It's an old journal. I'm hoping to find some kind of insight that'll give me something to look into while we're here."

"Find anything?"

"Not yet. Some weird similarities ... and some annoying differences."

"How do you mean?"

"Cressie has been blamed for holes in the ice when Lake Crescent freezes over. There's another cryptid, said to be responsible for holes in the ice that covers Lake Utopia in New Brunswick. Old Ned."

"That seems reasonable. Folklore often crops up to explain complex phenomena. For whatever reason, these holes appear, and if there happens to be a legend about a monster, the two coalesce."

"Here's something else. The Old Ned story also features an encounter involving an accident and 'eels thick as a man's thigh.' It looks like there could have been cross pollination."

Lindsay rolled onto her back and lifted one arm out from under the covers. She rested the top of her forearm across her face, concealing it from me, and took a deep breath. "Maybe it's time to stop viewing this as a zoological expedition and more like an ethnographic one. We tend not to think that North Americans of European descent have folklore all their own, but the ubiquity of lake monsters in North America and their similarities says otherwise.

"I took a class in ethnology when I was doing my undergrad, and the part I found most fascinating was the study of so-called urban legends. We read about a study where the subjects were asked to read an urban legend, rewrite it in their own words, then pass on their version to another participant. And so on. The researchers concluded that urban legends tied to survival themes stick more readily in a person's mind and carry on most accurately. Sex and nudity, snakes and spiders, anything tied to human survival and procreation."

"We'll probably have enough material for a book on why people believe in monsters by the time we're finished with this show," I told her.

Lindsay dropped her arm to the bed, turned to me, and smiled. "It really is fascinating. I think many academics are inclined to dismiss squatchers and the like, but I think it's interesting that such a culture can build up around monster sightings. It makes you wonder about religion, or any other faith-based group belief system."

"I definitely see a bestseller in your future," I said.

"We seem to be wired to create sea monsters that are a physical manifestation of the dangers of large bodies of water. Our powerlessness in water, our susceptibility to drowning, can turn something so necessary to our survival into a lethal monster."

"These stories are just oikotypes. Is that the right word? Whether it's wild men in the woods or serpents underwater waiting to attack the unwary, certain legends seem to evolve independently across cultures."

"Just look at the number of flood myths that exist worldwide."

"Exactly," I said. "Or even Cinderella stories."

Lindsay rolled over on her side, her eyes barely open. She yawned and buried her face into her pillow and, without saying another word, dropped off into sleep.

I turned off the overhead light and pulled up the covers to my stomach. White moonlight shone through the gaps in the curtains.

F O U R T E E N

On June 7, 1960, the Canadian Press described how four loggers had seen a monster in Lake Crescent, near Robert's Arm in Newfoundland. "Bruce Anthony of Robert's Arm," said the report, "thought it was a giant conger eel."

— John Braddock, "Monsters of the
Maritimes," *Atlantic Advocate*,
January 1968

THE TOWNSFOLK HERE EMBRACED CRESSIE the way the people of Loch Ness embraced Nessie. The creature was, alongside the fishing and the hiking trails, a pillar of the tourism industry. Mayor Dunlop, along with people like Beave, were Cressie ambassadors, often taking time to discuss the creature with anyone holding a camera.

When the expedition was still in its planning phase and I was contacting officials in Robert's Arm, Mayor Dunlop offered to give me a personal tour. I declined then, as Danny and I agreed that it wasn't the best use of our time, given our tight schedule. When she repeated her offer, at the inn, I glossed over it, rather than say no a second time. But Beave's disappearance had altered our shooting schedule, since he was supposed to take us around the lake and show us where famous sightings of Cressie had taken place. Suddenly, I had some free time. Spending some time with the mayor would give some context about what Cressie means to the town. But also, as much as I didn't want to admit it, Mayor Dunlop would be able to answer some of the questions about the townsfolk that had been eating at me.

Mayor Dunlop met me in the parking lot at the mouth of the Hazelnut Hill Hiking and Adventure Trail, near a part of the lake the locals called Muskrat Brook. She was wearing a pullover and khakis and had a backpack with the waistband clipped loosely across her stomach.

"You walked here?" she asked, as I approached her on foot.

"It wasn't far. Gave my legs a bit of a warm-up." I wasn't going to tell her that I had already jogged the trail.

She smiled. "We're lucky, it's still early enough in the season that the nippers haven't woken up."

"Nippers?"

"Sorry, mosquitoes. We grow them big out here. But they're nothing compared to stouts or, even worse, timber flies." She made her eyes wide like she was telling a ghost story. "Some summers have been so bad, feels like they're draining every last drop of blood. It's just over three kilometres to Hazelnut Hill. Another two and a half to Tommy's Arm River Bridge."

"Do you get a lot of hikers, nippers notwithstanding?" I asked, ignoring the fact that the parking lot was empty.

"We have the premier hiking trail network on the island, and the word is spreading. We expect up to a thousand visitors annually in the coming years." She slowed her pace and scratched the back of her head. "I hate to say it, but your show, and that skeleton, will probably do wonders for us. We need all the press we can get up here."

"I hope my show gets people interested in your town. As for the skeleton …"

"I know, dear, I know. It's a terrible thing. I've heard that you think it might be Sarah Tindall."

In a town with such spotty internet, it was hard to believe that word could travel so fast. But it didn't come as a surprise. I was sure many people around Robert's Arm were jumping to the same conclusion.

"I have no reason to believe it is or it isn't," I said. "My interest in Sarah Tindall pertains only to authenticating the claims that, after she fell through the ice, the divers attempting to recover her body encountered giant eels. Finding the skeleton was just an awful coincidence. But since we're on the subject … can you tell me anything about Sarah Tindall?"

"The trail takes us around what we call the lower part of Lake Crescent," she said in her tour-guide voice.

"I was just a teenager when she came blowing into town like a leaf in autumn."

"Did you have the chance to know her?"

"Not well, no," she said. "I knew enough to know she wasn't good for the town."

"How so?"

"She … I don't know how to say this…. She woke up something in the men in town," she said. "There are four different routes on this trail, of different lengths depending on how serious a hiker one is. The most popular route goes across the George Baker Bridge then up to the top of Hazelnut Hill."

She had two tones of voice, one for the tour and one for the gossip, as though there was the chance someone might overhear us.

"Are you talking about Lou Fenton?"

"It wasn't just Lou. It was half the men here. She didn't settle on Lou until she'd been around a while."

"Did you resent her for that?"

"Oh sure. I couldn't stand the sight of her for a while. Lou lived just up the hill from me. They cut a line through the bush to run the hydro wires to all the houses, and I could see Lou's bedroom window from mine. We were an item at the time, so we'd put candles in our windows to signal when our parents fell asleep. Then we'd sneak out. It was all innocent, you know, kids' stuff. We'd climb to the top of the hill and look up at the stars, or hold hands and walk along the water."

"That sounds nice," I said.

"It was. Lou was a nice man. Maybe too nice, where women were concerned."

"Sarah had several relationships here before Lou?"

"I don't want you to think I'm the town gossip, but yes, she had, let's just say, *relations* with a few of the boys around here. I don't care about things like that — I'm not old-fashioned — but I thought Sarah could be so self-absorbed. It was cruel. Especially to John."

"John?"

"O'Donahue. Sarah and him had a fling before Lou came into the picture. It was sad, really. See, John's wife had passed a few years before, and he was raising that boy of his by himself. He never smiled or nothing after Janet died. Then, all of a sudden, this flower child shows up and he's alive again. I think she thought that was quaint, him courting her. He was very proper, mind you. An old-fashioned gentleman. But when she moved on to Lou, he didn't take it well. I don't think those two boys spoke to each other at all after that — which is hard to do in a town this size."

"Lou and John were friends?"

"Certainly. John, Lou, and Beave were inseparable. Like the Three Musketeers. After the trouble with Sarah, Beave and John turned their backs on Lou. It was hard enough to find work back then as it was, with the mill closing up and the fisheries declining. But once you made it onto John O'Donahue's bad side, it was damn near impossible. The way Lou and Sarah carried on, so publicly, I'm surprised John didn't have them run out of town. I know how deeply it hurt him."

There seemed to be a contradiction in how Fern and Mayor Dunlop described the town and its economic prospects at the time of Sarah Tindall's appearance and disappearance, and the hopefulness John described. Maybe the opportunities were different based on gender, education, and other factors. Maybe the outcomes influenced their perceptions of the past — John obviously did well for himself in the intervening years. Or maybe John had something else to be hopeful about, something the others didn't.

The trees on the left began to thin out, and the lake was visible through a frame of birch trees.

"There's the RV park across the water," Mayor Dunlop said.

I took a step toward the lake, admiring the view but not losing track of the conversation.

"Did John have that kind of sway?"

"Oh sure. I'll tell you one thing, there's no way I could beat John O'Donahue in an election. If he still wanted this job, he'd have it. Even I'd think twice about voting for myself if he were in the race." She paused. "I don't mean to make him out as a bully or a tyrant. No one loves this town more than him, and he'll give you the shirt off his back if you ask. But Sarah hurt him, and he felt betrayed by Lou."

Back at the library, I'd asked John about Sarah, and he behaved as though he'd only had a passing acquaintance with her. Maybe he was hoping to leave those memories buried.

"If you don't mind telling me, how did Mrs. O'Donahue pass?"

Mayor Dunlop stopped walking. She hooked her thumbs under the shoulder straps of her backpack and stared out at the trees and the water down the decline ahead of us. The lake was like a pane of deep blue stained-glass with ripples across the surface. "Ever wonder why so many tall tales about men drowning involve women luring them into the water? Are rough water and high winds not enough?" she asked.

I thought about the sirens of Greek mythology, the rusalka of Slavic lore.

"I suppose there's no reason not to tell you. We've all moved on," Mayor Dunlop finally said. "Mrs. O'Donahue hanged herself."

"My god," I said. "That's terrible."

"John and his boy came home and found her there, hanging from a rope she'd tied to the bannister. That part hurt him a little more, I think. He prided himself on the restoration of the house, on how safe and sturdy everything was compared to when he bought the property."

"That's tragic," I said.

"The Showalter place was just about to collapse when John took it over. I, for one, was grateful that he did. Fixing it up was good for all of us, symbolically. Sir Leland Showalter was the pulp and paper industry on this part of the island. He built up this town and many like it. But he was a hard man who squeezed every penny out of his workers. He ruled this town like a colonial viceroy. We all grew up hearing the stories. That house started as a symbol of industry, but became a source of resentment after the mills closed. His heirs wanted nothing to do with the place. The land it rested on wasn't valuable, and the mansion wasn't worth maintaining if they were only going to use it once a year. After Sir Leland's son died at a young age, ownership of the family properties was shuffled around between lawyers, distant relations, and the courts, until the house was put up for sale. The Showalter estate was eager to be rid of it."

We stopped at the gazebo in the middle of the Tommy's Arm River Bridge and looked out at the winding river that led to the ocean. We continued on to the Sandy Point picnic area, the wind funnelling between the rising, tree-covered hills on either side of the river.

Mayor Dunlop's oral history of Robert's Arm filled in some gaps while raising new questions. The challenge was to keep her talking without seeming nosy. There was no telling if she might decide to turn off the tap. I'd hoped to better understand John's sense of optimism in the past, where the others I spoken to had felt pessimistic. Like everything about that man, there seemed to always be something churning beneath his calm surface.

"What did John do for a living back then? I take it he wasn't the mayor yet."

"Heavens, no. He worked in the Provincial Archaeology Office. He made sure all the proper procedures were followed before any development took place on sites with potential historical value. At that time, there was a boom in offshore oil, which meant the construction of oil platforms. All those men building the things needed somewhere to live, so we were seeing housing projects popping up all over. That kept old John busy, not to mention the dam project and the highway extension."

"Oh," I said. "He wasn't kidding when he told me he'd dedicated his life to the history of the island."

Mayor Dunlop smiled and nodded. "He also made some smart investments — in computers, I think. Made a fortune."

"Good for him," I said, "and good for the town. Even in a state of disrepair, that mansion must have cost more than a government employee could afford. I don't mean to be impertinent, but it seems lucky he had that windfall. I'm sure it's good for the whole town not to have the Showalter House crumble."

"It was no secret that half the town thought he was crazy for buying that place. 'You're going to go into debt so deep you'll never crawl out,' they said. 'It's a money pit,' they said. But John proved them all wrong. When he gets an idea in his head, there's no stopping him. And you're right, it certainly helps the whole town having the house in pristine condition."

From a clearing at the top of the hill, the town was visible to the northeast. The picnic area offered a panoramic view of the lake. There were what looked like the parapets of a medieval castle, except they were made of wood, not stone, and were too small to repel an invading army. This was Cressie's Castle.

"When did he first run for mayor?" I asked.

"Way back," she said. "In the nineties, I think." We had a clear view of the lake side of town, which was mainly houses, roofs sticking out among the trees. The inn was set too far back behind a wall of trees to be visible. Patches of the road leading up toward Pop Fitzcairn's place could be seen where it came close to the shore and the trees thinned out.

You know, it's a hard life out here, not simple like some people expect. You must wonder why the folks around here didn't kick up more of a fuss when word of the skeleton being found started to spread. Truth is, they've been pulling human remains out of the waters here for ages."

"I keep thinking that finding that skeleton was a good thing, that at least we found that woman's body. Maybe the police can identify her and give her family some closure…. Sorry, I don't mean to sound morbid."

"It's okay. On the bright side, Beave is back," she said. "Don't be too hard on him now. I know he was supposed to be in your show."

"Oh yeah?" I said, acting disinterested. My poker face worked. Mayor Dunlop didn't seem to sense my surprise. As far as I knew, only Sergeant Deloitte and I knew that Beave Cannings was in a hospital bed in Corner Brook.

"Yes, I ran into Claire Dooley on the way over here. She said she saw him when she drove past his house."

It wasn't clear to me whether or not Mayor Dunlop knew about his accident. It was still too early to tip my hand. I rolled this information over in my head: *Beave was unconscious, had been badly beaten, and then he suddenly regains consciousness, checks out of the hospital, and drives for hours, all within a day?* It didn't pass the sniff test. Sure, he could have been driven back, but by who? The police would have wanted to speak to him once he came around.

"I wonder if he still feels like doing an interview with us," I said.

"Go by his place and ask him."

"I will. Soon as we're finished here."

"I can take you there," she said.

"That's very nice," I said. "But I'd like to go to the inn first. Thank you, anyway."

By *go to the inn first*, I meant *call Sergeant Deloitte.* No doubt he'd like to be kept in the loop about Beave's miraculous recovery and return.

"I can drop you off at the inn," the mayor said.

"That would be great."

FIFTEEN

The Monster seems to have been fairly ac-
tive over the last decade or so. In the late
spring of 1990, a resident of Robert's Arm
saw a slim, black shape rise five feet from
a patch of churning water before sinking
out of sight.
> — Dale Jarvis, "What's in the Water?"
> *Telegram* (St. John's), June 2, 2008

WHEN I RETURNED TO THE INN, MARY AND
Fred were in the kitchen, speaking to each other like
two people still in love. I waved at them and headed
right upstairs.

In my room, I sat down on the bed and called
Sergeant Deloitte.

"Hi, Sergeant. It's Laura Reagan. Mayor Dunlop just
told me that Beave was back at his place."

"He's in Robert's Arm?"

"That's what she said. She didn't see him herself, but apparently Claire did."

"I'm in Springdale, I could give him a ring at his house, but …"

Obviously, an officer of the law would never ask a civilian to look into the subject of an ongoing investigation, or whatever the Beave situation was considered. And I wasn't going to offer. Not directly, anyway. "I'm gonna stop by Beave's place this afternoon to see if he's fit to do an interview," I said. "Nothing strenuous, of course. Should I let you know how he's doing?"

There was a moment of silence on the other end, then a long sigh. I could almost imagine the smell of coffee on his breath.

"Sure, that'd be fine," he finally said. "Take it easy on him. I'm on my way."

When I arrived at Beave's, Claire Dooley was standing on the porch peering into the front window.

I cleared my throat so as to not startle her, but did so, anyway.

She popped up and turned around, clutching her chest. "Oh goodness, you scared me!"

"I'm sorry, Ms. Dooley," I said. "Where's Beave?"

"I thought he was here. I saw him earlier today, when I was driving by; I'd know that hat and coat anywhere," she said. "I went back home, put the food in the ice box, and came right back here. I didn't doddle one bit."

"I'm sure you didn't," I said.

She went back over to the door and knocked again.

I jogged around the garage and looked in the back window. There was a pickup inside. I ran back, hoping Claire was still on the porch.

"You have your key, don't you?" I asked, getting a little ahead of the situation.

"I wouldn't want to invade his privacy."

I chose to conceal the fact that Beave's truck was sitting in the garage. "That's fair, but we should make sure he's all right."

I watched as she rolled my words around in her brain. Her mouth tightened and moved to the side. While the great debate continued in her head, I passed through the cloud of perfume encircling her and looked through the window. There were no signs of life inside.

"I guess it's okay," Claire said eventually. She went to the door and stared down at the lock, holding the key in front of her like it was a gun. She moved with the door as she pushed it open.

I crept in behind her.

Claire led the way, which seemed proper.

"Beave," she called out softly. Then once more, louder the second time.

We moved inside slowly, ears listening keenly for a reply. The fireplace didn't look as though it had seen any use since my last visit. The floorboards creaked as we approached the bedroom. I hadn't noticed how uneven they were on my first visit. Everything feels like a different world when you're trying to be quiet.

The door to the bedroom was open slightly. Claire put her face right up to the gap and peered in. A moment later, she stepped back and looked at me, her mouth open. She shrugged.

I pushed the door open. The empty, unmade bed told a story of its own. The drawers of the dresser were in various stages of openness. *Did the Mounties leave them like that on their previous visit?* I wondered. *Doubtful.*

"We should go," Claire said.

"You're right," I conceded.

Suddenly, we heard a loud thud, like something had fallen, but it sounded far away. I looked around before turning back to Claire inquiringly.

"I think it came from the cellar," she whispered. She motioned for me to follow her. At the open door to the living room, she pointed down, where the outline of a trap door was cut into the floor. The rug that had covered it was turned up. I couldn't believe I hadn't noticed it when we came in.

"I guess Beave's down there," Claire said uncertainly.

I took the poker from its stand next to the fireplace, then pointed to an old red flashlight by the front door. Claire fetched it silently without question and extended it toward me.

I shook my head. "You keep it," I whispered. "When I open the door and go down, I want you to kneel down and shine the light through the hole."

She looked at me quizzically, her confusion reaching a slow boil on its way to fear.

"Look, I have reason to suspect that someone else might be here, not Beave. I already called Sergeant Deloitte. He's on his way."

She nodded, her eyes wide.

Using the tip of the fire poker, I pried up the brass ring fastened to the trap door and pulled it open, the hinges squeaking. I looked over at Claire again and slowly exhaled. "If somebody pops their head up and it's not me or Beave, slam the door shut," I said quietly.

Claire nodded, her hand trembling a bit as she held the light for me.

Unhooking the poker from the ring, I brandished it like a baseball bat as I carefully placed my foot on the top step. The stairs were just thick planks with no risers. It would have been no problem for someone to reach through, grab my ankle, and send me toppling to the bottom. The stairs creaked with each step I took.

When I reached the bottom, I peered into the darkness, my eyes adjusting. The cone of light that Claire shone down diffused about a foot from the steps. I could make out a row of shelves in the centre and stacks of what looked like firewood around the perimeter. It was deathly quiet. Holding the poker out like a sword, I adjusted my grip to free up my left hand. I took out my phone and turned on the flashlight. I did a quick sweep of the basement. I caught my breath. Behind one of the shelves on the far wall stood a dark figure. Whoever it was remained still.

I took a step closer and held my phone high. The figure bolted. There was a loud screech as a shelf fell toward me. As the figure ran past me, I caught a glimpse of a monstrous face beneath a cap I recognized as Beave's. I staggered back against the wall. Footfalls rang off the stairs as the figure attempted to flee. A loud scream came from above, and the door slammed shut. In my surprise, I'd dropped my phone and it had skidded under the stairs. The home screen glowed ominously. There was the sound of footsteps again, coming down the stairs, then a creaking sound. A square of light appeared at the other end of the cellar, revealing a set of stairs that led outside. The figure lumbered up them and slammed the door behind them.

I got down on my hands and knees and grabbed my phone. I shone the flashlight in the direction of the doorway and ran toward it. It refused to open as I pushed against it. I stuck the poker under my arm and pushed with both hands. The door gave a little. It wasn't locked, but it felt as if there was a weight against it. I put my shoulder into it and gave it one last hard push. There was a snap and the door opened enough that I could squeeze through.

I reached the top of the stairs just in time to see the figure run past a woodpile at the back of Beave's property and disappear into the trees. Not only was the person wearing Beave's hat, they looked to be wearing the jacket he'd worn during our interview, as well.

My attention was distracted by the sound of banging on the kitchen window. When I turned to look,

Claire was pointing toward the figure, as though I had somehow missed him. I gave her a thumbs-up, then took off after him.

The face I'd caught a glimpse of was definitely not Beave's. And from what Constable Vance and Sergeant Deloitte had told me, Beave would be in no condition to run, even if he'd managed to make it home. Whoever it was moved well but not quickly. The terrain at the edge of the property was covered in dense brush and stubby evergreens, making it impossible to see more than ten feet ahead. Fortunately, the branches swinging back and forth indicated which way I needed to go.

I plunged into the brush. I could soon clearly hear twigs snapping and the sound of heavy breathing, and felt I was just a few steps behind.

When the terrain began to rise, I could again see the figure ahead. As he climbed, his plaid coat was snagging on branches. I dropped the poker and slid the phone in my pocket. I was going to need both hands for the climb.

The sounds of my own breathing, my boots hitting the earth, and the scraping of branches against my jacket had become a bubble of noise against the silence around me. The chase itself had given way to another goal: summiting the rocky peak.

Suddenly, a branch snapped out and hit me straight in the face. I fell ass over tea kettle, as my mom would say, and would've rolled all the way back down the hill if not for a sapling just strong enough to slow my fall.

Through tear-filled eyes, I looked up and saw the figure looking down at me. He, if it was a he, took a step toward me, then turned and continued to climb.

Aside from a few scrapes and impending bruises, I seemed to be fine. I rolled back onto my feet and continued making my way, more cautiously this time, toward the summit.

The figure disappeared over the top of the hill. I slowed down and, before cresting the hill, paused at the base of an elm tree to catch my breath. The exposed roots concealed a network of small burrows, and around me, game trails cut lines across the ground.

When I reached the top, he was gone. I stood still and listened, but there was only silence. *Was he lying in wait? Hidden beneath the boughs of an evergreen tree, maybe? Setting another trap for me?* Ahead, the hill sloped down before rising again, even higher, on the other side. Large rocks protruded from the soil. *Large enough to conceal a man from view?*

I was done. Like a dog I had growing up, I had chased just because my prey ran. If he was up there somewhere, just waiting, then I was going to force a confrontation I had no business getting into.

"Laura!" a voice yelled, the sound echoing over the hilltop like a yodel.

I backed up to the point where I first crested the hill and knelt down, taking one last sweeping look at the area before sliding back down the way I'd come.

Sergeant Deloitte, red-faced and breathing heavily, was waiting for me at the bottom of the hill. His hand rested on the grip of his pistol. "What in God's name do you think you're doing?"

"That's a good question," I said.

"Claire says you were chasing someone who broke into Beave's cabin."

"Yes."

"Did you see who it was?"

"No."

"No?"

"He was wearing what looked like Beave's hat and jacket. I didn't get a good look at his face. Only half of it, and even that was in the dark. He had an eye like a fish, big and round. It glistened when I shone my light on it."

"You're not making any sense," he said.

"I know," I said. "It could have been some kind of mask, I suppose."

"I called the hospital in Corner Brook. They assured me that Beave is still in his bed."

"Are you sure?"

Sergeant Deloitte pulled out his phone and turned the screen toward me, revealing a photo of Beave in a hospital gown, his eyes closed, his face badly bruised. "Pretty sure," he said. "And there's something else, though I'm not sure if it makes a difference. Pop Fitzcairn passed away. Nothing suspicious about it. It was just his time"

"Still," I said, "it definitely seems related."

"But it's not for you to worry about. You're done with this, you hear me? Stick to your lake monster and let me do the police work."

"Don't you want to know what the man in Beave's cabin was looking for? Whatever it is might still be there."

"And I intend to have a look around, once I call in Hodges and Anthony. And I'm going to need a statement from you."

"I'll be happy to give you one," I said. "I'll tell you everything as we go through the cellar."

"No," he said.

"Sergeant, you know I can help. You know I can be trusted. And I'm a hell of a lot closer than your constables. Let's just go back inside, and I can walk you through what happened."

"All right," he said, gesturing toward the house.

I felt better now that Sergeant Deloitte was there, even if he looked more like a high school soccer coach or a friend's dad than a tough cop. But I wouldn't have objected to more backup. A few more constables, maybe. Or Saad.

"Can't be too careful," Deloitte said, shining his flashlight around the steps that led down to the cellar, his other hand still on his pistol.

"Don't worry," I said. "You're going down first."

The intruder had shoved a wheelbarrow over to the cellar door, fitting one of its handles through the two on the cellar doors. I'd broken the door handles on my way out, but the wheelbarrow itself still partially obstructed the door. I moved it aside. Deloitte pulled the cellar door wide open with a flourish, like a colony of bats might fly out. He then pointed the beam of his flashlight into the musty cellar. I also shone the light from my phone around the opening, though I'm not sure how useful it was. Deloitte made sure to sweep his light over every corner before giving the okay for me to join him.

The hatch in the living room opened, spreading more light on the far end of the cellar.

"Hello?" Claire Dooley called out, her voice panicked.

"It's Deloitte. Just stay up there, Ms. Claire. We'll join you in a minute."

The contents of the shelf the intruder had pushed over were scattered across the floor. Now that I had time to look around, I noticed that the stacks of firewood ran the entire length of the west wall. An assortment of tools hung from the opposite wall and covered a workbench in the far corner.

When we turned around, Deloitte's flashlight fell on the wall with the door leading up to the backyard. An old trunk, which reminded me of a treasure chest, sat on the floor to the right of the door. Deloitte headed straight for it, careful to avoid stepping on any of the fishing tackle, jars of screws and nails, and other knickknacks that were scattered all over the floor.

"That must have been what we heard slam," I said.

"What?"

"The noise in the cellar that Claire and I heard. The only reason I came down here. I bet it was the sound of the trunk slamming shut."

The trunk was pressed so snugly against the wall that the lid wouldn't stay open. Sergeant Deloitte had to sit on the edge of the trunk and hold it open with his back just to shine his light inside.

As I was just about to cross the cellar and join him, I noticed a red toolbox on the floor. It was an ordinary thing, unusual only because it was located far from the tools and other toolboxes, which sat collecting dust by the workbench. I flipped up the clasp and opened the lid. Inside was a tray filled with an odd assortment of tokens, buttons, bullets, patches of fabric, fishing lures that looked a hundred years old, and a small cross pendant. There were also some old coins, though not the gold kind. I lifted the plastic tray to reveal the compartment underneath, which held a large cigar box.

"Sergeant," I called out, "I think I may have found something."

Deloitte got up, catching the lid of the trunk before it fell.

I stood up and held the cigar box out, using my thumbs to open the lid.

He shone the flashlight inside and exclaimed, "Oh dear!" He tucked his flashlight under his arm and pulled a pair of latex gloves from his pocket. Then he reached into the cigar box and lifted out a thick stack of cash. He examined it closely, twisting it around in the flashlight's beam.

"This money's from the eighties," he said, pointing to the year the bill was printed, which was written in small print to the left and slightly below a picture of a middle-aged Queen Elizabeth. He ran his thumbs along the edges of the bills as he counted, then poked around in the cigar box with his gloved finger. "There's five thousand dollars in this stack, twenty thousand in total." He then flipped over the stacks.

"Would you look at that," he said, tilting the box down so I could see the gold coins lining the bottom.

It wasn't what I'd call a pirate's treasure, but it was a hell of a lot more than you'd expect to find tucked away in someone's basement. Math was never my strong suit, so I took out my phone to use the calculator app.

"How many coins is that, Sergeant?"

He was quiet for a moment while he slid the coins around the bottom of the cigar box. "Fifteen," he said finally.

"Coins identical to these ones have sold for twelve thousand British pounds each. So, times fifteen, that's a hundred and eighty thousand. Plus the cash, that's an even two hundred K."

Sergeant Deloitte let out a long whistle. "That's a lot of money for a man like Beave."

"I imagine even just twenty grand in cash went a long way around here in the eighties."

There was nothing else inside the box, but maybe the exterior held some important piece of information. I switched on my phone's camera and held it up.

"Do you mind?" I asked Deloitte.

He shook his head, then held the cigar box up so I could examine its exterior. He turned it over slowly so that I could photograph it from all angles The words *Hecho en Cuba* were stamped into the bottom. "I guess we know what that person was looking for."

Deloitte shook his head. "You find a lot of strange stuff on this island," he said. "We have a long history. One gold coin, well, that's one thing. But a boxful? That's something else altogether."

"Do you know anything about Jack Brill?" I asked, putting some of my credibility on the line. "The pirate."

"I've heard some stories," he said, gesturing toward the stairs.

Claire was in the living room, hovering around the trap door, when we came up from the cellar. Deloitte smiled and her, resting his free hand on her shoulder reassuringly, the cigar box tucked under his other arm. She looked as though she might cry.

"Go on home, now, Ms. Claire. We'll get everything sorted out here and I'll call on you later," he said.

We went back outside and Deloitte put the cigar box in the trunk of his cruiser. We then went inside and did a light search of the rest of Beave's cabin. Between the gold coins and the cash, though, I thought we had found enough.

"I think maybe we should have a look around Pop Fitzcairn's place next," I said when we were back outside the cabin.

"We don't have any reason to," Deloitte said. "I don't want you to think I play fast and loose with the law."

Now seemed like the right time to lay all my cards on the table.

"The coin we found on that body, and those that we found in the cellar, are rare and valuable. It's highly unlikely that they could both appear in Robert's Arm through unrelated circumstances."

"Maybe not," Deloitte said. "You mentioned that pirate, Jack Brill. Now what if he hid his gold around here. Beave may have dug some up and someone else may have stumbled across that other coin, not realizing its value."

"That type of coin has only been found twice on the island —"

"That we know about," Deloitte said. "I admit it looks suspicious, and I will pursue it, but we can't jump to conclusions."

"I'm not. I'm just formulating a hypothesis and then testing it against the facts," I said. "What if the skeleton we discovered was Sarah Tindall?"

"That's a big *if*. I thought you weren't going to jump to conclusions?"

"I'm just speculating. Let's say it was Sarah Tindall. You see the way she was wrapped up in that tarp. There's no way she went through the ice on a snowmobile. Which means maybe Lou Fenton didn't go through the ice either. The accident had one eyewitness: an old man, a fair distance away from the scene, at night."

"You think Pop Fitzcairn was wrong about what he saw?"

"I think he was lying."

"Why?"

"I think he wanted this whole town to think Lou Fenton and Sarah Tindall were dead."

Sergeant Deloitte took a half-step back, put his hands on his hips, and looked down at the ground. He chewed his lips. His index fingers tapped on his belt. "If that *is* Sarah Tindall we pulled out of the water, how do we know it wasn't Lou who killed her?" he asked. "When a woman is murdered, nine times out of ten it was by her partner."

"Pop had to be in on it if he gave a false statement. Beave must know something, too. Maybe they were in on the murder together. Maybe that's why Beave took off."

"You've given me a lot to think about, Laura," Deloitte said. "But like I said, you're done. I can't have you getting hurt on account of this."

"You know the difference between the coins we found in Beave's cellar and the one we found on the skeleton?"

"That one was bent, the rest were flat," Deloitte said.

"Exactly, Beave's were flat. Men used to bend coins like that as tokens of love. Leaving a coin like that on the body meant something. As far as I know, Beave was never in love with Sarah Tindall."

"As far as any of us know. But who really knows what was going on in Beave's head? It wouldn't be the first love triangle that ended in murder. From what I've heard, Sarah Tindall got around. Maybe she moved on to Beave, and Lou couldn't handle it."

"Beave told me he was living in St. John's at the time of the snowmobile accident. He may not have even been here when Sarah was murdered."

"What's all this have to do with Pop Fitzcairn's place?"

"With this place compromised, where else could our Beave impersonator hide?"

"You're sure this 'impersonator' is from out of town?"

"If he was truly wearing Beave's hat and coat, and I assume Claire knows what they look like, it wouldn't make a whole lot of sense that someone followed Beave out of town, jumped him to take his clothes, then come back to burgle Beave's cabin. The whole point of the disguise must have been to get through town and into the cabin unnoticed. A local would have probably just come over the hill and broken in through the back."

Deloitte's gaze travelled to the tree-covered, rocky land that rose around Robert's Arm. "Okay then, assuming he's not a local ..." Deloitte said. "He could be hiding anywhere."

He was right. A man raised out here could survive among the trees with the right supplies. It wasn't too cold at night to stay in a tent with a good sleeping bag this time of year. If he bundled up, he could go without a fire, so as to not give away his position. And who knows how many shacks and blinds there were around here. There were probably plenty of places to take shelter besides Pop Fitzcairn's dilapidated shack.

"I'm not saying your guess is a bad one," Deloitte said. "I'll run by Pop's place later. But we just don't have enough manpower out here to keep an eye on that house on a hunch."

I nodded. "I understand, Sergeant."

"Are you sure you don't want to be checked out by a doctor?"

"I'm fine. Just a few scrapes."

"Then let's get you back to the inn."

S I X T E E N

In Indigenous folklore, a Cressie is a trickster, a shapeshifter able to appear to men as a seductively beautiful female. She would lure them into the depths, and fill their minds with lurid images. Cressie was both feared and revered as a spiritual being, able to transcend to the upper and lower realms at will, bestowing both vengeance and grace upon humans.

— Louie Sperber, *The Esoteric Codex: Cryptozoology*, 2015

WHEN SERGEANT DELOITTE DROPPED ME OFF at the inn, the crew was once again serving up Chinese takeout on the dining room table. Eating a third of my meals out of Styrofoam or cardboard containers was just a fact of life on the road.

"Are you all right?" Saad asked. "You're walking like a zombie."

No doubt — the stiffness from my fall was setting in from my lower back downward.

His look of surprise turned to worry. "And your face …"

I ran my fingers down my cheek and felt scratches, probably from the pine needles. It was like a cat had taken a swipe at me. "It's a long story," I said.

Danny looked uncharacteristically stern. "Why were you getting out of that cop's car?"

All the heads in the room turned in my direction.

I stared down at a container of steamed rice. "That's an even longer story," I said.

"There's nowhere I have to be," Danny said, keeping his eyes locked on me.

"I'm not in any trouble. The show will go on, just like you want. There's nothing to worry about."

"I worry about you," he said, then paused. "And be sure to use enough concealer to cover up those marks. I don't want to see them on camera."

Danny's concern just about floored me. I knew that he looked at me more as an asset than a human being, but still. As Saad slid the General Tso chicken across the oak tabletop, I could almost hear the questions that he wasn't asking me.

We settled into dinner after that. Danny ate quietly. Chris and Saad discussed the transition from analog equipment and magnetic tape to digital everything. Lindsay cast glances my way when she thought

I wouldn't notice. It was almost like being in college again.

Mary then made a pot of tea, and while the rest of the crew stayed downstairs, I went up to my room. I had an impulse to do something I hadn't done in a long time: I called my mother.

The phone rang and rang, and as it did, I composed a voice message in my head in case no one picked up. We spoke so rarely that I didn't know what to expect. Would she be happy to hear from me, absence making her heart grow fonder? Or would lack of communication lead to nothing but resentment?

"Hello?" She sounded tired.

"Mom."

"Laura! Oh gosh, how are you, sweetie?"

"I'm fine, Mom."

"Where are you?"

"Robert's Arm."

"Where on earth is that?"

"Newfoundland."

"Is everything all right?"

"Yeah, Mom. Everything is just fine. I just wanted to chat a little before bed."

"Bed?"

There was a pause. I could practically hear her counting backward in her head, calculating the difference in time zones.

"How have you been?" I asked.

"I'm just so tired all the time."

"I'm sorry to hear that."

"How is your show coming along?"

"Mom. Can I ask you something serious?"

"Certainly, sweetheart."

"Have you forgiven Dad? Is that even possible?"

There was a long silence. Eventually, she cleared her throat. "It's easy to say I forgive your father. After all, it's been a long time. But that would be superficial. But if he were to show up on my doorstep, then who knows? You never know what you'll do when the past bubbles up to the surface."

The floorboards outside my door creaked. A shadow appeared beneath the door, one pair of legs shifting back and forth. I said goodbye to Mom and told her I loved her. Then I walked slowly to the door and opened it.

Saad was standing in the hall, his fist held up ready to knock but frozen in the air.

"Hey," I said.

"Um, hi."

"Come in," I said, stepping back and pulling the door open wide.

Saad sat down in a small chair against the far wall, leaning forward with his elbows on his thighs. I could tell he was nervous, a few degrees shy of agitated. I wanted to rest a hand on his shoulder but thought better of it.

"Is everything okay?" I asked.

He continued to stare at the floor. "I'm worried about you," he said, finally.

"Don't be."

"Why did the sergeant drop you at the inn?"

"I've stepped in something," I said. "I just don't know what it is."

"It has to do with that skeleton, doesn't it?"

"It's a long story," I said.

Saad leaned back in the chair, resting his right ankle on his left knee and folding his arms. It was the pose of a man not going anywhere for a while.

I may have smiled, though I tried not to. "I heard from the mayor that Beave was back. So, I went over there. His housekeeper was out front. We went in and found someone else there."

"I thought Beave was still in the hospital, unconscious?"

"He is."

"Then who …?"

"I don't know; I didn't get a good look. I chased him for a while, but he knew the terrain better than I did."

"You chased him? Why?"

"I don't know why. It's like I'm lying down in the middle of a canvas, part of a bigger picture, but I can't see it."

"It's none of your business," Saad said.

"I've heard that before."

"Sorry, I just mean … you're not the police. I worry about you."

"You don't have to."

"But I do."

"I can't help it, Saad. When I see something like this, I have to help if I can. It gnaws at me."

"But you don't have to do it alone," he said.

I smiled.

He smiled back.

"You don't know what you're getting into," I said.

"What else is new?" he said, stifling a yawn. "Sorry. I haven't slept well since we've been here."

"Me, neither."

The door opened and Lindsay came in. "Oh," she said, keeping her hand on the doorknob. "Secret meeting?"

"We're fighting crime," Saad said.

Lindsay raised her eyebrows. "I see. Deal me in." She walked between Saad and me and sat on the edge of her bed. "Let's start with what happened to you," Lindsay said to me.

"Laura chased a man people thought was Beave out of Beave's cabin and into the wilderness," Saad answered for me.

"Whoa," Lindsay said. "He got away, I assume?"

"He did," I said. "But that's not the most important part." It might have been a betrayal of Sergeant Deloitte's confidence to reveal these details, and I wasn't sure what his expectations of my silence on this matter was, but I didn't have a choice. I realized that I couldn't rely on Deloitte anymore. He had said it himself: he was just spread too thin. I needed my own people involved. "We found more of those Portuguese gold coins hidden in Beave's cellar along with a large stash of money."

"So, you think Beave is connected to the remains we pulled from the lake?" Lindsay said.

"We can't be a hundred percent sure, but his disappearance after the skeleton was recovered and his possession of those coins seem very incriminating."

"What about Pop Fitzcairn? Maybe he knows something," Saad said.

"If he did, he took it to his grave," I said. "Sergeant Deloitte informed me that he died yesterday. Nothing suspicious about it, but he won't be any help to us. It doesn't look like Sergeant Deloitte will be much help going forward, either. I get the sense that he's had about all he can take of my interest in this."

"Or he's trying to keep you safe after your encounter with a would-be burglar," Saad said.

"Right?" Lindsay said.

"There's that. I figure the man at Beave's must have been looking for the gold coins and the money."

"It's got to be Lou," Lindsay said. "Beave would have just taken the money and the gold with him ..."

Lindsay had just blurted out what I was thinking, what my gut was telling me yet my brain prevented me from saying. I felt certain that Sarah Tindall and Lou Fenton didn't go through the ice that night.

"Not to mention Beave's still in the hospital in Corner Brook," I said.

"And Pop is dead," Lindsay said. "Process of elimination."

"There's no hard evidence that Lou ever died," Saad said. "And now there's the money we have to consider. I'm not sure where it fits."

"If Lou Fenton is really alive, that money would be his only motivation to come back, right? Why else would he risk being recognized? Maybe he waited for Beave to visit Pop, jumped him, and masqueraded as him to get into Beave's house and steal that money," I said.

We sat quietly as we each played out different scenarios in our heads.

"The money was from the eighties, which means whatever Beave did to get it happened decades ago, before Lou's 'death.'"

"And he never spent it?" Lindsay said.

"Or he had more of it and that was just what's left," Saad said.

"Maybe it was guilt," I said. "Maybe he didn't want to spend it because of how he got it."

"So, where would Lou go if he's still alive and didn't get his hands on that money?" Lindsay asked.

"Probably back to wherever he's been hiding all these years. But he doesn't have Beave's truck anymore. He left it in Beave's garage. So, I'm not sure how he'd get back."

"What if he doesn't know that you and the sergeant found the money?" Saad asked.

"I was just thinking that," I said. "He might go back to Beave's to look again, or to steal the truck. I'm guessing he still has the keys. Another option would be to steal another car, or a boat, and skip town."

"Where would Lou go if he's lying low in town?"

They both looked at me. It seemed as if their gazes weren't going to let up until I came up with an answer.

"My money's on Pop's house. He knows it, he used to live there, it's isolated enough. He just has to go in through the back to avoid Mrs. Flynn. I already suggested as much to Sergeant Deloitte, but he says he can't commit resources on a hunch like this."

"We can," Saad said.

"Sure!" Lindsay said with genuine enthusiasm.

"The trail cams," I said. "We can set some up around Pop's cabin and behind Beave's. If anything moves around there, the cameras will be triggered and we'll have video evidence."

"I'll go ask Chris about them," Lindsay said. "We should get them set up as soon as possible."

"Is that the RCMP file from the night of the snow-mobile accident?" Saad asked once she'd left the room.

"Oh yeah," I said. "Sergeant Deloitte gave it to me yesterday. I haven't finished it yet, but I didn't see anything that we don't know already."

He opened it, flipping through with casual interest.

Lindsay came back minutes later, no signs of enthusiasm left on her face. She closed the door and stood with her arms crossed. "Chris didn't bring the trail cams."

"Why not?" Saad asked.

"He didn't think we'd need them, since we're here to film aquatic fauna, not terrestrial."

"He didn't use those words, did he?"

She managed a smile. "He said 'lake monster' and 'Bigfoot,' but his point was clear."

"Everybody hunts around here," I said. "It can't be too hard to find a store that sells trail cams."

"I'll look into it," Lindsay said. She sat on the bed and logged on to her laptop.

I turned to Saad. "Let me know if the file mentions the names of the divers who looked for the body. Maybe we could track them down. I doubt we'd have time to go out and interview them, but they might be good for a quick phone call. If they did see abnormally large eels, we could at least get a soundbite for the show."

"Hang on," he said, "there's a second witness statement here." Saad laid the folder down in his lap. "I thought only Pop witnessed the accident."

"That's a strike against your hypothesis about Pop Fitzcairn making the accident up," Lindsay said to me.

How had it become *my* hypothesis? It seemed we'd all agreed on it. But I didn't bring that up. "Move over, Hitchcock, we have a new master of suspense," I said. "Who else witnessed it?"

"Maureen Dunlop," Saad said. "She was walking her dog along the road by the lake, apparently."

"I guess it makes sense that they wouldn't rule two people dead on just one person's say-so," Lindsay said.

"The mayor," I said. "Can I see it?"

"She wouldn't have been the mayor then," Saad said absently.

"Of course not," I said. "But I wonder, who was she? Was she a credible eyewitness? Did she have a reason to make a false report?"

Lindsay gave me a puzzled look. I shrugged my shoulders, not wanting to commit my suspicions to words. I guess I didn't have any real suspicions, it was that my hypothesis seemed to be crumbling.

"Where does this leave us?" Saad asked.

"I'm not ready to drop our hypothesis just yet," I said. "I spoke to the mayor this morning. She didn't mention anything about the snowmobile accident. But we know the remains we found were not those of an accident victim."

"We don't definitively know whose remains they are," Lindsay reminded me.

"We know something about that coin spooked Beave. And we know that he had more of the same coins. We know somebody was in Beave's house, likely looking for them. So, what does that all mean? The pieces only fit together if Lou is still alive. Even then, I don't see the full picture. Pop Fitzcairn is dead. Beave is unconscious. We're not getting any answers out of them."

"We can't stick with our plan if we don't have any trail cams," Saad said.

"The hardware store just around the corner from the library apparently sells trail cams," Lindsay said. "Shit!"

"What?" Saad and I said at the same time.

"They close at seven thirty."

The glowing green numerals on the clock radio on my nightstand read seven seventeen. I rose quickly, trying to remember who had the keys to the van. Saad stood up a second later and Lindsay stepped onto my bed to get to the door rather than go around.

"Chris has the keys," she said, as though responding to what must have been a searching look on my face.

We made it to the hardware store with three minutes to spare. Lindsay pulled the van right up to the front doors and parked between two pallets of firewood, charcoal, and road salt. I hopped out of the van and hit the ground running, Saad close behind.

"We're closing," the lady in the blue vest behind the cash said. She was probably in her late thirties but looked a decade older, her tattoos, scars, and burst capillaries betraying her life story.

"We won't be long," I said, moving deeper into the store. "Where do you keep the trail cams?"

"Far wall," she said, pointing.

The two trail cams they had dangled from a long steel hook, nestled among the tackle gear and fishing nets. There was something ironic there, the fact that we'd left our trail cams stateside because we were hunting a giant eel, and here the cameras hunters used to locate game were displayed among the implements used to catch fish. I didn't put those thoughts into words but ran back up the aisle with the trail cams under my arm like the cash register was the end zone.

"Only two?" Lindsay said as we sat down in the van.

"It's all they had," I said. I turned to Saad in the back. "Hand me a multi-tool and some AA batteries, please."

"So, one for Beave's place and one for Pop's? Or should we double-down on one location?" Lindsay asked as she unclasped the lid of a storage tote where the batteries were kept.

We sat thinking, listening to each other's breathing and watching the tube lights dim inside the hardware store. The woman in the blue vest watched us through the door as she locked up.

"Both," I decided. "We'll have a camera covering the back of each house, at the most likely point of entry."

The sun was due to set in about forty-five minutes. Beave lived on the bayside of Robert's Arm; Pop's cabin faced the lake. Although Lou, if it really was him, would likely wait until nightfall before moving around, we'd also need to conceal our actions. If we waited too long, we'd likely draw attention to ourselves as we bumbled through unfamiliar terrain in the dark, our flashlight beams a dead giveaway, like the beacon atop a lighthouse.

"Hand me my backpack please, Saad."

I took it from him and loaded a trail cam inside.

The Fitzcairn house was the obvious starting point, mainly because I'd never been behind it and I would need the waning daylight. We drove down Crescent Avenue, following it to Tommy's Arm Road, stopping where the concrete became gravel and the road split. Lindsay pulled the van onto the shoulder, the passenger-side tires on the grass, and killed the headlights. Between two young jack pines on the right, we watched as the still lake turned from blue to purple. Soon it would be black.

"Wait here," I said, "I won't be long."

"Shouldn't I go with you?" Saad asked.

"Two people are easier to spot than one."

"Remember what happened at the Johansson cabin back in Roanoke Ridge" Saad reminded me.

As if I could forget. It wasn't often I was held at gun-point and had to drag an unconscious forest ranger out of a burning cabin.

"Don't worry, I'm not going inside."

"Still …"

"He's right," Lindsay said. "It's too risky to go alone."

Exiting the van, I closed the door most of the way, then leaned on it until it clicked shut. Saad did the same, albeit with a little less finesse. Everything echoed around the lake, especially as competing noises ceased. There were no boats on the water, no ATVs chewing up the countryside, no chainsaws and axes chopping trees or firewood. I took a moment to get my bearings and plan a route, then I slipped around the van and across the road. Hiding behind a mountain alder, I waited for Saad to join me. We moved together into the bush, following a small game trail that cut through the trees.

It was slow-going as we navigated around each tree and shrub, careful not to give ourselves away by stepping on twigs or snapping a branch as we pushed ahead. We soon reached the small clearing where Pop's cabin sat.

I crouched behind a small tree. Saad lowered himself down beside me. We scanned the yard. It was empty. The back door of the cabin was shut and there were no obvious signs that anyone was there. The screens on the windows looked untouched, and there were no lights on inside the house. Still, I worried someone could be inside. Perhaps at this moment peeking out one of the windows. Or that a more experienced hunter and tracker than me might have concealed himself among the shrubs and pine trees, watching and waiting for the cover of darkness. Though Mrs. Flynn's house was not that far away, the trees between the two properties, and Mrs. Flynn's poor hearing, meant there was no one nearby we could count on for help.

Tapping my hand against my pocket, I felt for the reassuring heft of my compact folding knife. It was there, right where it should have been. I surveyed the yard and settled on a row of red pines that lined the corner of the property. I could fasten the trail cam to one of the trunks and get an almost panoramic view of the back of the cabin. The location would also make the camera hard to spot, especially in the dark. I just hoped that the "no-glow infrared" feature was as good as advertised and that the trail cam could take good video at night without giving itself away.

It would be dark soon. There was no time to waste. I motioned to Saad to wait for me there. Staying low along the tree line, I hurried to the stand of red pines. I picked one in the centre, set slightly farther back from the others. We didn't have the security cover and chain that we normally used on our own trail cams, so the camera could be easily stolen or damaged, but that was a chance we'd have to take. I strapped the camera to the trunk, tightened the strap as best I could, and returned to Saad the same way I'd come.

The shadows seemed alive as we started back toward the van. It was about the right time of year for black bears to wander out of caves or hollow logs, groggy and hungry. They'd stick to the woods and feed on roots and leaves until the berries came into season. Newfoundland was known for its berries: blueberries, partridgeberries, and cloudberries, which the Newfoundlanders called *bakeapple*. When it came to bears, I wasn't worried they'd try to eat me, but I was concerned that if the cubs were on one side of the road and Momma Bear on the other, it wouldn't be so good for us to be standing in the middle.

We heard the sound of tires on gravel as we approached the road. Pausing, we watched as a pair of headlights illuminated the road and the van. A rust-patched Toyota pickup was headed back toward the centre of town. Once the tail lights, like two smouldering embers, disappeared, Saad and I crossed the road and hopped into the van.

"Next stop: Beave's," I said.

Setting up the second trail cam took a quarter of the time. Before we got there, I could already picture the perfect tree to attach it to, a red maple behind the garage. Whether the man we were calling Lou came back for the gold coins or the truck, the camera would get him.

"That's it?" Lindsay asked as I reached over my shoulder for the seatbelt.

"That's it," I replied, "for now."

Lindsay parked the van in front of the inn and leaned back in the driver's seat. She seemed in no rush to go back inside; neither was I. The waxing gibbous moon cast silver light on the lawn.

"What's next?" Lindsay said after a while.

"Business as usual," I said.

"Do you always speak in clichés?"

"Only when there's nothing else to say. Now we have to go inside and pretend we didn't go out and do something crazy."

"I don't think Danny will even have noticed we were gone. And Chris is pretty chill," Lindsay said.

"True," I agreed. "But Danny wouldn't be happy with me meddling if he found out. And recruiting you two won't help my case."

"It's a risk I'm happy taking," Lindsay said.

"Me, too," Saad added.

"Hold on. Let me record you guys saying that," I said, reaching for my phone.

Saad laughed quietly.

"So, now we just wait and hope the cameras get something?" Lindsay asked.

"We have one full day left here, so it's a longshot that we'll get anything," I said. "But I think I'm going to see if our invitation to John O'Donahue's home is still open."

"Why?" Saad asked. "I mean, what does that have to do with this?"

"Mayor Dunlop will be there," I said. "I'd like to ask her about the snowmobile accident. Maybe she'll be less guarded after she's had a few drinks."

"She is the one person getting in the way of the *Lou is alive* hypothesis," Lindsay said.

"That's right," I said. "So, what's our cover story when we go back inside?"

SEVENTEEN

And in St. Andrews, New Brunswick, Dr. Carl Medcof, a research biologist with the Fisheries Research Board's Biological Station, gave me this warning: "One thing! We should not make light of the stories or the people who tell them. There is a sound basis for monsters. I feel sure it is we who are the fools if we laugh at them. Our job is to find out the basis for the stories."

— John Braddock, "Monsters of the Maritimes," *Atlantic Advocate*, January 1968

AT BREAKFAST THE NEXT MORNING, MARY hovered more than usual. I felt her glances on the back of my head as she set out freshly baked banana bread, cereal, milk, and coffee. Her fingertips lingered on the bowl of sugar cubes. When the table was set, she said,

"Something came for you," and disappeared into the kitchen. When she came back out, she was carrying a small bouquet of flowers.

"For me? Again? This is a personal best."

The bouquet was lovely, an arrangement of purple irises. A little pink envelope was taped to the side. It said *Laura* in beautiful, looping cursive.

"Ooh la la," Chris said, before taking a bite of banana bread.

I opened the card: *Please be careful. Yours, John.*

"I think old John's taken a fancy to you," Mary said as she leaned in to read the card.

"Old is right," Chris muttered.

"Oh, he's harmless," Mary said. "He's just the chivalrous sort. I'll tell you one thing: I haven't seen him this much in ages."

Saad and Lindsay walked into the dining room just then, and Saad gave me a puzzled look as he sat down.

"What do we have here?" Lindsay asked.

"Apparently, taking a branch to the face gets you flowers," I said.

"Is that two bouquets since we've been here?" Lindsay smiled.

I set the flowers down on the edge of the table and proceeded with breakfast without answering her. The less attention on them, the better. What would I do with them anyway? Ship them back to the States?

"Fascination or respect," Danny said as he walked into the room, fixing his Bluetooth headset into his ear. Everyone turned to look at him. "That's what purple flowers symbolize," he said. "What? I send enough bouquets to women — I know what they mean. Purple is a royal colour that conveys charm and elegance. They can also mean love at first sight."

Saad and Lindsay both looked at me, the three of us on the edge of laughter. It was hard to imagine Danny as a sensitive romantic. I bit into the banana bread and stared at the pattern on the plate in front of me, two large bluebirds opposite each other, a pair of smaller ones on either side, together forming the points of a compass. I wanted to talk about the trail cams. I'm sure they did, too, but we carried on as though the impending day out on the water was the only thing on our minds.

Lindsay followed me up the stairs as we went back to our room to grab our gear.

"We could probably sneak over to Beave's cabin to check the trail cam before we go out on the water," she said. "Pop's place is just too far."

"I think we should wait awhile," I said quietly.

After the hearty breakfast, and more coffee than was prudent before a day on the water, our team drove into town to meet Captain Phil by the dock. Danny was the only person who didn't come, deciding instead to stay on dry land to teleconference and email.

After we parked near the dock, Chris and Clyde opened the vans' back doors. Along with Duncan and Dr. Willoughby, they stood there debating which pieces of equipment they needed for our final day of filming aboard the *Darling Mae*. Saad intercepted me before I joined the others. Lindsay, sensing something was up, made it a trio.

"Should we check the trail cams when we get back?" Saad asked.

"We don't want to give the game away," I said. "I'd rather leave the cams there a while longer. If we go back and forth too much, someone'll spot either the cameras or us."

"We only have one night left," Lindsay said.

"Exactly. I want to use it. If we're right about Lou, he may not have made any moves last night. He might be gun-shy after the encounter with me at Beave's. We can pick up the cameras tonight, after dinner at John's. Danny and the others won't notice. Plus we'll have the cover of night, so we won't have the neighbours asking questions. Besides, the best time to hunt is at dawn or dusk."

"You guys want to lend a hand, or what?" Chris called out, only his legs visible behind the open van door.

As we boarded the boat, our arms full of gear, our single-file line diffused along the deck, taking up our favourite vantage points. Captain Phil merely plucked the brim of his hat at us. It seemed we were already too familiar for formal greetings.

It was our last day of shooting and we still had no evidence of Cressie on camera. But we did have footage of locals telling tall tales, we had Dr. Willoughby's traps and the juvenile eels we'd caught and measured, and we even had footage of the conger eel that, despite what Jimmy O'Donahue claimed, had definitely been caught in the ocean.

The purpose of today's trip was to collect two-litre samples of lake water at various depths and locations. That was the real reason Dr. Willoughby was working with us. Anybody could have helped him sample eel populations through traditional methods. But what he wanted was to use environmental DNA, or eDNA, technology. Environmental DNA analysis was used to detect traces of DNA in a given environment, to get an idea of what species lived there as well as approximately how many individuals of those species were present. If there was an unknown species of eel in Lake Crescent, it would definitely leave a DNA trace. Though we only wanted data to confirm Cressie's existence, all that information would come in handy for Dr. Willoughby and significantly contribute to his overall study.

As we launched, Dr. Willoughby sat at the little table-top in the cabin of the *Darling Mae*, poring over bathymetric surveys of the lake. I went over to observe. The images, printed on glossy paper, were beautiful. Each was colour-coded to indicate the depths of the lake: pale blue for shallow water, purple for the deepest parts.

We still needed more underwater footage, so Clyde and Duncan knelt in the aft section, unclasping the latches on the containers of equipment and flipping the lids open. Clyde took a cloth and wiped down the ROV.

"Have you met our new neighbour?" I overheard Duncan ask Clyde.

"The biker? Sure. He was out smoking first thing this morning. He and that girlfriend of his sure are ... loud."

"I could hear their music," Duncan said.

"Be thankful that's all you heard," Clyde said.

Lindsay stood at the mouth of the cabin, leaning over the railing and looking out at the water. "This reminds me of that show *Voyage of the Mimi*," she said to me. "Did you ever have to watch that?"

"Yeah," I said. "In fifth grade."

"Same for me," she said.

"What are you talking about?" Saad asked.

"It was this educational miniseries about a ship called the *Mimi*, some kind of research vessel studying humpback whales. That's where I first learned about flukes, the patterns on the underside of a whale's flippers, unique and identifiable, like fingerprints."

"It was cool," Lindsay said.

"And it starred Ben Affleck," I said.

"Really?" Lindsay said.

"Yeah," I said. "He was the little boy."

It was difficult to reconcile that boy, his golden-blond hair and his optimistic smile, with the brooding, scowling man I was familiar with onscreen. It made me think of my father, of how far his plans had deviated over time.

"I didn't know that was him," Lindsay said. "It was so long ago."

"I'll have to check it out," Saad said.

The engine turned on and the propellers dug deep into the emerald water as we pulled away from the dock for what would be our last outing on Lake Crescent.

Clyde and Chris revelled in their final opportunity to play with all the gear. Duncan stood over Dr.

Willoughby's shoulder, pointing at and tapping on the bathymetric data.

Captain Phil took us toward the far eastern part of the lake, the same area the two doctors were debating over. Part of me wanted to stand with Lindsay and Saad and just watch the scenery pass by, feel the wind against my face. But being on the water, doing the job I was being paid to do, started to feel confining. It wasn't that I felt trapped — just that my mind wouldn't stay focused on the task at hand. As we travelled across the lake, filming, checking the traps, deploying the side-scanning sonar, I replayed the chase at Beave's house over in my head and found myself gritting my molars.

Hours later, when the *Darling Mae* drifted slowly back into the harbour, I moved anxiously on the dock side of the boat, like a dog who'd been locked inside all day. There was a symphony going on behind me: footsteps on the deck, cases being closed and latched, polyurethane-coated fabric scraping against polyurethane-coated fabric.

"I've always been troubled by the prehistoric survivor paradigm," Duncan suddenly said to me. "This idea that lake and sea monsters are actually ancient creatures that escaped extinction. It tends to defy what we know about the fossil record. Not to mention, the reported descriptions of these sea monsters vary so widely. It seems unlikely that witnesses are encountering dozens of different species of aquatic megafauna from the distant past."

Working on a show like ours, with a group like ours, I'd gotten used to non sequiturs that would strike a random passerby as batshit crazy.

"Fascinating," I said, my thoughts and eyes focused on dry land. "You'll be joining us at the St. George's Day dinner tonight, right?"

"Indeed," Duncan said. "I look forward to our culinary expedition. It's my understanding that Dr. Willoughby and Clyde won't be joining us."

"They're both leaving town tonight," I said. "Since they live on the island, there's no sense in making them stay away from their own beds another night."

He considered my words and nodded.

"And what of Chris and Danny?"

"They were both invited," I said. "Danny made out like he has something more important, and I got the impression Chris just wanted time to himself."

"I thought perhaps my British charm had won me the invitation over the others."

"Yeah, let's go with that," I said, smiling. "We'll swing by the motel and pick you up this evening."

E I G H T E E N

Dr. John M. Castleman, biologist at Queen's University at Kingston, has studied eels for decades, and also investigated Native American legends of serpents. He claims that the serpent legends of the Algonquin do not refer to snakes, but something much more.

— Denver Michaels, *People Are Seeing Something: A Survey of Lake Monsters in the United States and Canada*, 2016

WE FOLLOWED THE OTHER VAN AWAY FROM the harbour, down Main Street to Pilley's Island Road, and watched them turn into the Robert's Arm Motel parking lot. Chris careened slowly in behind them so that we could say our goodbyes.

"I can't say this wasn't eventful," Dr. Willoughby said.

"Let's do it again some time," I said playfully.

"Count me out," Clyde said. "I don't like untangling dead bodies from my gear."

"Fair enough," I said.

Both men stood waving at us from the walkway that ran the length of the motel as we drove out of the parking lot. They disappeared into their rooms as we turned out onto the road and drove toward the inn.

We got back about an hour before John O'Donahue expected us. Lindsay and Saad hurried upstairs to clean up and get ready. I wasn't one to get gussied up for dinners, and with the attention and flowers John had been giving me, I thought it best to look professional but not as though I was trying to impress. Having reached that decision, I realized that it made no difference. I hadn't packed an outfit suitable for a dinner party.

I found Mary drinking a cup of tea in the kitchen. The rising moon was visible through the window, partially hidden by the trees and looking ghostly in the twilight sky. She seemed mesmerized by it.

I stood awhile in the doorway, and when she didn't react to my presence, I knocked gently on the white doorframe. She looked at me with raised eyebrows, half in a dream.

"Hi, Mary."

"Oh, hello, my dear."

"I just wanted to thank you for everything."

She smiled, swatting my thanks away with her free hand.

"Can I ask you something?"

"Certainly," she said, coming alive.

I took my phone out of my pocket and opened the notepad app. "I've heard a few words lately, Newfie words you could say, and I'm not sure I understand them."

Precision, in matters of science or murder, was everything.

"Don't fret about that, dear. Happens to all the mainlanders."

"Can you tell me what *low-minded* means?"

"Feeling depressed."

"I see. And *batty*?"

"A large catch of fish, a boatload," Mary said. She pointed in the direction of the lake. "What all the boys out there are praying for."

"Okay," I said. "Thank you."

I slipped the phone back into my pocket, rolled my shoulder off the doorframe, and turned toward the staircase.

"*Batty* could also mean a large sum of money," Mary added.

"Ah, I see," I said. "Thank you."

Mary followed me out of the kitchen, grabbing hold of the doorframe where I'd just been leaning. She didn't speak, so I let my hand rest on the bannister, and we just stood there. It was so quiet I could hear the water running upstairs, either Saad or Lindsay in the shower, getting ready, as I should have been.

"You were talking to Mrs. Flynn, I take it?"

I nodded. "She seems like an authority on all the goings-on in town."

"That's the God's honest truth, I tell you that. She must have more stories than our library and know more of our secrets than the parish priest."

"That wouldn't surprise me. She has a certain … bluster, but I think she really cares about the town."

"Did she have much to say about Sarah? And Lou?"

"She pointed me in the right direction," I said.

Mary looked around the living room, then back over her shoulder into the kitchen. "I'm thankful my Fred never fell in with those boys, Lou and Beave. They were always up to something. I know old Pop tried to keep them working. When boys like that get restless …"

"Not John?" I asked.

"Well, John turned out fine. He always wanted more out of life."

"Sometimes all anybody needs is a little direction," I said.

"Look," she said, stepping forward and clasping her hands together in front of her. "I hope you don't think … given what happened … what you found …"

"Nothing happened here that doesn't happen everywhere else."

Cressie was good for the people of the town, but the team and I had dredged up something different from the bottom of Lake Crescent. *Does this make me two for two? When I come into a little town and start poking around, do I leave it worse off than if I'd never come at all?* My ego was not so swollen that I blamed myself for finding the skeleton in Lake Crescent. It was entirely random, and it was good that we brought it to the surface. But I wondered if there was a price to be paid when you set out to debunk the local legends that help feed a community.

"We'll see you at the party, okay?" I said.

NINETEEN

The very fact that people associate "monsters" — giant, weird, dangerous creatures — with large and sometimes not-so-large bodies of water is probably the one crucial, core component of the lake monster mystery. As anyone who has grown up or lived close to any large body of water can attest, a collection of vague ideas, concerns and half-remembered stories are forever associated with such places.

    — Dr. Darren Naish, *Hunting Monsters:*
Cryptozoology and the Reality
Behind the Myths, 2016

THERE WAS NO HOT WATER LEFT WHEN I took my shower, but the cold water woke me up. It was a different type of cold than the wind off the ocean that spritzed us with sea water and made me want to curl up under a comforter. The cold water numbed the stiffness that had set in from my chase the day before and invigorated me.

When I came out of the bathroom, I found that Lindsay had moved the chair from the corner of the room to face the dresser. She had propped up the mirror of her compact on the dresser and was applying eyeliner.

"Should I wear my glasses or contacts?" she asked.

"Just be comfortable," I said.

The bathroom mirror was opaque with condensation. I could feel the scratches on my face but hadn't seen them since coming out of the shower. I had no reason to think they looked any different than before, but for some reason I thought they might.

"What's the plan?" Lindsay asked.

"Not much of a plan," I said. "I just want to get the mayor alone and ask her about the snowmobile accident."

"Then we check the trail cams?"

"Sure," I said. Then, after a few seconds' thought, "Actually, why don't you two leave early to check the cameras?"

She looked at me curiously, setting down her eyeliner and picking up her lipstick.

"Mayor Dunlop will probably feel more at ease in a smaller group, though we'll need someone to run interference with John and the other stragglers —"

"I could do that," Lindsay said, turning back to her mirror.

"I want you to go with Saad. It's a two-person job. It's too risky to go alone, remember? If you two find that our hypothesis is correct, that there is someone either squatting at Pop Fitzcairn's place or that someone has broken into Beave's cabin again, you can text me and let me know. That will change how I handle the mayor."

"And we'd call Sergeant Deloitte, right?"

"Of course," I said.

"We could ask Duncan to run interference. He seems keen to help out." Lindsay reached up and unwound the towel, her long black hair clumped together in thick, damp strands. She raked her fingers through it, looking around the room for her hair dryer.

Our last night in Robert's Arm couldn't have been more beautiful. The full moon shone a pure, clean glow over the harbour and the houses nestled among the spruce trees. The peaks of waves kissed the moonlight as the water ebbed gently. It was so quiet, as if a dome had been lowered over me, blocking out all other sounds. World War Three could have been half over and I wouldn't be the wiser.

"I was thinking about our little game the other night," Duncan said as the van approached John's house.

"Yeah?" I said.

"You'd tell me if you'd become more involved in the matter of the skeleton, wouldn't you?"

Saad, who was driving, watched Duncan and me in the rear-view mirror.

"That depends," I said.

"On what?" he asked.

"A few things, there's —"

"On whether or not you can help get to the bottom of it," Lindsay said.

"If there was anything I could ever do, it would be a pleasure," Duncan said.

"Well, Duncan, now that you mention it ..."

Minutes later, we arrived at Showalter House. Two lines of cars were parked in the driveway that stretched past the house and curved around it. John O'Donahue came out onto his wraparound veranda and stood between the two Victorian-style light fixtures on either side of the door. He rested a hand on one of the white beams, watching me as I approached. When I got halfway up, he extended his hand as though to guide me up the last two steps. Usually I'd refuse a gesture that implies a certain incompetence at navigating stairs, but I was trying to act casual, which I was not necessarily a natural at, and John had a charm that could make it easy to forget why I was there.

"I'm glad you found the place okay."

"It's hard to miss." I laughed.

He smiled, then opened the door and ushered me inside with a sweep of his arm. Saad, Lindsay, and Duncan followed.

Immediately inside the doorway was a vestibule adorned with stained glass. A Persian rug lay at our feet. It was as though we had stepped back in time. Voices echoed down the hall, carried from the other room. It didn't sound like a large gathering but a few hat and coats more than intimate.

"That's the original stained glass," John told us. "I've restored some of the wood panelling, but I've tried to keep the vestibule the exact same as it's always been."

It felt as if we were in an art gallery. Paintings lined the burgundy walls, basking in the glow of the track lighting. The hardwood floors seemed perfectly flat and did not creak underfoot. A wide staircase rose to the second floor, making a sharp turn to the left partway up.

John led us through to the living room, where a bay window provided a view of the water that made my heart beat a little faster. The cold dark waters seemed so dissonant with the warmth of that room, it was like gazing upon the savagery of the wilderness from the pinnacle of comfort.

"You have a beautiful home," I said.

"Thank you. It took me years to restore every last inch of the place. I didn't finish it until Jimmy was off at university."

Fred and Mary stood in the corner of the living room, near a stereo playing soft jazz. Fred raised his glass to us as we entered. Mary kept her red wine at waist-level, offering a polite smile instead. Mayor Dunlop stood with them but faced the stereo, examining the records on the shelves on either side. Fern Devonshire was there with a man I didn't recognize.

She waved, and I waved back while checking her left hand for a wedding ring. Jimmy O'Donahue slouched in an armchair on the far side of the room, a tumbler of what looked like whisky resting on his stomach. He gave me a half-hearted salute as I glanced over at him.

"Help yourselves to drinks," John said, pointing to a small bar he had set up.

"Did you always want to live here?" Lindsay asked John.

"I used to live in a small cabin on the other side of the bay there. Six kids in one bedroom. But that's how it was back then. When I was a boy, there was an old man living here, a mean old sod who did nothing for the town or the church. My grandmother was his maid. I didn't think you could get to live in a place like this without being a man like that."

I pictured Lionel Barrymore's character, Mr. Potter, from *It's a Wonderful Life*. It was easy to see a wealthy man living in that house like a king, losing his mind from being so far removed from the other residents, or maybe from his humanity. It wasn't just maintaining a house that size, but maintaining the status of the owner, maintaining that sense of being above all of one's neighbours. Alienating oneself just to prove superiority.

"The man's father, a lumber baron from the old days, had built it. The father's fortune dried up with the lumber industry, and when the son died, the house fell apart. You should have seen the place when I took it over."

"You have done a brilliant job," Duncan said.

"I thank you, sir," John said. "Dinner should be just about ready. This way."

We walked down a long corridor, John running the fingers of his left hand against the wood-panelled walls. His collection of paintings was as impressive as it was extensive. I didn't think the Louvre would be calling him asking to borrow any pieces to exhibit, but it was clear these oil paintings were not picked up at a local garage sale. At the very end of the hall, flanked by sconces and beneath the ornately carved cornice, was a portrait of John, a woman I presumed was his late wife, and little Jimmy. The clothes, the cold stares, and the dark background all gave the impression that the portrait was Victorian, but the cheekbones and the deep, sad brown eyes of the man were unmistakably John's.

"What changed your mind?" I asked.

"I beg your pardon?"

"What made you think that you might one day live here without being cruel or heartless?"

"Love," he said.

"Love?"

"I was always in love with this house. There was no denying it. It sounds silly, but as a boy I'd look across the water and see this place half-hidden among the trees and say to myself, *One day you'll marry the prettiest girl in town and live in that house*. If anything could break the curse of this place, it was love. A home is what you make it, what you fill it with."

"Not too many people make their childhood dreams come true," I said.

"I know," he said. "I certainly didn't. A place like this is a curse for just one man and his son." His voice broke a little, and the words hung in the air between us.

John kept walking, the scent of his cologne leaving a faint trail to follow.

"This house is an example of the Queen Anne Revival style of architecture that was fashionable among the grand old homes of Atlantic Canada in the late nineteenth century," he said. "There aren't many of these old places left on the island."

The dining room was almost large enough to be considered a dining hall. An oil-rubbed bronze chandelier hung down from the high ceiling above the table. Wood crackled in a fireplace. It wasn't a cold night; the fireplace seemed to be stoked more for the effect of the smoke and embers rising than for warmth. A long burnished wood table was waiting for us, a dozen settings already laid out. John took a seat at the head of the table and offered me the place at his right.

By no means did the food on the table look completely foreign — it wasn't like the monkey brains scene in *Indiana Jones and the Temple of Doom* — but I couldn't identify any specific ingredient aside from boiled carrots.

"This all looks so delicious," I said. "But what is it exactly?"

"I have a few traditional Newfoundland dishes for you this evening," John said, like a head chef serving esteemed guests. "One of them is my own recipe, but I won't say which one until you tell me which was your favourite." He reached over the table and began to point at each dish, starting with the nearest one. "Here we have all the components of a Jiggs' dinner," he said. "Salt beef, boiled carrots and cabbage, meatless pease pudding, and a duff for dessert. There's also fried cod tongues and scrunchions, which are made from pork, I'm afraid. That over there is the stewed moose meat and boiled potatoes. Don't mind their bluish colour; that's just the variety we grow around here. We also have toutons, which are typically served at breakfast, but I thought you'd like to give them a try. Traditionally, they're fried up in pork fat, but I thought, given the circumstances, butter was a better choice. One pork dish was enough." He looked at Saad sitting beside me and bowed his head a little.

"Thank you," Saad said.

John must have assumed Saad was Muslim, based on his name and skin tone, since I doubt they had a chance to discuss Saad's religious upbringing, if they spoke very much at all, when we first met at the inn. Perhaps he was trying to show us how cultured and worldly he was. However, he had no way to guess what Lindsay's dietary restrictions were and I'd forgotten to mention them when I said we could attend. As a pescatarian, she was limited to the boiled vegetables, the toutons, and the duff. If I were her, I'd fill up on the latter two.

"I beg your pardon," I asked. "Did you say cod tongues? Surely you don't mean the actual tongue of a fish."

"It's not quite the tongue of a cod, but the squishy piece of flesh found on the underside of the cod's chin and at the back of the throat," John said. "I do hope you're not a vegetarian."

"I draw the line at Meatless Mondays," I said.

During the meal, I noticed a painting above the fireplace. It was of a white lighthouse with a red lantern room and a weathervane on top. Clouds crowded the sky like rush hour traffic. It captured both beauty and loneliness. I wondered if John saw himself as that lighthouse, standing alone on the edge of nowhere.

After dinner, we exited the dining room and came back to the foyer. Again, I thought of John's wife, hanging from the bannister along the second floor. Fred and Mary decided to call it a night, and I didn't blame them, since they would no doubt be busy getting the inn ready for its next guests after we departed. John made sure the rest of us each had a drink in our hands before leading us on a tour of the house. Saad and Lindsay both opted for sparkling water. I brought the wine from the dinner table that I'd barely touched, more just as a prop. John led the way, his prideful voice echoing through the corridors of his beautiful old home.

Jimmy went on ahead to the study. I watched the mayor nervously, looking for signs that she, too, might leave, but the only other people who chose to break away were Fern and her partner. *Don? Dan?* We said our goodbyes and stood admiring the stained glass until John continued the tour.

Eventually, we came to the study. It was as grand a room as any in the house, the kind of place you could envision Sherlock Holmes interviewing a Bavarian count about the particulars of some stolen jewels. The oak desk, the armchairs across from it, the bookshelves lining the walls, the divan in the corner were all from the nineteenth century. The study had its own fireplace, which burned in front of a red rug and two wingback chairs. The paintings on the walls were darker than in the rest of the house. They were almost gruesome, images of shipwrecks and tempests, sirens leading sailors to their deaths.

John put on a record of Newfoundland folk music and began pouring liquor from a crystal decanter on a small bar near the wall that was entirely covered by bookshelves. There was even a rolling library ladder that had been slid to the side of the room farthest from the bottles.

"So many of these songs are about death," I said to the mayor as she sidled up to me.

"It was a hard life out here for so many of our ancestors," Mayor Dunlop said. "Death was around every corner."

"You don't need to tell me," I said, "after what we discovered this week."

"That was a tragedy," John said, handing the mayor some sherry.

We sat in a bubble of silence.

"It's a pity that we need a monster to drag camera crews and tourists to our little town," John said. "There's so much history in and around these waters."

"Maybe it's cold comfort," I said, "but we intend to show the story of Cressie in a cultural context, to showcase the island and its people. Tales of sea serpents are only fascinating if the viewers are invested in the people and the culture that spawned them."

The mayor raised her comically small sherry glass. "We certainly have no shortage of culture here."

Lindsay waved off John's offer of a drink, as did Saad, who never drank alcohol. Duncan more than made up for the other two with the glee in his eyes as he took a Scotch from John and thanked him warmly. Duncan had joked about his possessing "British charm," but John seemed to eat it up. Maybe it was something a person develops a taste for when living in a mansion built by an English lord.

"I think it's time we head back to the inn," Lindsay said to both John and me. "Saad and I haven't packed yet, and I still have some work to do."

I saw John look at me out of the corner of my eye, but I didn't acknowledge it. "All right, I'll see you two back at the inn."

"I can come back and pick you up," Saad offered.

"I'll see Ms. Reagan home safely," John said. He smiled and bowed his head a little as I faced him.

"You don't have to," I said.

"It would be my pleasure." John looked over at Duncan. "And of course, I haven't forgotten about you, Dr. Laidlaw."

Mayor Dunlop and Duncan sat in the wingback chairs by the fire and were soon laughing. Duncan was keeping the mayor pinned down for me, but John didn't seem to want to leave my side. Hopefully, Duncan and I could swap dance partners at some point. The mayor would be more open to questions in a one-on-one setting but I couldn't see how to engineer that.

Jimmy stood by himself. He rolled up his sleeves before pouring himself a Scotch, as though it was part of some ritual. Drink in hand, he stared absently at the books lining the wall-high shelves. The thought of Jimmy being the lord of that stately old manor put a smile on my face. I watched as he looked down into the amber liquid before swishing it around the glass. There was a look of melancholy on his face for a split second, like a frame of film spliced into the centre of the reel, which made me think that perhaps he'd grow into his father despite how different they seemed at that moment. He looked up as I approached.

He changed, right there in front of me. Whatever reminded me of his father vanished. He straightened up, pulling his shoulders back and sticking his chest out, but the alcohol made him a little loose and unsteady. He gave me a long appraisal. "You're pretty fit," he said.

"Yeah, thanks," I said, parrying the comment and hoping that was the last of it.

"Fittest girl in town," he said. "Do you have a boyfriend?"

There were bruises on his wrist and forearm — the defensive kind.

I took a step back. "No, and I'm not looking for one."

His lower lip was split in two places, a day or two old. They weren't so severe that they stood out unless you were in close proximity and face-to-face, and that was certainly where I did not want to be. The marks definitely hadn't been there the last time I saw him.

Jimmy noticed me staring. "Yeah, my old man wasn't pleased with the eel gag," he said. "He's got quite a temper on him."

It seemed like a lie, the way he said it so matter-of-factly, like he wanted to take his father down a peg in my eyes, to his own level. I let that comment slide, too; maybe I shouldn't have. He ran his fingers back through his hair and laughed a little. "The old man's pretty adamant that I return that five grand," he said.

"My boss seemed happy to part with it," I said.

"You wanna tell him that?" Jimmy asked. "He'll listen to you."

Jimmy set his glass down on the top of the waist-high bookshelf and put his hands in his back pockets. The gestured stretched his shirt taught over his muscles, which I assume he thought were an asset. For the first time, I felt genuine sympathy for him.

I took the last sip of my wine. "I'll talk to him," I said.

He leaned in my direction and I took a step back and brought my left hand up.

"Relax," he said. "You're fit, but you're not that fit." He reached for his glass, somewhat unsteadily, draining it in one sip. It seemed clear that he wasn't going to remember the finer details of our conversation, or of the evening as a whole, so I decided to get creative. I had nothing to lose, after all.

"Danny didn't tell me that he put you up to the eel stunt beforehand," I said. "He wanted things to play out naturally."

He looked at me suspiciously while plucking the crystal stopper off one of the decanters on the tray and pouring more Scotch into his glass. But he didn't deny it.

"Could you pour me one of those?" I asked.

"You got it," he said. With tremendous concentration, he poured the whisky into a crystal tumbler. He left it on the tray and turned to me, taking my wine glass then handing me the tumbler. The idea of setting his own glass down to make the process easier hadn't occurred to him.

"You did your part," I said, "so I'll be sure you get to keep your money."

He smiled while bringing the lip of his glass toward mine. I brought the glass up to my mouth slowly, breathing in the aroma of the Scotch before taking a small sip. Jimmy was past the point of ritual and gulped his down.

The view of Lake Crescent outside the massive front window of the study was like a landscape painting, breathtaking. I tried finding our van in the darkness. The odd pair of headlights was visible around the harbour. If Saad and Lindsay went to Beave's first, there was a chance I could spot the van coming or going, but Pop's place was on the other side of Robert's Arm, impossible to see from Showalter House.

"I thought I was royally screwed when that skeleton turned up," Jimmy said. "Me *and* Danny. That cop Deloitte might have thought I had something to do with it. What are the odds that we'd try our ... prank in that exact spot. Had he tried putting the screws to me, I'd have to tell him the truth."

That bastard, I thought, picturing Danny sipping tea and staring down at his tablet, cozy in the inn's dining room.

"Why that spot? I mean, that was one hell of a coincidence. I know you didn't do that on purpose," I said.

"It was just a spot, you know? My dad took me there as a kid. It was where he went to get away from everything. We could pull the boat up close to the rocks where nobody could see us; that way, nobody could say that we didn't catch the eel there. I mean, how would they know?"

"Wow," I said. "Talk about bad luck."

He looked down at the marks on his arms. "Tell me about it," he said. "I've seen the old man mad before, but that was a new record."

My pocket started vibrating. I set my glass down on the bookshelf and plucked the phone out. Saad's name appeared at the top of the screen. I raised a finger to Jimmy and stepped away from him.

"Hello."

"Hi, Laura. Well, we can't be sure who it is," Saad said, "but we have video of a man prying off the window screen and breaking into Fitzcairn's house. Last night."

I could hear Lindsay talking to someone in the background.

"Did you call Sergeant Deloitte?"

"Lindsay's doing that now."

"Great."

"There's also footage of the man leaving the house." Saad hesitated. "He had a gun."

"A rifle, like for hunting," I heard Lindsay say.

"What's the time stamp on that video?" I asked.

There was a pause. "That was about half an hour ago," Saad said. "We must have just missed him."

"Be glad that you did."

There was a beep, and when I looked down at my screen, I saw that Sergeant Deloitte was calling.

"Saad, Deloitte's calling. Go back to the inn and lock the doors, just in case."

"We're coming back to Showalter House," he said.

"Fine. Call Chris and have him lock the doors. And isolate the best frame you can of the man and email it to me, please. Bye."

I switched calls just before Sergeant Deloitte got my voice mail. "Sergeant?"

He didn't seem to hear.

"Sergeant," I said louder.

"I just got a call from one of your … associates."

"Yes, I know. They're coming here now."

"Where's here?"

"Showalter House."

"I'm less than an hour away," he said. "I want to see that footage."

"We'll forward you the files," I said.

"I'm still on my way," he said. "All I know for sure is that your friends have video of a man breaking in to another man's house and stealing a gun. Now that man is armed and loose in Robert's Arm. I've called this in. Any units in the area, either Mountie or constabulary, have been notified. Stay put. I'll be in touch."

John stood backlit by the fireplace, holding a tumbler. He was watching me. I turned to see both the mayor's and Duncan's faces peering around the wingbacks at me. I realized how loud I had been speaking.

"Do we have you back, Laura?" John asked, flashing an empty smile.

"Yes, I think so," I said, putting the phone back in by pocket.

"Is everything okay?" Mayor Dunlop asked slowly, seeming to sense something was wrong.

I noticed Jimmy was also watching me. Everyone's attention was on me, in fact. I moved close to the centre of the room, onto a thick Afghan rug. I could see the headlights of the van cutting through the night as Saad and Lindsay drove back along Orlando Avenue.

"I'm not sure how to answer that," I said.

John came closer. "Perhaps you'd better tell —"

"No," I said, "things are definitely not okay. I'm just not sure where to start." I turned to face Mayor Dunlop. "Maybe we should start with why you lied about seeing Lou and Sarah fall through the ice that night back in 1988?"

Mayor Dunlop didn't feign surprise or outrage. John turned to her, and she maintained eye contact with him, as if he had asked the question and I had faded into the background.

That didn't work for me, so I pressed on, not about to be ignored. "I was sure Pop Fitzcairn was lying about the snowmobile accident, but then I saw your witness statement, which made me think I was wrong. But Lou Fenton is alive, so I guess I was right."

The pieces were starting to fit together in a way that I hadn't seen until I was standing in the centre of that room, in the middle of the beautiful house, with its crackling fireplace and its ghosts.

"Jimmy, could you lock the outside doors, please?" I asked.

He looked at me like a toddler deciding whether to cry after scraping his knee. Then he looked at his father.

John raised a hand, stopping him in his tracks. "Laura, I think you'd better tell us what's happening. Right now."

"Jimmy," I said firmly. "Go. Now."

His mouth tightened a little and the look on his face said *you're not the boss of me*. But to my surprise, and relief, he projected that look toward his father, not me, and moved unsteadily toward the door.

"Laura —"

"Lou Fenton is in town," I said. "He's already put Beave Cannings in the hospital, and now he's armed and may be on his way here. I know people don't lock their doors around here, but I'm not willing to take that risk."

John looked back at the mayor. Neither of them looked shocked, which confirmed what I'd feared.

Duncan rose from his chair, circling around the perimeter of the room until he was beside the door.

I glanced out the window again but saw no headlights. Lindsay must have shut them off, the equivalent of silent running for them.

"Laura, you must be mistaken," John said.

I took out my phone again. There was an MMS from Saad. The picture was black and white. The man in the image wore Beave's hat and coat and carried a rifle. The face wasn't clear enough that I could match it with the photograph in the article about Lou's death, but people who knew him would recognize him, even after all the years and apparent injuries.

"This is him," I said, showing the video still to John and the mayor. "It was taken outside Pop Fitzcairn's place forty minutes ago."

The mayor stood up, put on her glasses and took a closer look at the image.

"I know that you knew Lou was alive," I said to her, "but I'm a little surprised about John." I turned to look up at him.

I was momentarily distracted by a glimmer of what might have been the moon reflecting off a windshield outside the window. A vehicle had pulled up under some trees across the street.

"I haven't seen Lou in ages, since before the accident," John said.

"I know, but you must have surmised that he was alive when Sarah came back."

Mayor Dunlop looked sharply at John and took a step back.

"This is fantastic," John said. "Absolutely fantastic."

My phone vibrated once more. It was Saad again. "Hello."

"Lindsay just saw someone going behind the house," he said.

"I *thought* I did," she qualified from beside him.

"Shit," I said. "Go back to the inn. Call Deloitte."

"What is it?" John asked.

"Lou's here," I said. "Hopefully, Jimmy got the doors locked in time."

I opened up the audio recording app on my phone, hit record, then slid it back in my pocket upside down, leaving the mic exposed.

"Jimmy!" John called out. He crossed the room and peeked out into the hallway. "Christ!" Pulling himself back into the study, he slid the door closed, turning the little brass switch to lock it. He backed toward us. Duncan was watching him so intently that he didn't seem aware of his own position.

I yelled, "Duncan, back away from the do—"

There was a loud bang as a bullet ripped through the door, sending slivers of wood flying. Duncan, the mayor, and John ran back, taking cover by the wing chairs.

The barrel of a rifle poked through the bullet hole and slid the door back into the wall.

The man I'd chased the day before stood there for a moment, still wearing Beave's hat and jacket, then stepped into the study. He surveyed the room, then settled his gaze on us. In the light of the study, I could see his black eye and bruised cheekbones, the scratches all over his face. He and Beave must have had a real scrap. He cradled a Remington 742 Woodmaster, like the one Dad used to have.

"Looks like you had a real nice to-do here, Johnny," he said.

"Christ, Lou! Did you hurt Jimmy?"

"He's out, but he'll be fine." Lou took a few more steps forward, scanning each of our faces. He seemed to relax when his eyes landed on the mayor. "Maureen, you look lovely, m'dear."

"Thank you," she said rigidly, the trepidation palpable in her voice.

"And you," he said, gesturing toward me with the rifle, "you gave me quite the start. I'm sorry I had to bushwhack you like that."

"I've had worse."

He leaned forward and squinted at me. "I'm sure you have." He straightened up. "Don't know buddy over here."

"That's Dr. Laidlaw," I said. "A scientist who works for me."

"More like *consults* for you, but why split hairs," Laidlaw said under his breath.

"Why don't you put the gun down and we can …" I abandoned that sentence and let it fly away. "Never mind. Keep the gun."

Better to let him feel in control. He wouldn't have given it up, anyway. He was there to use it.

"I want to talk with you, though," I said steadily.

"'Bout what?" he asked.

"About Sarah Tindall, about the gold, about when you and Sarah and Pop cooked up the idea of faking your deaths."

He let out a laugh from deep in his belly, as though he'd been saving it for years. "Y'do, do you? Well, that's something. I didn't come here to talk."

"You came here to make John pay, right? For killing Sarah? Why don't you tell us about it?"

"Can't make him pay by talkin," Lou said.

"That's the best way," I said. "Take everything away from him. His pride, his position in the community. Expose him for what he is. If you shoot him, nobody's going to understand why."

"That doesn't matter."

"It does matter. Beave's gonna wake up, and it'll just be his word against yours. And if you shoot John and run, or shoot all of us, it'll only be Beave's version of events."

He seemed to consider my words. He stared long and hard at me, the corners of his mouth twitching a little. White stubble grew on his cheeks, his skin like a worn baseball glove. "I'm not going to shoot anyone … 'cept him." He pulled the slide back, chambering another bullet. I hadn't noticed after he fired that first shot through the door that he hadn't reloaded. Lou raised the gun and pointed the barrel in my direction, waving me aside with it before bringing the butt of the rifle to his shoulder and staring along the sight.

"Step over there, girlie," he said. "I want this to be over with."

"Can I ask you one thing first?"

He lowered the gun and looked at me. "What?"

"How long after you and Sarah left Robert's Arm did she leave you?"

It was a risky question to pose, but I wanted to get him thinking about something other than pulling the trigger. More importantly, I wanted to get him talking.

He readjusted his grip on the rifle. "Years," he said. "Years later. We had nothing. We left everything behind the night we left."

"You didn't keep any of the gold, did you?" I asked. "You turned it all over to John. You just wanted the cash."

"I couldn't do nothing with that gold, and I didn't want nobody seeing me with it. I just needed the money."

"But John found out about you and Sarah. He didn't pay you."

"We just wanted to be left alone," Lou said, then turned to look right at John. "But you made it impossible for us to stay here. No one wanted to hire me. You told everyone that I was a thief, that I didn't pay my debts. All I had was my word, and it meant nothing in this town after you were through. You burned my goddamn house down. Even after we left, Sarah was so afraid of what you would do if you found out she was alive."

"You should have stayed away from Sarah!" John yelled, his voice breaking. The noise was like firecrackers popping beside my head.

Lou flinched, bringing the gun up again like might shoot through me to get to John. But then Lou smiled, lowering the barrel again. Seeing John finally lose his composure seemed to make Lou genuinely happy. "Easy, Johnny, easy. Your temper will get you into trouble again."

Maybe Lou wasn't intending to shoot John and flee. Maybe he never intended on escaping. Lou wanted to savour the moment.

"What gold?" Mayor Dunlop asked.

"Portuguese coins, worth about twelve thousand British pounds each," I said. "Beave had over a dozen of them, which I assume is what you were looking for when you broke into his house, Lou. Were you looking for them because you wanted the money, or did you want evidence?"

Lou lowered the gun completely, holding it in just one hand. He pulled Beave's cap off his head and dropped it onto the rug before wiping his hand over his bare scalp. His age and frailty showed, as did the bruises on his knuckles. "Beave told me he didn't spend all his share, he couldn't bear it, because of what happened. He tried to use it to buy me off."

Mayor Dunlop sidled up behind me. "I still don't understand," she said.

"I'm not sure I get it all either," I admitted. "I mean, I get that John must have used his position at the

Provincial Archaeology Office to plunder at least one site, a pirate hideaway, maybe. He couldn't do it on his own, so he enlisted his childhood buddies and their surrogate father to help excavate the site and take everything of value. Sometime between getting hold of the gold and finding a buyer, John found out that Sarah had fallen in love with Lou. So, he kept Lou's share. It's not like you could take him to court over it, could you, Lou?"

Lou sneered. "He had me over a barrel."

"But you still had Sarah, and John couldn't stand that. He used all his influence to ruin your reputation in Robert's Arm. Maybe it wouldn't have been so bad if you and Sarah weren't so public about your relationship, but John wasn't only hurt, he was humiliated."

"You always did think you was better than the rest of us," Lou said, glaring over my shoulder. "You thought you had breeding. I remember when we was kids, you saying you thought you had some Showalter blood in you because your gran worked for Sir Leland. Well, I guess you got your birthright. But it didn't mean Sarah fancied you. She got to hating you."

"And where were you when she needed you?" John asked, his voice as cold as the icebergs floating around the mouth of the bay.

"We had a horrible fight before she left," Lou said, his voice trembling. "She said I wasn't man enough to get back what I was owed. I didn't know she came here. I thought she was gone for good, that she threw me over like she did you."

"She came back for the money," I said. "She came back for your share of the gold sale."

"And he killed her for it," Lou said, raising the rifle again.

"I didn't know it was her! My son was asleep in the next room and there was a burglar in the house. What did you expect me to do?" he yelled. "It was dark. So, I hit her hard. I didn't even know it was a *her*."

"Dear God," Mayor Dunlop said.

"You didn't know?" I asked her.

"What? Certainly not."

"I thought maybe you did; I thought maybe that's what you had on John to make him not run against you for the mayor's job."

"I saw him," she said. "The night of the fire at Lou's, I saw John in the woods between our houses. I couldn't prove anything —"

"But he didn't want to risk it. I get it. John would rather just live here and be the elder statesman, not risking his reputation. That's also why you lied about seeing Lou and Sarah go through the ice on a snowmobile."

"I resented Sarah for taking Lou from me, but after the fire at Lou's, once I understood what John was willing to do, I knew I had to help Lou and Sarah. I didn't know how I could. Then when I heard what Pop had told the police, I thought I'd say I'd seen the same thing. I knew it wasn't true. I was out by the lake just like I said I was in my statement. There was just no accident."

"So, you corroborated the story to give Lou and Sarah the second chance they'd never get so long as John thought they were together," I said. "And it worked for a while. John had enough money to restore his dream house and stay out of debt, Beave lived comfortably on top of his pile of money, Pop was paid enough to keep quiet, and Lou and Sarah started a new life. All of this, and John got to play the role of village elder in the intervening years, pretending to care about the history he profited off."

"In my day, we didn't speak on matters we didn't understand," John said.

I turned around. The charm was gone; the easy and sincere smile had vanished. The years came rushing back to John and hit him like an express train. I hardly recognized him. Hurt, loneliness, and rage did more to his face than a plastic surgeon could. "Your day is done," I said.

Lou moved closer; I could feel the vibrations through the floorboards even with the thickness of the rug. I turned to face him, my hands up, open but in a defensive position. That's when I felt John's hands on my shoulder blades. He pushed me violently toward Lou. I grabbed the Remington as Lou shielded himself with it and tried to sidestep away. But I held on tight and fell to the floor, pulling him down with me.

John swung a fire poker downward and hit Lou in the shoulder. Lou tilted the barrel of the rifle toward John. I tried clapping my hand over the trigger guard to stop Lou from getting a shot off, but the loud bang and the flare from the muzzle told me that I'd failed.

John fell to the floor.

My ears were ringing after the shot. I clung to the rifle so hard that Lou let go as he struggled to his feet and staggered to the door. John lay trembling on the floor, his sweater changing colour as the blood covered more and more of his body. When I realized that I still cradled the rifle in my arms, I pointed the barrel toward the other side of the room and cleared the chamber of cartridges.

Duncan took off his sweater and pressed it down on John's wound while the mayor called for an ambulance. A voice told me to get up and go after Lou. It wasn't my voice, or Duncan or Mayor Dunlop, but I heard it all the same. I was up and out through the doorway, running toward the front door. I found Jimmy lying in front of the door, blood trickling down his forehead.

"Jimmy? Jimmy!"

He awoke, groggy, his eyes looking everywhere but at me.

"Are you okay?"

"No, I'm not," he said, like a child waking from his nap. "My head hurts."

"Your father's been shot. He's in the study."

"I went to school … to be a firefighter," he said. "I trained in first aid."

"Just worry about yourself right now. If you can help your dad, then go right ahead, but take it easy."

I helped him to his feet. He got his bearings and zombie-walked toward the hallway, bracing himself against the wall, upsetting one of his dad's paintings on the way.

"Hey," he said, looking back at me, his hands patting his pockets. "That guy took the keys to the boat."

Lindsay met me in the driveway. She was clutching a large black Maglite, brandishing it like a club. "We heard a gunshot," she said. "I called the cops."

"Where'd he go?" I asked.

She pointed toward the water with the end of the flashlight. "Saad's gone after him," she said.

"Damn it!" I said.

I took off running down the sloping driveway. The lights of the RCMP patrol cars and an ambulance flashed red and blue against the houses and trees of Orlando Avenue. They were still a few minutes away. Up ahead, in the glow of the moon, Saad's shadow had a life of its own. I heard the sound of a puttering engine, the gurgle of water being churned by rotors. A dark silhouette was crouching on the dock in the distance. He was taking Jimmy's boat.

The whole lake lit up as Lou backed the *Tide Queen* away from the dock.

I knew I was too late to stop him, but I kept running, anyway. At that point I wasn't running after Lou, but Saad, who was already racing along the dock with speed I'd never seen from him. When he got to the end, he flung himself across the gulf between the dock and the boat. He landed hard against the railing.

Lou ran across the deck toward Saad, who was struggling to pull himself on board. Lou swung a fist at Saad's face, but Saad dropped down onto the buoy fastened to the gunwale, clinging to it as his legs were sucked down into the dark water. Lou ran back to the bridge, turned the boat toward the open ocean, and pushed the throttle forward as far as it would go.

White foam kicked up from the rotors and the boat sped away, Saad still clinging to the buoy, his lower body completely submerged. All I could think was, *He can't swim!*

The RCMP cruisers skidded onto the grass by the steps leading down to the dock. I saw that the ambulance was pulling into John's driveway. Lindsay must have been directing them.

Sergeant Deloitte and his entourage piled out of the cruisers and ran down to the dock, their boots *clip-clopping* over the wooden boards.

I made up my mind and ran toward the van, which was parked on the other side of the road and fortunately not blocked in by any of the first responders.

"What are you doing?" Lindsay asked, holding her glasses steady on her head as she caught up with me. I was already in the van and turning the engine. Lindsay quickly got in the passenger seat, slammed the door, and buckled her seat belt. I put the van into reverse, backing off the shoulder and onto an unkempt lawn, before turning around in pursuit of the *Tide Queen*.

"What's the plan?" Lindsay asked, panic stalking the edges of her voice.

There was no plan. I watched out the windshield as the *Tide Queen* sailed toward the centre of the bay. In my side mirror, Deloitte and his officers ran back along the dock toward their cruisers. The *Tide Queen* was careening straight toward Harbour Island. Saad was hidden from view. I expected Lou to turn starboard and make his way for the mouth of the harbour and open ocean, but the vessel didn't turn.

Sirens filled the night, echoing through the harbour and the hills around it. The inside of the van filled with light as the cruisers' high beams caught up to us.

"Let's just pull over," Lindsay said.

I brought the van as close to the edge of the road as possible so the cops could pass. I wasn't trying to get in the way, but Saad was half-immersed in the freezing water. The police would have their hands full with Lou; Saad could only count on me.

Then it occurred to me: If Saad let go, would we even be able to see him in the black water? Would we be able to hear his cries for help and thrashing over the sirens and the sounds of our engines? He just had to hang on.

I turned onto a small unmarked road that ran parallel to the shore. The *Tide Queen* looked to be cruising straight for the harbour. The boat disappeared from sight as it passed behind Harbour Island.

When it reappeared, it drifted straight into the rocky shore of Robert's Arm, crashing into a small shed, ploughing through it and an overturned canoe just beyond it. I slammed on the brakes and the van drifted along the gravel, sliding to a stop beside a white shed.

"Flashlight!"

Lindsay handed me the Maglite.

I got out and ran toward the water, shining the beam over the aft section of the boat. Lindsay joined me with a second brighter beam from a big yellow floodlight. The police cruisers slid to a halt behind our van, headlights beaming. Car doors slammed, boots pounded the ground, Deloitte shouted orders.

"Saad!" I called out. "Saad!"

"Here! Help!" His voice sounded weak.

I slid down the bank, over the rocks and into the water, lodging the flashlight into the rocks and swimming out to grab Saad. He wasn't far and the water wasn't very deep, but he struggled to keep his head up, his muscles must have been practically frozen. I pulled him to shore and climbed up the rocks around Saad so that I could give him a hand up.

Three Mounties climbed aboard as the *Tide Queen* began drifting back down the bank and into the water. Deloitte was on shore, his sidearm trained on the bridge of the receding boat. Flashlight beams danced wildly in the night air as the cops searched the vessel.

"There's no one here, Sergeant," a constable called from the deck.

Lindsay came over with her jacket and laid it over a shivering Saad.

"Crank the heat up in the van," I said.

As Lindsay hurried back to the van, Deloitte ran over. "What the hell were you thinking?"

"I asked myself, *What would Laura do?* Then I did it," Saad answered sheepishly.

Deloitte stood over us, his shadow huge in the van's headlights.

"That's rarely a smart move," I said. "Trust me."

Saad looked up at me and smiled.

"Is he okay?" asked Deloitte.

"He's freezing, Sergeant," I said. "Can you give me a hand getting him to the van?"

"Was he piloting that boat?" Deloitte asked.

"Are you nuts?" I asked. "No. It was Lou Fenton."

The constables continued to search the boat and the water around it.

"I'm gonna to need some proof of that," Deloitte said.

I reached into my pocket and produced my phone. There was a crack in the screen that split the lower half into a row of sharp teeth. It wouldn't turn on as I pressed the button.

"Damn! I threw the phone into the back of the van. I'd recorded everything. Well," I said. "Call the mayor. She saw everything."

"Stay here," he said. "I'll get a blanket."

Sergeant Deloitte came back and wrapped a thermal blanket over Saad's shoulders.

"I can only think of one place Lou might go," I said. "Back to Beave's. It's close enough to walk to, and if he still has the keys to Beave's truck, he can make his getaway."

Lights in nearby houses were being turned on. Silhouettes in housecoats stood in doorways, watching. A pair of constabulary cruisers pulled up and parked in a V formation. Deloitte jogged over to the driver's side of one cruiser and directed the driver to head to Beave's. The other officers got out and joined the Mounties in their search around Harbour Island.

Saad sat shivering in the passenger's seat of the van. Lindsay pointed the vents toward him. Standing arm's length from the passenger door, I looked for Sergeant Deloitte, who'd headed over to the *Tide Queen* to join his men in the search. We needed to get Saad inside and out of his wet clothes.

"Ya think if I just drove your van into the bay, then all the proof that I'm still alive would be gone," Lou said from behind me. His back was to the water, shielded from view of the street by the van. "It's only a few feet away." He stood holding a club-sized piece of wood. "Have to kill you three, too."

"You could try," I said, putting some bass into my voice. "But I can think of only three ways that would go. And none of them would work out well for you."

Circling away from the van, I made sure that Lou had to choose between lunging at me or lunging at the van. *Why give him a two-for-one deal? Better to have him with his back to Harbour Island and the Mounties searching it.*

"You sure have a mouth on you, girlie."

He smiled the kind of smile that morphed into a sneer easily.

"I like my chances against a tired old man like you," I said. "Not to mention I have a trump card I'm just waiting to play."

I glanced over at the *Tide Queen* and couldn't see Sergeant Deloitte or his constables. The beams of their flashlights that had once been beacons of their positions were now gone.

"S'pose you tell me what you mean?"

He took a step closer, his hands coming away from his sides. I bluffed and he called. After everything he'd been through, I liked my chances in a fight with him. But there was something cold in his face. Behind the bruising on his face, I saw a look in his eyes that told me he had nothing to lose. I stepped back with my right foot, lifting both heals off the ground and raising my hands to my jawline. If Lou wanted a fight, I'd give him one.

Lindsay, behind the steering wheel, reversed the van and swung its nose around, blinding Lou in its headlights. She laid on the horn, spelling S.O.S. in Morse code. Lou turned and looked through the windshield; his clenched teeth with their spit-sheen caught the glow of the headlights.

"Lou Fenton!" Deloitte called out as he came around the *Tide Queen*, the authority in his voice cold and hard like concrete.

He dropped the piece of wood onto the gravel, looking around and weighing his options. Suddenly, Lou dashed between the van and me, hoping to exploit the gap I'd left for him. Disappearing behind the church or among the houses was his best bet until he could make it to the trees that bordered the town. I swung my left leg out, not hitting the femoral artery above the knee, as I was trained to do, but hitting his ankle with my shin, tripping him up and sending him down on the ground.

"I'll talk tough to anyone when there are three cops pointing guns at them," I said, standing over him.

"I know I'm a fool. There's no more running, anyhow," he said. "I got nothing left."

"That's not true," I said. "You have the power to set the record straight, to talk about Sarah, to tell the truth."

Deloitte closed the distance, slowing to a jog as Lou just sat there in the dirt.

"When I saw the news about the body, I asked myself, *Is that Sarah?* All these years, I thought she'd just left."

Lou turned toward Deloitte, raising his empty hands.

"Then you visited Pop in the hospital, and Beave showed up. Beave was afraid Pop might start talking about the gold and everything after it, if he had nothing left to lose."

"Up," Deloitte said, his constables arriving and flanking him.

They helped Lou to his feet and guided his hands to the top of his head.

"I had left the room for only a few minutes when I came back to find Beave sitting by Pop's bed. See, Beave was the only one who got all his money from John. Pop got enough to keep him quiet, and I got nothing. Anyhow, Beave thought the news of a skeleton being found would spook Pop into making a deathbed confession. It might have, too. He thought it must have been Sarah that you found, just like I did. The spot where they said she was found, it was John's special spot. I knew it had to be her."

The Mounties patted Lou down from head to toe.

"Everything about the way the body was wrapped and disposed of seemed sentimental."

"He wouldn't let her go, even after he killed her."

"What did Beave say to you?"

"Beave thought he'd seen a ghost. Y'see, he thought John musta done away with both of us. He was afraid that Pop might tell someone about the gold and they might piece it all together and pin the murder of me and Sarah on John and Beave both, since they both still had some of the gold. Beave told me all about his share of the money. He said he'd share some with me if I'd just go away again. But I wasn't going away. I was back now and I was going to make sure that King John in his mansion there paid for what he did to Sarah. I just needed some proof, but Beave wasn't about to give it to me. So, I took his clothes, his keys, his truck. I just had to get close without being spotted."

"It's all out in the open now," I said. "We just need you to tell your story, and Sarah can be buried somewhere other than John's special spot." I said. "Let's make this right."

Deloitte read Lou his rights while handcuffing him. It was very civil, very Canadian. Lou knew that anything he said would only incriminate him further, but it was his opportunity to get things off his chest that had sat there so long his ribs must have buckled and bent under the pressure.

"For as many times as I thought about the night Sarah left me, I must have thought twice as much about the night the boys and I snuck onto that construction site and dug up all that gold. We were all so happy, but I was twice as happy because I knew Sarah loved me, and the money we'd get from all those coins would be enough to get us out of here and give us the life we wanted."

In that moment, I was genuinely sorry it hadn't worked out for him and Sarah. Despite the laws they broke and the valuable archaeological knowledge that had been lost, I still had a bit of a soft spot for two people in love trying to make a better life for themselves. Sergeant Deloitte didn't seem to share my sentiment. Deciding that Lou had said enough, he escorted him to the back of his cruiser.

Minutes later, I sat by the docks with a blanket over my shoulders and a warm cup of coffee in my hand. Saad was in an ambulance being checked out. He was exposed to that cold water for a long enough time they couldn't rule out hypothermia.

I couldn't help but wonder how John had found out about Sarah and Lou, and when. Had he known when planning to loot the site but kept him along anyway? Then it occurred to me: What if it was Mayor Dunlop, who, having seen Lou and Sarah together in the woods near her house, was the one who told John about the affair in the first place? Was it guilt that motivated her to lie to the police about the snowmobile accident? Maybe I was just tired. The adrenalin was wearing off, and I was crashing.

Shortly after, the other van pulled up. Danny and Chris got out, and Lindsay came over to lead Chris to where we'd left the van. He seemed less concerned with the van than with the equipment inside it, his expression that of a dog kicked by its master. He knew, as well as I did, that some of his cool stuff must have broken during this episode.

"Sorry about the —" I began, and he raised his hand to cut me off before disappearing down the trail.

"You're a magnet for drama," Danny said, sitting down next to me.

"Don't expect me to believe that you're worried about me," I said.

"I'm worried about my job," he said. "One of two things is going to happen sooner or later. Either you're going to seriously get hurt, or —"

"Or?"

"Or you're going to have my job."

"I'm not crazy about either of those outcomes."

"Just be careful, okay?" he said, patting my knee.

"Sure, Danny," I said.

He stood up, stretched his lower back, and looked out at the lake. The water beyond the glow of boat lights was black. He checked his watch, then looked at me and smiled before heading back toward the van.

"Danny," I yelled after him, "I could never replace you."

He turned and smiled but kept walking.

"You know why that is?" I asked.

At that, he stopped and took a step back toward me, his hands on his waist. "Why?"

"I could never be a cheat."

Danny looked off to his left, scratching his bottom lip with a curled finger.

"You paid Jimmy O'Donahue for that conger eel stunt. Probably before we even got here. It takes time to get a conger of that size, and I doubt Jimmy would have gone to the trouble if it wasn't a sure thing. Look me in the eye and tell me I'm wrong."

"I think all this excitement is getting to you," he said.

"Maybe. I'm suspicious of everything now," I said. "How about you just show me your phone and prove that you haven't been talking to Jimmy?"

He bent at the waist and looked directly at me. Then he smiled. "We can't let viewership drop off, Reagan, and I didn't think I could count on the chaos you seem to attract twice in a row."

"I don't think you have to worry about that," I said, gesturing at the sirens flashing over the countryside.

"I still owe you that twenty bucks," he said.

"Let's call it even," I said. "You knew you'd lost the moment you made that bet."

"And think of it this way. Because of what I did, we ended up solving a real mystery."

"I wouldn't expect any medals if I were you."

Danny glanced at Sergeant Deloitte, who was approaching us but not yet within earshot. "Keep your answers short, and get some sleep," he said, turning up the collar of his jacket. "Next time, we're going someplace tropical."

"Count on it," I said.

Danny turned and walked away.

Sergeant Deloitte followed Danny with his gaze as he came over to me. He adjusted his hat. "What a mess. I should have never let you get involved. You could have been killed."

"All's well that ends well," I said.

"I still don't see how you put all this together," Deloitte said. "John's not talking, but maybe that'll change once he realizes he has no choice but to cooperate."

"Maybe Lou or Beave could fill in the missing pieces. John must have been the brains of the whole thing. In his position in the government, he would've known of any artifact smuggling networks were operating in the area. I doubt Beave and Lou were anything more than muscle. The fact that Beave had so many coins left makes me think that John was the fence, and that he could only move so many of these coins at one time without attracting the wrong kind of attention."

Deloitte nodded. "I still need you to come down to the station to give a statement. When are you leaving town?"

"We fly out tomorrow," I said.

"I hope you have some answers for me," Deloitte said. "I have a long list of questions."

Answers, I thought. *I don't have any answers.* Only more questions, which seemed to be my natural state of being.

TWENTY

As with other reported lake monsters, it's a mistake to look for only one explanation for all the Cressie sightings. In truth, there are many things in the lake — living and otherwise — that might double as large lake creatures.

— Ben Radford, *Lake Monster Mysteries: Investigating the World's Most Elusive Creatures*, 2006

WE LOADED THE REMAINING VAN AND FILLED Fred and Mary in on what they missed the night before. Danny spent some time on the phone with the network's travel adviser and changed our tickets to a later flight to accommodate Saad, who had been taken to the hospital for observation. Danny and Chris drank coffee in the dining room while Lindsay and I were back upstairs, trying to get some rest before we started for home but not succeeding.

"Have you heard from Saad?" Lindsay asked from under her comforter.

"He texted me earlier, but now I think he's doing what we should be doing: sleeping."

I looked at my phone again to make sure I hadn't missed anything. "I should be there with him."

"It made more sense to come back here after the police station, you can't criss-cross the whole island after what we just went through."

Maybe Lindsay was right, or maybe she was just saying what she thought would make me feel better. I tried to tally all the footage in my head of our Cressie hunt, and the conger eel examination, splicing it together in my head, trying to envision the finished product in my head. As hard as I tried to focus, my thoughts always drifted back to Saad and how he'd thrown himself into danger without a second thought. He was turning out to be another mystery in the long line of mysteries that defined my life.

Lindsay and I decided that it was futile to stay in bed any longer. The four of us who remained could sit around Corner Brook and drink coffee just as well as we could in Robert's Arm. With the two of us applying pressure, Lindsay and I convinced Danny and Chris to hit the road earlier.

Driving away from Robert's Arm was like waking from a dream. Showalter House, pirate treasure, the search for a giant eel, it all seemed so unreal and that it all might vanish from memory the farther we drove down the highway. I sent Saad a text telling him we were on our way, and he promptly replied with a smiley emoji. Cressie, too, was smiling — at least the statue of her to my left, standing guard over the road leading to town and the lake itself. There was something about the water that made me think that beneath it, among the rocks and shipwrecks, an eel larger than average undulated across the lake bottom. But Danny was right: *Next time, we're going someplace tropical.*

ACKNOWLEDGEMENTS

This project would be nothing without the belief and support of my agent, Kelvin Kong, and my publisher, Scott Fraser — most people would have laughed me out of town for proposing a cryptozoological murder mystery series. I would also like to thank my dear friends who supported this book and its author from the very beginning: Neil Springer, Vivian Lin, Bryan Jay Ibeas, and Mandy Hopkins. I would also like to acknowledge the research and work of Dr. Darren Naish, Dr. Joe Nickell, and Ben Radford, in bringing science and skepticism to the world of lake monsters. And, finally, most importantly, this book would not have been possible without the love and support of Sheeza Sarfraz, who always has my back.

ABOUT THE AUTHOR

 J.J. Dupuis writes fiction, poetry, and satire. His work has been published in magazines and journals such as *Valve*, *Foliate Oak*, *Spadina Literary Review*, and *University of Toronto Magazine*. J.J. is the founding editor of the *Quarantine Review*, a literary journal born out of self-isolation. He lives and works in East York, Toronto, and is an avid outdoorsman and martial artist.

Mystery and Crime Fiction from Dundurn Press

Victor Lessard Thrillers
by Martin Michaud
(Quebec Thriller, Police Procedural)
Never Forget
Without Blood
Coming soon: *The Devil's Choir*

The Day She Died
by S.M. Freedman
(Domestic Thriller, Psychological)

Amanda Doucette Mysteries
by Barbara Fradkin
(Female Sleuth, Wilderness)
Fire in the Stars
The Trickster's Lullaby
Prisoners of Hope
The Ancient Dead

The Candace Starr Series
by C.S. O'Cinneide
(Noir, Hitwoman, Dark Humour)
The Starr Sting Scale
Starr Sign

Stonechild & Rouleau Mysteries
by Brenda Chapman
(Indigenous Sleuth, Kingston, Police Procedural)
Cold Mourning
Butterfly Kills
Tumbled Graves
Shallow End
Bleeding Darkness
Turning Secrets
Closing Time

Tell Me My Name
by Erin Ruddy
(Domestic Thriller, Dark Secrets)

The Walking Shadows
by Brenden Carlson
(Alternate History, Robots)
Night Call
Midnight

Creature X Mysteries
by J.J. Dupuis
(Cryptozoology, Female Sleuth)
Roanoke Ridge
Lake Crescent

Birder Murder Mysteries
by Steve Burrows
(Birding, British Coastal Town)
A Siege of Bitterns
A Pitying of Doves
A Cast of Falcons
A Shimmer of Hummingbirds
A Tiding of Magpies
A Dance of Cranes

B.C. Blues Crime
by R.M. Greenaway
(British Columbia, Police Procedural)
Cold Girl
Undertow
Creep
Flights and Falls
River of Lies
Five Ways to Disappear

Jenny Willson Mysteries
by Dave Butler
(National Parks, Animal Protection)
Full Curl
No Place for Wolverines
In Rhino We Trust

Jack Palace Series
by A.G. Pasquella
(Noir, Toronto, Mob)
Yard Dog
Carve the Heart
Season of Smoke

The Falls Mysteries
by J.E. Barnard
(Rural Alberta, Female Sleuth)
When the Flood Falls
Where the Ice Falls
Why the Rock Falls

CPSIA information can be obtained
at www.ICGtesting.com
Printed in the USA
LVHW020436190821
695591LV00004B/374